A FOUNDATION OF GRAVESTONES

Published by Clockwork Dragon, LLC
www.clockworkdragon.net

First Printing, August 2020

A Foundation of Gravestones is a work of fiction. People, places, and incidents are either products of the author's mind or used fictitiously.

ISBN: 978-1-944334-57-4

STARDRIFTERS BOOK 2

A FOUNDATION OF GRAVESTONES

LEE FRENCH
JEFFREY COOK

This book is dedicated to the Cummings family, for their amazing support and kindness, and Ken in specific, for their boundless enthusiasm and willingness to use their multitude of artistic talents for the joint causes of both good and awesome.

Also to Ghost Ship Games and Coffee Stain Publishing for providing Lee with a much-needed distraction in the form of *Deep Rock Galactic*. Rock and stone!

CHAPTER 1

MADISON

The cable plugged into Madison's cybernetic eye socket fed raw information from the ship's systems to her brain. With the direct neural interface, the ship supplanted her flesh and became her body. Combining that with her hands on the manual controls, she piloted their stolen luxury spaceship toward the prison planet's stratosphere.

Pilots using only their two hands rarely stood a chance of keeping up with her.

Next stop, reuniting with her uncle's Stardrifter ship, the *Wayward Star.*

Hopefully.

Images piped into her brain from cameras mounted on the outside hull gave her pause. Though Kirehe and her big dragon had cleared the atmosphere-based pursuit ships for them, the space-based ones lurked ahead. Behind, a few smaller ships like theirs launched and followed.

She activated the ship-wide intercom with a thought. A microphone near her head turned on. "The Oligarchy has extended another invitation for us to stay indefinitely on Rikor Six. When I indicate our negative response, I believe they might object. If you're not already strapped in, this is a good time to fix that problem."

"What's going to happen?" Lylla asked with a gulp. The wispy preteen girl sat in the navigator seat, a swivel chair bolted to the floor behind and to the right of the recessed cockpit. She hugged herself and strained to watch the front viewscreens while ignoring the navigation console.

Anyone else saw a starfield. Madison knew an Oligarchy cruiser lurked there with several support ships. The viewscreen, though, showed only a vague area with no stars.

"She's going to maneuver the ship to avoid weapons." Jaco sat opposite Lylla, in a seat intended for a co-pilot. Madison's adopted little brother had plenty of training with weapons control, but this ship had no weapons to control.

Lylla whimpered and covered her face.

"Oolaang!" Madison continued to shift their angle of ascent so they headed anywhere other than directly at the cruiser.

As long as they stayed out of short-range weapons range, everything would work. They'd escape the planet and they'd find Captain Wayward.

She could dodge the long-range weapons. No problem.

Their engineer sprinted into the control pod. "What do you need?" the small man said as he gasped to catch his breath from running. Half the height of a human, he had four arms and wore dark-lensed goggles to protect his large, sensitive eyes from bright light.

Like everyone else on the ship, he wore the standard plain clothing of a Rikor Six slave. Functional and easy to clean, the shirt and pants hung from everyone's bodies, somehow managing to fit poorly no matter their physique.

Madison intended to change that as soon as possible. She missed her Wayward blue uniform. Among other things.

"This ship has minimal shields and zero weapons," Madison said as if she spoke about the weather or a passing tourist sight, "and we have incoming. The controls are also a little mushy. Whatever you can do to upgrade, like right now, would help a lot."

"On it." Oolaang whacked Jaco in the arm. "Come help me."

Jaco unbuckled and hopped out of his chair. The two men left.

Madison's escape planning had more or less ended the moment they climbed into a ship capable of leaving the planet. She'd strapped herself into the pilot seat with a vague idea about where to go and what to do.

Of course, she knew how to pilot a ship. She'd flown her uncle's much larger ship under stressful situations for the past three years. His smaller scouting ship too.

By sneaking away with his scout craft and a sizable fraction of his crew, she'd taken a lot from him. At least they'd succeeded at the mission.

Sort of.

She had not intended for that mission to include capture, several deaths, and imprisonment in a gladiator pit.

"What should I do?" Lylla asked with a sniffle.

The poor kid had lived her entire life in the gladiator pit as the child of a renowned fighter. She'd never even seen a spaceship before.

Madison shrugged and set her expectations low. "If you can figure out how to run the navigation console, I need a jump to anywhere that isn't here. Otherwise, try not to distract me too much or fall out of your chair."

"I'll try." A thread of brave conviction ran under those two small words. "What are all these numbers?" Lylla faced the screen, number keypad, and switches of the console.

Shmar rushed into the control pod. Jaco or Oolaang must have sent him to help with navigation. Though he had the build of a security team member, he'd joined the Wayward nav team a few years earlier.

"Here, I know how to do that," he told Lylla.

At least Madison didn't have to try to explain anything.

Maximum speed for the craft failed to impress her. Their flight took forever. Pursuit craft closed the distance.

"Do *not* make her get out of that chair," Madison said. The ship registered weapons firing. The stupid thing couldn't detect targeting system activity, but it could detect ionizers and explosive things. "Kut. Hang on."

This dumb ship couldn't do anything about weapons firing at them.

Madison could.

She closed her one real eye to focus on ship data. In the background, she heard Shmar speaking, though he kept his voice down. Maybe he'd knelt beside Lylla to hold onto the chair. Whatever he did, Madison could ignore his voice as nothing more than another flavor of engine hum.

Her cybernetic interface teased the data streams into usable information for a certain part of her brain. Uncle Christopher had explained it as accessing the part of her brain most directly responsible for piloting.

Even as a child, she'd shown an unusual aptitude for piloting. As her sole remaining guardian, Uncle Chris had given her the tools to use it better than anyone.

The ship peeled off its trajectory in response to Madison's commands. She noted the cruiser launching a twelve-member wing of star-shaped fighters.

Twelve.

For one little luxury yacht.

Viriok, the owner of the prison planet who'd just suffered a humiliating defeat live on screens across Oligarchy-controlled space because of Madison's actions, wanted them dead.

A lot.

"We may have a slightly larger problem," Madison said as she tracked a steady stream of plasma beams and torpedoes from all three of their small pursuit craft. The cruiser had yet to fire, at least. "I need a jump, Shmar. I need it now."

"I don't have one. This pokken system is—" He growled his frustration.

She snorted. The data shifted as if Madison had moved an inch to the left. She suddenly had more information than before.

Bravo, Oolaang.

Five of the fighters already had targeting locks on their pokken ship. Did they mean to board? No. She had their range now. They needed to close the distance a hair more.

She needed more speed. This bucket had no more speed to give.

If she couldn't have speed, she'd have to stress the maneuvering thrusters.

Madison flexed her control over the craft, testing its limits while she dodged a series of incoming torpedoes. Plasma blasts streaked in a straight line. Torpedoes could turn.

"Out of time," Madison said as she flipped the ship and headed toward the fighters.

Twelve targeting systems locked on. Madison dipped and spun the ship. The computer system did the math to weave the ship through the plasma blasts. Pilots with only their two hands lacked any ability to react fast enough to use that kind of information.

Lylla squeaked in fright.

"Calm down," Shmar said. "If there's one thing I trust Madison to do, it's keep a ship in one piece."

In the time it took Shmar to offer Madison a compliment, she reached the scattering line of small fighters and pivoted to avoid letting them chase her to the cruiser.

To her satisfaction, a torpedo slammed into the fighter directly behind her. Those zippy two-man craft had no defenses against a torpedo half the size of their ship. A short-lived explosion shattered the fighter. The pieces scattered at high speed.

Madison winced as shrapnel slammed into the shields. Oolaang hadn't accomplished anything with them yet. The shields managed to incinerate or deflect all but three larger pieces.

One scrap of metal plunged into the outer hull, causing a breach. Fortunately, the ship had an inner hull. A breach in the space between them caused no serious harm.

Another shard of the destroyed ship scraped along the outer hull, leaving a furrow. Probably only cosmetic.

Probably.

The third hit one of Madison's four down-thrusting space maneuver jets. This one mattered. She had to compensate for the loss.

"Shmar," Madison said as she spun the ship, "I need a jump. I can't stay on the same trajectory. Deal with it."

"I can't calculate that! I need at least half a minute without deviation."

"Try." Madison led a torpedo into a line of plasma blasts. The explosion rocked the ship forward and knocked two fighters together.

Three down, nine to go.

"It's not possible!"

Madison rolled her eye under its lid. "Escape from Rikor Six isn't possible either, but here we are. Escaping from Rikor Six."

"What does this button do?" Lylla asked.

"Bad things," Shmar said.

"Oolaang, where's my shields?" Madison bellowed into the intercom.

Plasma drilled through the shields to burn a hole along the underside of the craft. Madison rolled to evade three more beams.

Still no inner hull breach. Good.

"What kind of bad things?" Lylla asked.

Shmar sighed. "It initiates an FTL jump. If we jump without plotting the course, we can hit a star or a planet, which means we all die. It takes complex math, and it's even harder when you aren't using regular jump points. We need the computers to calculate it, and they need a steady ship. Human brains can't do that."

"Can you explain quieter?" Madison asked. She flipped the ship again and wished Jaco could shoot the fighter in front of her. Or the one behind her. Either way.

At the last moment before the fighter peeled off, she dumped the nose down and introduced the fighter in front of her to the fighter behind her. Violently.

"Not without getting out of this chair," Shmar snapped. "If you're going to keep flying like that, I'm not getting out of this chair."

"Fine, just be less distracting."

Madison's camera feeds fuzzed with crackling static. "Oolaang, what did you do to my cameras?"

The Oligarchy cruiser loomed ahead, much closer than Madison liked. A little closer and they'd zap the little ship's engines to death.

She hadn't piloted toward it. That meant Viriok had ordered it into pursuit. Once they got going, cruisers could move a lot faster than little ships.

They had a minute at most.

She muttered a few choice curses under her breath. "We need a jump. Now. Or we're done."

"It won't work like this," Shmar wailed.

Seven fighters circled Madison, having learned from their comrades' mistakes. They flew like electrons around a nucleus, gnatlike and annoying. No fighter crossed another's line of fire, and they avoided chasing. As soon as Madison pointed the ship at one, it veered to the side and found another place to circle.

That stupid offline down thruster meant plasma crashed into the shields. Unlike before, they held and kept the hull safe.

Oolaang had boosted the shields at the expense of camera clarity. She could live with that trade-off. Literally.

They could fix it later.

Assuming they got a later. Madison could tell she'd expend all her thruster fuel if she had to keep weaving and twisting through their tight lines of fire.

At least the pursuit craft from the planet had backed off to let the fighters handle it.

Not that it mattered with the cruiser picking up speed. The big ship loomed like an asteroid on a direct line path to blot out the nearest star and roll over them.

"Pick a path," she snarled at Shmar. "Any path. Make up some numbers! Anything. A short jump is fine!"

"A path?" Lylla asked. "I know how to find paths."

"Fine," Shmar snapped. "Punch in numbers there. We can die spectacularly."

"I'm pushing the button!" Lylla announced.

"What?" Shmar shrieked. "No! I didn't mean it!"

Someone smacked the console.

The ship jumped.

CHAPTER 2

KIREHE

Nihan, Kirehe's bonded krata dragon, kept everyone in place with his leathery green wings and large, bone-white claws anchored to the walls and floor while the ship rolled and tumbled like a leaf dancing on the wind. Kirehe, Rho, Gordy, and all the dragons had remained in the cargo bay. They huddled together for safety.

Despite this effort, nearly all of them had sustained at least a few bumps and bruises in the mad, chaotic scramble to avoid bouncing across the cargo bay repeatedly.

Gordy bled from a cut above his eye. Kirehe ached everywhere. Rho cradled their hand though Kirehe saw no sign of serious injury. All the dragons grumbled at their predicament. Even Skila, the tiny kukiri covered with bright, cheerful feathers, whined incessantly.

No one but Kirehe could understand any of their cranky chirps, rumbles, and whistles.

The ship shuddered with a groan and stopped tumbling. Kirehe's stomach flopped without causing her serious distress. Engine noise, a constant hum neither Kirehe nor the dragons liked, dropped. Another noise like hundreds of leaves tearing at the same time rumbled through them.

Her mara dragons growled and grumbled, squirming against Nihan's huge body.

Skila pressed against Kirehe's belly where she huddled in Kirehe's hands. The kukiri's wordless whining shifted to wordless wheezing.

Gordy groaned and held his stomach. "I almost forgot what FTL jumps feel like."

Kirehe understood he'd spent multiple years in the gladiator pit, though she had no idea what the human had done before his capture.

Rho, the lone survivor of the slaughter of their macrica clan, covered their mouth and nodded. As a nucri member of their clan, they had wide hips good for squatting and a pouch for carrying their remica's young.

Once again, the ship shuddered. Kirehe's stomach churned again. The leaf tearing noise stopped. All the dragons groaned. Engine noise returned.

"What is FTL jump?" she asked, looking between Gordy and Rho.

"Faster Than Light," Gordy said. "The ship moved really, really fast. Fleshy bodies don't like it so much."

"I'd like to congratulate everyone for successfully completing our escape plan." Madison's voice bounced off the walls. "We jumped away from the planet. We have no idea where we are. Working on a course to someplace useful. Unless someone managed to get a lock on us before the jump, which I doubt, we're done with the evasive maneuvers and will jump to someplace useful in a few minutes."

"This means safe?" Kirehe asked. She understood the language they all used though she still had difficulty with many of the words. All of them spoke too fast.

"For now," Gordy said.

Kirehe whistled and chirped at Nihan. "No more tumbling. Let us go."

The krata dragon removed his claws from the ship and hunkered to take up as little space as possible for something of his size. Kirehe wished they could jump from the back of the ship so she could fly on his scaly green back again, but she understood the concept of space.

Her mara dragon pack, a group of four wingless, bipedal creatures about two-thirds her height, slumped against the wall in a pile. They laced their necks, tails, and legs together to form a mass of black and brown feathers and green and brown scales. Maras rested like this when they wanted to comfort each other.

Kirehe understood.

"I sure hope this boat has plenty of food," Gordy said. He lifted his arm and winced. "And medical supplies."

"We should look into that." Rho raised their hand and moved their fingers one by one. They grimaced as they bent the smallest one. "How much do your dragons eat, Kirehe?"

"Much. Unless do nothing and stay warm. Then, not much." She rubbed her hand under Nihan's broad chin. "Not like do nothing."

Rho nodded and waddled out of the cargo bay, heading deeper into the ship.

"No one likes doing nothing," Gordy said. "We won't stay on this ship forever, though. Even if it has plenty of supplies, it'll need fuel soon. Stardrifter outposts are usually small. There shouldn't be major problems letting them out to run around when we land."

"Good." Kirehe turned to her dragons. She whistled, chirped, and growled to communicate with them. Her people, the Iwans, called her a dragoncaller for this gift. "We have to stay in this room for a long time and with small food. But not forever. Rest. Heal. Together."

"Sleep!" Skila chirped. "Nest?"

"I'll find you something to nest with," Kirehe said.

"Noisy." Rila, the lead mara said this. The others agreed. So did Nihan.

Kirehe agreed too. "This is normal now. Maybe we can fix it. I will talk to the small man."

Her assurance she would try to do something about the annoyance made the dragons content enough.

"You bleed," Kirehe said. She pointed at Gordy's forehead.

He swiped his hand across the spot and checked the blood smeared across his skin. "Yep, I sure am bleeding. It stings a bit. We won't have all the fancy medical care here. I'll miss that. Nothing else, but definitely that."

Kirehe nodded. She'd noticed the advanced medicine their captors used, especially when they'd used it on her. Gladiators who healed fast fought more. More fighting meant more money. Arena Master Viriok, a member of the lakhan race, liked money.

She had no idea why Viriok prized money so much. He and his kind frightened everyone, which gave them enough power to rule everything.

Nihan had crunched Viriok in jaws capable of snapping through a tree trunk as big as the circle of Kirehe's arms.

This had not killed Viriok.

Kirehe had watched him get up afterward. Either his kind could repair their bodies, or they could withstand massive injury. Perhaps both.

Not sure what else to do with herself, Kirehe sat with her back against the mara pile. Nihan wriggled closer and put his head next to her. She laid her hand on his head and idly rubbed over his eye ridge.

"That is probably the most terrifying thing I've ever seen," Gordy said.

Some of Kirehe's tribe would agree with him. She shrugged. "They no harm you." Patting the ground to suggest he sit with her and let the maras bask in his warmth, she asked, "Tell about lakhans?"

Gordy gave the mara pile a suspicious frown. "They're gods." He took a hesitant step closer.

Kirehe understood him. Standing near a creature capable of ripping him apart, he could handle. Especially with their mistress nearby.

Sitting where they touched him crossed the line into scary.

"Gods of what?" Kirehe's tribe knew the concept of gods, though they worshipped none.

Jaco stepped into the cargo bay and scanned the room as if checking for someone. At least he hadn't come looking for Kirehe. She still wanted to kill him. His betrayal lingered in her mind.

Gordy crossed his arms, radiating discomfort. "Not that kind. They're immortal. They live forever and can't be killed."

"Captain Wayward says that's jetwash," Jaco said. He remained by the door to the rest of the ship, not taking even a single step closer. "No such thing as someone who can't be killed."

"Captain Wayward is a madman," Gordy said with a roll of his eyes and shake of his head. "No one's ever killed a lakhan. No one ever will."

Jaco opened his mouth. His gaze flicked to Kirehe and back to Gordy. "You should know we're headed to find Captain Wayward. It's his ship we're looking to rendezvous with."

"Right." Gordy sighed and flicked a hand to dismiss Jaco, who left immediately. "Of course. I suppose it's better than staying on Rikor Six."

The exchange puzzled Kirehe. She knew the lakhans hated Madison and her uncle but had no idea why. "I do not understand. Why this is bad?"

Gordy rubbed his face and sat close to Kirehe without touching the maras. "It's complicated."

Kirehe shrugged. She needed Madison to explain complicated things because Madison could speak her native language better than Kirehe could speak their alien one.

Rho returned with a small red case marked with a white cross. White tape bound their injured finger in a straight line. "I found at least a few things to treat our wounds. That cut looks minor, but let's cover it to prevent infection. Kirehe, are you hurt?"

"Small only," Kirehe said. "Sleep and fine."

Rho squatted beside Gordy, also not touching the maras. They opened their case and retrieved a white square. "Good. I found some food. I'm hoping there's another stash someplace. We only have enough for two days with this many people, assuming I can count the dragons each as one person's worth of food."

Kirehe considered the dragons' eating habits and how to translate to how much a person needed. "When still, one person is one mara for one week. Two person is Nihan for one week. Skila…" She frowned at the tiny dragon. "Very small bites but many."

"We'll try offering her the food and see how much she'll eat." Rho cleaned Gordy's wound and applied a small bandage. "How much the other dragons need will help a great deal, though. I hope we're only out here for a few days before we can find fresh supplies."

Gordy touched the bandage, pressing on the edges. "The bad part is we have nothing to trade."

"I expect Madison will have some kind of plan before we reach anyplace." Rho nodded at their handiwork. "Do you have any sharp pains anywhere?"

"No, just general aches." He waved for Rho to leave him alone. "I'm fine. Go fuss over the others."

Rho huffed and turned their attention to Kirehe.

"Bruises only," Kirehe said before the macrica could pester her. Every muscle in her body complained, but she needed no medicine. "We are used to a beating, yes? Tough bodies." She knocked on her chest and grinned.

"Warriors." Rho snorted. "Lunatics, the whole lot of you." They shut the case and stood. "Come see me if you notice anything serious later."

Gordy smirked. "Sure, one of us could have a broken rib pretending to only be a muscle ache."

Kirehe laughed. Her entire body protested, but she liked feeling that she could enjoy something.

Rho stuck out their tongue and swatted at the air above Gordy's head, making him duck. "Smartass. The point is, I have all the medical supplies. If I find any more, I'll take charge of that too." They turned to leave, but stopped. "Oh, and there aren't enough private rooms for everyone to sleep, so most of us will have to double up."

"I stay with dragons," Kirehe said. "This helps?"

"It helps, yes. Thank you." Rho offered her a weary smile and took the case out of the cargo bay.

Kirehe hoped Madison would come stay with the dragons too. Or maybe she hoped Madison stayed in her own room.

She needed to decide which was better because both sounded terrible.

CHAPTER 3

MADISON

Shmar remained in his chair, panting as his panic eased. He held one hand over his chest like he'd suffered a heart attack. Madison wanted to slap him. She chose to stay in the cockpit instead.

They'd popped out of FTL completely safe with a brown planet between them and a nearby red dwarf star.

"You're telling me you just got numbers in your head?" Madison asked Lylla.

"Sort of?" Lylla kept staring at the navigational console. "It's more like I flashed through a lot of math and somehow just knew."

"She somehow just knew," Shmar whimpered. "Like magic."

"Shut up," Lylla said. She leaned to the side and punched him in the arm. "You wouldn't have gotten out of that pit if I hadn't somehow just known how to find the path. Space is bigger, but it's not different."

Madison cranked her body so she could see Shmar. The guy had annoyed the hell out of her on Rikor Six, but he'd always served her uncle with loyalty.

If she wanted to understand anything about Lylla's interesting ability, she needed to get him out of the control pod. "Hey Shmar? Why don't you go check on Oolaang? See if he needs anything or has some kind of estimate on when he thinks he can get me some kind of weapon?"

"Sure." Shmar moved like a man who'd seen his own ghost. His fingers fumbled as he unbuckled his harness and his legs stumbled as he lurched out of the pod.

"What's wrong with him?" Lylla asked.

"He knows a lot about navigation and exactly how it can go wrong." Madison shrugged. "You scared the kut out of him."

"Oh." Lylla lowered her gaze to her boots. "I didn't mean to."

"I know. He'll figure that out eventually. Shmar can be an idiot, but he's not dumb." Madison needed a navigator and she had one if she could figure out how to explain things well enough to Lylla. The girl had some kind of gift. "Tell me more about this stuff in your head? Because we need to get to an actual jump point so we can path to a Stardrifter hideout for supplies and information. And we should do that as soon as possible."

Lylla nodded. "When you said you needed a path, I realized what you were trying to get. Shmar didn't really explain anything. He kind of wanted me to get out of the way so he could work, I guess. Except he couldn't work because the ship kept turning." She pointed to the screen. "After you said it was a path, things sort of clicked into place. Everything made sense. I punched in all the numbers, waited for the moment the ship was pointed in the right direction, and hit the button."

Ship computers couldn't do that, as far as Madison knew. A nav calculator needed the ship to point in a particular direction the entire time while it calculated. It couldn't make adjustments for changing trajectories or decide when the ship had reached the correct trajectory to engage the FTL system.

"Wow." That little word felt stupid and small compared to the treasure she'd discovered in the navigator's seat. "I've never heard of anyone who could do that before."

Lylla blushed bright pink.

Though she hated to think in such mercenary ways, Madison thought maybe her uncle might forgive her a little bit easier when she brought him a living nav calculator.

Jaco stepped into the control pod. "I checked on everyone else. They're banged up but fine. Rho found medical supplies and food.

Oolaang says he's boosted the shields, recalibrated the data matrix for your interface, and fixed the camera fuzz problem caused by the shield boost.

"He says there's no way to give this ship a weapon without mounting one. It doesn't have enough power. Also, we're low on thruster fuel. He's adjusting something with the landing struts right now. I guess there was damage, maybe from the fight before liftoff."

"Thanks." Madison beckoned for him to sit. "I have a few things to say to you. But first, we have to decide where to go. If you had to guess where we might find Uncle Chris, where would you say?"

Jaco gulped and sat dutifully. He clasped his hands between his knees like he always did when he expected a scolding. "Uh. Veriscova Four or Dridi Prime, probably? Those are his favorite places when he's prepping to yell at you."

She wanted to disagree with his premise. But odds were good Uncle Chris would want to beat the kut out of her for what she'd done. Knowing she'd escaped would mean he'd expect her to come looking for him.

He'd get ready to unleash anger at his only living link to his lost wife and brother. At the girl he considered a daughter.

Madison expected to find him drunk or doing something stupid. Maybe both.

She sighed. "Yeah. You're right. Let's try Veriscova Four. If he's not there, we'll head to Dridi Prime. Show Lylla how to find those on the screen so she can plot a route."

Jaco shifted to take a knee beside Lylla and show her how to use the star map.

While he did that, Madison checked the scans of the local system. Two blips appeared at long range, which caught her attention.

Mining ships sometimes traveled in pairs. So did smugglers.

And Oligarchy scouts.

"Can we speed this up a bit?" Madison asked.

The two ships turned toward the yacht. Madison knew the

thruster fuel level. They couldn't afford to engage in evasive maneuvers.

Madison noted targeting scans without locks.

"I got it," Lylla said. She smacked the button.

The ship jumped. Madison found the sensation of FTL shifting unpleasant yet bearable. It made her want to drink tea to soothe her stomach.

They slid out of FTL beside a jump point buoy.

Madison had never seen so many Oligarchy ships lurking at a jump point. She counted one flagship, one cruiser, one carrier, fifteen scouts, twelve interceptors, and seven frigates.

Jaco made a stupid noise that echoed how Madison felt.

Lylla squeaked and smacked the button again.

They jumped.

"The time for this jump is thirteen hours and seventeen minutes," Lylla said. Her voice shook.

Madison panted to catch her breath from the brief flash of panic. "Great."

"Did you see all that?" Jaco asked.

Their quick escape meant the Oligarchy ships hadn't had time to tag them. No one would follow.

"We jumped into the middle of an armada," Madison said, still stunned by the swift series of events. But never mind that. They had things to do. "And then we jumped out. Because Lylla is awesome."

"An armada." Jaco's voice grew shrill and breathy as he continued. "There was an armada at the jump point. Why was there an armada at the jump point?"

"Calm down." Madison unplugged the cable from her eye socket and climbed out of the cockpit. The ship needed nothing from her and she got nothing useful from it while they traveled in FTL.

He knew why they'd discovered an armada at the jump point just as well as Madison did. Viriok wanted them dead. Subjugator Cradok also wanted them dead. He'd shipped them to the prison planet for execution in the first place, after all.

If two lakhans wanted to kill them, Madison considered it reasonable to assume all lakhans wanted to kill them.

"Calm down? Are you kidding?" Jaco covered his face with both hands and giggled like a lunatic.

Lylla stared at the front viewscreen, her eyes wide and shocky.

"Lylla?" Madison set a hand on her shoulder, trying to shake the girl out of her stupor without scaring her. "Why don't you go talk to Rho? They're always happy to have your company, and I think maybe you could use something to eat."

"Okay." Lylla removed the chair's harness and stood. She stared forward.

Madison prodded her shoulder. "Definitely eat."

"Eat. Yes. Good." The girl shuffled out of the control pod.

As soon as she left them alone, Madison turned to Jaco. "Okay, dumbass, we're going to have a conversation. No one is listening, no enemies lurk in corners, and we're not running for our lives. Not with our legs, anyway."

Jaco's shoulders slumped. He swore colorfully while still covering his face.

Madison sighed. She popped her cybernetic eye into the empty socket and engaged it while waiting for Jaco to settle down. Since Lylla had vacated the navigator seat, she sat in it and faced Jaco.

"I'm not going to shiv you."

He lowered his hands and stared at the floor between his feet. "I'm happy to hear that."

"I know you took a big risk by doing what I asked for the escape plan. That counts for a lot." She looked at her hands, not sure where to take the conversation. They needed to talk but she hadn't seen a good plan for how to handle it.

Planning never seemed to work with family anyway.

She had no idea what she'd say to her uncle either. In a lot of ways, she stood in Jaco's position for that talk.

Months ago, she'd persuaded twelve members of his crew of

seventy-five to sneak off the ship with her for a daring, insane mission. Only three had survived. Her betrayal came with no less of a sting than Jaco's when she looked at it that way.

Maybe it even made her worse.

"It was always about you." Jaco sounded tired and beaten.

Madison nodded. "They picked you because they figured out you were the weak link. The one most likely to agree to something you should've known better than to believe. Those pharedimi on Rikor Six know how to play people."

The race of zealots serving the lakhans, the pharedimi, thrived on cruelty and had found more ways to inflict it than any human could. All with minimal physical violence. They impressed Madison with their attention to detail, but nothing else.

Jaco grimaced and said nothing.

"I still trust you, Jaco. It's just hard to have faith in your judgment."

"That's rich, coming from you." Before the capture, he would've said that with a snort or a chuckle. After everything they'd suffered through, he sounded hollow. Empty.

She hated to hear that in him. No matter how much he'd disappointed her, she still cared about him. He was still her little brother, the desperate orphan they'd picked up on a backwater dump eight years earlier.

"This from the guy who tried to pick Uncle Chris's pocket, of all people."

Jaco's gaze flicked to hers long enough for him to see her small smile. "This from the girl who tried to catch me."

"I would have if not for that cat I tripped over."

"Sure, blame the cat."

The old teasing felt distant and strange yet comfortable like a beloved pair of worn gloves.

Madison offered her hand. He took it.

"I'm sorry." Jaco held her hand with a gentle squeeze.

"I'm sorry too. Have my back when we find Uncle Chris?"

"Always."

"Apologize for real to Kirehe?"

He grimaced again. "I already did, but I'll do it again. And again. And again until she doesn't want to murder me in my sleep anymore."

"Good." Madison stood and tugged him to his feet. "Don't do anything stupid to try to make this up to me."

Jaco hugged her. No matter how she felt about him, she relished an embrace in his strong arms. He cared, she cared, and if she'd ever found boys attractive, she would've jumped him in a hot second.

"Stupid is my department, though. How will I run my department?"

"The key word is delegation." She grinned as they pulled apart and poked him in the chest. "Get other people to do it for you. Then you're above the fray and blameless. Unlike that pokken cat."

He matched her grin. "My department is small, but I think I can manage that." He leaned closer and whispered, "I bribed the cat with meat."

"I knew it!" Madison poked him in the arm, acting like she'd never heard this revelation before. "Uncle Chris never believed me when I told him the cat was on the take. No, I was just clumsy. 'Stick to flying, Maddie, you're good at that.' Like I don't know how to run properly."

Jaco shook his head and draped an arm over her shoulders. "You do alright nowadays. But you were kind of pathetic then. Compared to a real professional such as myself, I mean."

"C'mon, let's get some food before we drop out of FTL. I'm starving. You can talk to Kirehe. It'll be fun."

CHAPTER 4

KIREHE

The food was not what Kirehe had expected. She'd assumed a ship in space would have strange food designed for space. Not that she had an idea what this would mean.

It tasted good. Like real food.

Kirehe fed strips of light pink meat drenched in a brown sauce to the maras. She had no idea what type of animal had produced them. It tasted like risi dragon slathered in oranges and salt, though, and the maras ate it without complaint.

Nihan had inhaled an entire meal in two seconds. He'd worked hard before landing inside the ship. She doubted he'd noticed the flavor.

Skila had a white plate with four different kinds of food, none of it touching. She circled the meal, sniffing everything and prodding it with her tiny claws. One green feather dragged through the brown sauce. For the next five minutes, she struggled to reach the feather and preen it.

The rest of the crew also dined with them.

Jaco sat against the wall with his meal. Gordy sat beside him. Shmar sat on his other side. All three men seemed tired yet still wary of the dragons. Especially with food. As far as Kirehe could tell, Gordy acted as a buffer between Jaco and Shmar, who still wanted to growl at each other.

Kirehe also wanted to growl at Jaco. He had, after all, stabbed her.

Rho and Lylla leaned against the maras. Unlike the men, they had approached and sat with only minor hesitation. They'd followed Madison's lead.

Oolaang, sporting a new bandage across his temple and another on one of his four hands, sat beside Rho. His hip almost touched a mara. Almost.

Madison herself lay on her stomach beside the maras with her feet in the air, crossed at her ankles. Her shoulder touched Kirehe's leg and she waved a leaf with white sauce at Skila while stuffing pieces of meat into her own mouth.

Skila took the leaf and nibbled the edge.

"What that armada means is the Oligarchy is serious about catching us," Madison said around a mouthful of food. "Given the chance, I'm pretty sure they still want to publicly execute me. But I think their priority is me dead, so we can't count on them trying to catch us instead of blowing us up."

"Which means we haven't finished escaping yet," Gordy said.

"You could look at it that way, I guess." Unable to shrug in her position, Madison bobbled her head. "We're heading to Veriscova Four right now, looking for Captain Wayward. I think we should avoid leaving the ship unattended while there."

"If I remember right," Gordy said, "Veriscova Four has one of the larger Stardrifter settlements. Doesn't that make it dangerous for us?"

"If Uncle Chris is there, it shouldn't be an issue. If he's not, we won't stay long." Madison cocked her head at Gordy. "What did you do before they caught you?"

"Deputy for the veiligbaas on Pichet Three."

Though Gordy sounded casual about this statement, Jaco, Oolaang, Shmar, and Madison all frowned in the same way. Kirehe thought they'd heard of whatever terrible thing had happened there.

Madison leaned closer to Kirehe. The contact distracted Kirehe because she hadn't yet decided how to feel about it.

According to Madison, she did these things out of affection. Kirehe also liked Madison. She had never liked anyone before. Not this way. Others of her kind, dragoncallers, had a kind of friendship among them. It never rose to this level.

As a welcome respite from this swirl of distressing thoughts, Madison spoke in Kirehe's native language. No one else on the ship understood much more than a few words of it.

"We keep our settlements on the small side so they don't attract attention with a lot of ships coming and going. They're mostly on worlds too difficult or annoying to colonize, or out of the way of trade routes.

"The place he mentioned, Pichet Three, is the world Jaco's from, and it has a nice climate. Lots of trees and some delicious little snail things. Interesting birds. We used to visit once in a while for a kind of vacation.

"About four years ago, the Oligarchy swooped in. They killed or captured everyone and we're pretty sure they check on it now and then in case anyone tries settling again, like bait."

Kirehe bared her teeth. "They're a blight."

"Yes." Madison sighed. "They're also in control of everything that matters."

"And difficult to kill." Kirehe scowled. She and Nihan had tried so hard to kill Viriok. Failing left a bitter taste on her tongue. "He got up."

"I know. They always do." Madison shook her head. "That other word he used, veiligbass, is what we call the head of security for a settlement. He was a guard and helped keep people safe."

Kirehe frowned. "Does this mean he is to blame for the Oligarchy attack on the planet?"

"No." Madison nodded to Oolaang and switched to their language. "You always know everything. She's interested in why Pichet Three fell."

The corners of Oolaang's mouth tugged upward. "I don't always know everything. But I do know the answer to that."

"Because a man was an idiot," Gordy grumbled. He flexed his fingers like he wanted to strangle someone.

"That's true," Oolaang said. "Captain Orsino of the *Grand Bear*, specifically. He conducted a raid on a supply ship carrying a variety of perishable foods from Planaçais Seven. The raid was successful but when the ship jumped away, he accidentally left behind his scout ship, *Little Bear*."

"I like small man," Nihan rumbled. "Good voice."

Kirehe agreed. He had a pleasant, melodious quality when he spoke on a subject he found interesting.

"Instead of heading to their usual rendezvous point," Oolaang continued, "he jumped back to the raid location. Orsino later admitted he panicked because his lover was on the scout. An Oligarchy cruiser had arrived at the location already, probably by chance. They detected Orsino's ship. His navigator plotted the first course they could, which took them to Pichet Three. The cruiser was able to tag the jump and follow."

The foolishness of two young men had caused Kirehe's capture. She could well imagine such an event on a larger scale.

"Boys," Madison said with an annoyed grunt.

Kirehe glared at Jaco, who kept his head down. He had also caused larger problems by doing something stupid for love.

"If you ever want to know anything else about Stardrifter history," Oolaang said with a broad smile, "I'll be happy to tell you. I've studied it quite extensively. That goes for anyone else here too." His smile dimmed. "A great deal of it is tragic, of course. But it's still interesting and worth learning if you're going to be part of our society."

"Thanks, Oolaang." Madison set aside her empty plate. "We'll get you back to Captain Wayward's archives soon. In the meantime, we have about twelve more hours before we reach Veriscova Four. This is a good chance to grab some sleep."

Everyone except Kirehe stood. She watched them all stretch and shuffle deeper into the ship.

Madison picked up plates around Kirehe. "Do you want to share with me?" She smiled with welcome and something more that Kirehe couldn't grasp.

Jaco glanced back too fast for Kirehe to interpret his expression. Lylla waved with a sleepy yawn and took Rho's hand.

In some ways, Kirehe wanted to accept Madison's offer. They would share warmth and spend time together. Alone. It seemed like a good chance to take Madison's help to try to understand all the things she felt.

But her dragons needed her. They'd fled their home and everything they'd ever known.

For Madison, this strange place felt more comfortable, not less. She traveled to reach her home.

Kirehe and her dragons had left their home, probably forever. Nihan would never mate again, and neither would Skila. They would live and die apart from their kind. The four maras, two brothers and two sisters, had no options for mating either. If they tried despite their pheromones, their offspring would have strange physical problems. Kirehe had seen that happen.

"I will stay with the dragons. They're scared and confused." Much like herself.

Madison's face shifted to disappointment. She nodded. "I understand. Get some sleep."

Kirehe wanted to apologize, though she couldn't say for what. "Will they be able to leave the ship and run on this Veriscova Four?"

"Probably." Madison backed toward the door with her hands full of plates. "Unless the *Star* is orbiting the planet in the open, which they almost never do, we'll have to head to the surface to figure out if he's there or not. We should be able to land on the outskirts and you'll be able to take them for an hour or two."

"I see." Kirehe had no idea how something as large as a spaceship could hide, but assumed the answer would involve many other things she had no frame of reference to understand.

How spaceships worked mystified her at least as much as her feelings for Madison.

"If you want some cushions or blankets, there are probably extras.

Just ask anyone." Madison ducked out of the room.

As if Kirehe would ask someone other than Madison.

The dragons provided plenty of cushioning, though. She doubted she'd want anything else.

"Kiki and Madad need hut," Skila whistled.

Kirehe rolled her eyes. "Skila needs sleep." She rubbed Nihan's head with one hand. With the other, she reached for the mara alpha, Rila, and scratched the feathers under her chin. "All need sleep."

"Story," Heetay, one of the male maras, chirped.

Kirehe huffed at them. "Sleep. Story later."

"Story?" the other male, Wooni, begged.

"Story story story story," the second female, Fobi, chanted.

Rila lifted her head. "Story."

Nihan laughed at them, the whistling sound echoing in his chest and off the walls.

"Fine. Story." Kirehe had, thus far, used simple stories to help them understand how to behave like normal mara dragons.

Their treatment in the slave pits meant they had no chance to survive in the wilderness without other wild maras to protect them. At least she'd turned them into a functioning pack. That had helped a great deal already.

She had no more stories of that type to offer. They already knew everything she could teach about how a pack of maras survived and thrived. Repeating one to emphasize it felt wrong in this situation. Though they craved comfort and familiarity, she thought they needed to hear about living on a spaceship.

After all, they had left their homeworld to do that very thing.

With Madison.

"Kirehe?" Jaco leaned into the cargo bay, only his head and one arm and shoulder visible.

She raised her brow, not sure she cared what he wanted.

"I'm sorry. I'm genuinely sorry. I only thought about myself and Madison, though I'm still trying to understand why. What matters is..."

He sighed. The way he met her gaze felt like a challenge, but not to her. A challenge to himself. "You're part of our family now. I will never betray you again."

Kirehe could see how much it cost him to say such a thing. She still felt the phantom wound in her side, though. Not as pain.

The sting of treachery.

"Prove it," she said, careful not to add bite to her words. If he wanted her loyalty, he had to earn it.

His face fell. He nodded and looked at the floor. "I will."

Jaco left the cargo bay.

"I doubt that," Kirehe murmured in his absence. "But for Madison, I will allow you the opportunity to try."

She settled with the dragons, ready to teach them how to avoid insanity from boredom.

CHAPTER 5

MADISON

The FTL jump put them on the star side of Veriscova Four. By the time the ship left the jump, Madison sat in the pilot seat again, as well-rested as possible when she had to sleep on a solid bed instead of in a hammock.

Lylla sat in the navigator seat, ready to get the ship out of the system as needed.

Ship sensors fed Madison data about the system, including an anomaly on the other side of the planet. *Wayward Star* might cause that kind of oddity, but it could've been anything. Including a different Stardrifter ship.

As far as she knew, Oligarchy ships didn't cause that kind of thing. They trundled along in the open. Why hide when you can beat everyone?

Madison tried to keep her hopes low. They might have to visit fifteen planets before they found Uncle Chris.

He had to know she wanted to find him at this point, so she thought he'd try to make that easy. Unless he hated her too much. Anger might make him abandon her, even if it also meant abandoning Oolaang, Shmar, and Jaco.

His anger might also blame those three anyway.

Yep, this reunion would be fun.

She angled the ship to cross into the planet's atmosphere. Where debris and plasma bolts had hit the hull, the ship registered damage from the entry. They'd have to survey the ship to determine if it needed repairs to leave the atmosphere. Oolaang would have to fix it.

Once through the outer atmosphere, she scanned for signals. Some planets had continuous, passive messages broadcast for incoming ships to guide them to a landing. Others had people actively monitoring the space. Some switched back and forth. As far as Madison understood, the difference related entirely to the amount of available manpower.

Nothing.

The ship flew through the planet's airspace. Madison couldn't remember where exactly to find the settlement. She'd expected to rely upon the broadcasts to find it.

Someone needed a swift kick in the butt to get the stupid broadcast running.

Sensors picked up enough garbage to find the place, at least. She aimed toward a bunch of clashing signals, a sure sign of civilization.

With a thought, she activated the intercom. "We're nearing the settlement. Prepare for landing."

"So everything is fine?" Lylla asked.

"More or less. No one is running their broadcast, but that could just be some idiot forgetting to flip a switch."

As soon as she said that, she worried. Stardrifters didn't forget to flip switches. Not that kind.

Sure, they sometimes forgot frivolous stuff, and sometimes did stupid things like Captain Orsino. The people on the ground, though, depended upon the goods coming in with the ships. They needed things from other parts of the galaxy.

Stardrifters stole for survival, not for fun.

They happened to enjoy doing it, of course. If not, they would've come up with alternatives a long time ago.

"I was going to land on the outskirts anyway for Kirehe. Now I think I'm going to put the ship down a little outside the town. We'll have a hike to get into the port, and we'll probably have to move it to resupply, but I don't want to risk the ship."

Madison scanned the area and found a clear space outside the town. She set down the ship there.

The moment she shut down the engines, Madison unbuckled her harness and scrambled out of the cockpit. Lylla followed her as she strode through the ship. Others fell in behind her.

She felt like she led a posse.

"Bring weapons," she said as they reached the cargo bay. "Never hurts to be armed, especially when you're us."

Kirehe stood with Skila on her shoulder.

Gordy cleared his throat. "We should stick together. No one harasses a large group."

"Yes." Madison hit the button on the wall to open the cargo bay door. "Kirehe, meet back at the ship in about two hours."

Kirehe whistled and chirped to her dragons.

Nihan rose and lumbered out of the ship, sniffing the air. The four mara dragons followed him, staying in a close group.

"Two hours," Kirehe said, holding up two fingers. She turned and jogged down the ramp.

Madison watched her dragon warrior princess from behind, admiring the view.

If she couldn't touch Kirehe yet, at least she could watch.

As soon as the dragon cleared the space, Madison led her crew down the ramp.

The pleasantly warm and dry air smelled like damp earth and wood. Their ship's arrival had added a touch of burnt fuel and metal.

Outside the ship, Madison sent Shmar to check as much of the hull as he could while she and Oolaang walked around the ship in the opposite direction. Jaco climbed onto the topside.

Gordy waited with Rho and Lylla, keeping an eye out for anyone approaching. Eventually, someone would come to investigate the unexpected luxury yacht in their backyard.

Oolaang and Madison stood under the plasma blast scar on the underside of the ship.

"There's a score up here," Jaco called to them.

"I've got a big hunk of metal jammed through the hull back here," Shmar called.

So far, they hadn't found anything surprising.

With one of his four hands rubbing his chin, Oolaang said, "This should be fine for our exit here. It'll probably break apart if we try to land on another planet, though. If they have any of that crappy carbon filler here, I can patch it enough to get us a few more entries and exits. Get, oh, ten cubic meters should be enough for three problems of this size and a few smaller ones."

"I'll see what they have," Madison said. She cupped her hands around her mouth and shouted up. "Jaco! Anything else?"

He stepped into sight on the edge of the hull. "A few small marks, nothing worth worrying about. The big one up here, though, I can stick my hand through it. We're lucky it didn't fall apart on entry. Exit…? Maybe it'll last through exit. I'd want Oolaang to check it first. I'll come down and check that one to compare."

Whatever else she thought about Jaco lately, Madison knew she could count on him for this. They'd both done these inspections with her uncle for years. Jaco knew the difference between a big problem and a little problem. So did Shmar.

"Oolaang, have Rho help you check what's inside the ship to see if you can get anything done while we're gone. This one doesn't look as bad as Jaco thinks the other score is, so that one's the priority." Madison returned to the cargo bay ramp.

Rho held a rifle as they squatted beside Lylla. Gordy held a rifle slung across his body and Viriok's spear.

"Oolaang and Rho stay behind," Madison said. "The rest of us are heading into town."

Jaco climbed down the side of the ship, using the cargo bay opening for handholds. He jogged under the ship and stood with his hands on his hips as he scrutinized the score on the underside.

"The one above is definitely worse than this," Jaco said. "I'd expect this one to be fine for one more pass-through, maybe two or three."

"I'll see what I can do about the one on the topside," Oolaang said. "We might take apart some of the guts to patch it if I can find enough rivets."

Madison nodded. "Do what you need to do. Comfort is a distant second place to survival, and we'll at least have to get off this ball of dirt."

"The debris in the back needs some attention," Shmar said as he reached them. "It's not too bad, though. Cut it off and seal the hole, and it'll last as long as the rest of the ship. I could stay behind and do that if we have anything to seal it with."

Oolaang shrugged. "If we don't, you'd be better off going with them to help carry stuff back. And odds are good we don't have anything to work with anyway."

Shmar nodded like he didn't care, which he probably didn't. "I'll go, then. Is there at least a cart or a hand truck in this pokken piece of kut?"

"Didn't see one." Madison grinned. "We should be able to rent or borrow one with the money we stole from the owner of the ship."

Lylla gulped. "Do I really need to go? Because I could stay here."

They had three strapping men, all capable of both fighting and carrying things. Madison knew what to buy and had access to the accounts. Lylla might get in the way.

"You can stay if you want," she told Lylla. "I thought you might like to see a settlement and other kids your age, but it can wait if you'd rather stay."

Lylla nodded so fast her head bobbed like it might fall off. She scurried into the ship and out of sight.

"Poor kid," Madison murmured. "But we need to get moving. Let's go, guys."

She led Jaco, Shmar, and Gordy into the trees. Bright green foliage blocked the blue-white light from the nearby star. They marched at a swift pace, their boots crunching through fallen leaves and releasing a woody fragrance into the air.

"Why didn't we land at the dock?" Jaco asked.

"In case it might spook Uncle Chris." She lied to him casually and effortlessly, a thing she hadn't found quite so easy before. Why? Because she could?

Because she didn't want him to panic.

"There's no way to know what kind of reception we might get anywhere," Gordy said. "They could've met us with guns pointed in our direction because they saw the escape match. There's probably a description of our ship on blast everywhere, and I wouldn't be surprised if the Oligarchy put a bounty on Madison."

"They already had a bounty on me," Madison said with a sniff. "I was a properly high-value criminal before Subjugator Cradok caught me, thank you very much."

Gordy snorted at her. "Excuse me, Your Illegalness. I'm just saying we shouldn't expect to find a friendly welcome anywhere. The lakhans really, really don't like to lose."

"Hey, you know what else is new and exciting?" Jaco asked with fake enthusiasm. "Water is wet!"

Shmar laughed.

Madison chuckled, but she sobered as they neared the outer ring of the settlement. "Shut it, guys. It's time to pretend we're serious."

Like many Stardrifter settlements, this one had a huge outer wall made from local materials. In this case, they'd used tree trunks reinforced with sharpened stone stakes pointing outward. Clumps of earth filled the spaces between the upright logs. Living trees grew along the line to provide cover from visual sweeps.

In most cases, they built the walls to protect the inhabitants from wandering creatures. Such a barrier provided no impediment to ships or the Oligarchy's hevit troopers.

One wide archway offered entry. Though Madison couldn't see it, she knew a door of some sort slid from the side or cranked down at need. For whatever reason, they left it open here. Maybe they only had problems with marauding critters at night.

No one stood sentry, though.

With an open archway, they should've heard noise. People talking in a settlement, even small ones, always offered a baseline murmur in these places.

A few birds screeched in the nearby trees, but no other animals made a sound. Most humans liked pets of some kind. *Wayward Star* had a small menagerie of cats, dogs, and flying things kept by various members of the crew.

No scents hit her nose either. As they passed through the archway, Madison expected to smell food. Animals. Sweat. Waste. Industry.

Nothing.

They stood on the other side of the archway, facing wooden buildings of one and two stories. Dirt paths formed straight lines between them. Trees grew as corner anchors for most buildings. Laundry rippling in a light breeze hung on lines strung from one building to another. Leaves rustled. Insects buzzed.

"Does anybody else feel like we should turn around and leave right now?" Gordy asked.

Jaco gulped. "There's definitely something not right here."

"Where is everyone?" Shmar asked.

"An amazing number of horrifying stories start like this," Madison said with a nod. "Let's not become one of them. Back to the ship. We picked the wrong planet."

They turned around.

The gate clanged. A metal grate fell from the ceiling of the archway.

Everyone swore. No one tried to beat the gate to the ground.

CHAPTER 6

KIREHE

The air smelled strange yet glorious. Kirehe ran with her mara pack, devouring distance at high speed. They surged over fallen trees and under low branches.

These maras had never run in the wilderness before. They shrieked their joy in high-pitched whistles.

Skila flew overhead, swooping between trees and circling trunks. She chirped out her name over and over, probably expecting other kukiris to respond.

Above them all, Nihan swerved through wide gaps between trees. He streaked forward, circled to return, flipped, climbed above the canopy, and plunged into it again.

Kirehe directed the maras, pointing to keep them from running too far from the ship. Despite the two hours Madison had given them, she wanted to stay relatively close in case anything happened. If the ship needed to lift off suddenly for some reason, she had no desire to stay on this foreign planet with its unknown dangers.

No, that was a lie.

Running unfettered for the first time in months, she wanted to stay on this planet forever. The dragons all loved it.

Come nightfall, though, they would have to tend to the routine concerns of food, shelter, and safety. This planet could have nothing more dangerous than a kukiri, or it could have predators to rival Nihan.

Her krata called to her as he returned to them, swerving among the tree trunks. "Machine hum," he rumbled.

"Slow," Kirehe whistled.

The maras slowed to a walk around her. Kirehe turned her head and listened. She heard the soft, high-pitched whine of hevits nearby.

The man-sized creatures, capable of shifting their feathers to create perfect camouflage, emitted a hum she and the dragons hated. Among her people, this ability on the part of all dragoncallers had kept them safe from enemies with mechanical vehicles.

Why these creatures, the Oligarchy's elite stealth troopers made a similar sort of hum as machines, Kirehe had no idea. That hum, though, allowed her and all the dragons to detect them without sight or smell. She welcomed the anomaly.

"Skila, scout." Kirehe pointed in the direction of the hum. "That way."

The tiny dragon shot through the air without a sound.

"Rila," Kirehe said to the mara alpha, "hunt. Kill the ones you can't see."

Rila chirped her understanding. The four maras crouched low and stalked forward, using the trees and shrubs for cover.

They left signs of their passage in the form of heads too high, shifting branches, and cracking twigs. Considering their background, they did an exceptional job.

She would teach them better.

"Nihan, come get me!" she whistled.

The mighty dragon flipped in a sinuous wave and slowed to land beside her. His wings picked up every leaf and stick nearby. Kirehe ignored the whirling storm to leap onto his back. He jumped into the air, bounced off a tree trunk, and flapped to shoot through the canopy.

They soared through the air unhindered.

On her homeworld, flying above the treetops had carried too much danger to do it for long.

"Nice here," Nihan chirped.

"Yes. Go below. Watch the maras."

He dove into the trees again. They swerved and slipped around trunks at high speed. Ahead, the mara pack devoured their kills.

Nihan flew around the pack as slowly as possible, watching them.

Kirehe counted four hevit heads. Bits of wires and metal sparked and glinted among the flesh and feathers of the avian warriors. Part lakhan machine. She figured that might explain why no one could see them, but they hummed like the ships.

As they swung in a wide arc, Skila plowed into Kirehe's chest. The tiny dragon had no hope of flying as fast as Nihan. She'd chosen to fly at him instead.

"Big machine! Big machine! Big machine!"

"Where?" Kirehe covered the kukiri with her hand, holding Skila in place.

"No trees. Near."

Hevits had come from a big machine in a clearing. "Big machine like ours?"

"Yes! New big machine, same size."

An Oligarchy ship had landed on this planet. Kirehe still knew little about their tactics, but she suspected they rarely sent only one ship to a place. Even if they did, she'd gotten the impression people on one ship could speak to people on another ship.

She wished to check with Madison yet lacked any means to do so without leaving the area. If she left, she thought the hevits or their handlers would discover the corpses and report about them. Such a report would bring reinforcements.

"Find the big machine and attack it," she told Nihan.

Kirehe regretted not bringing her spear.

"Do not kill big machine, only disable. Maybe food inside."

Nihan roared for the maras to follow him. He flew over them and kept going.

They burst out of the trees to discover a clearing filled with a blocky spaceship near the size of their own stolen ship. Though she saw no one, she heard not only the larger ship but also several hevits.

Someone laughed. Perhaps others had brought the hevits.

Could hevits fly spaceships?

Nihan flew at the top of the ship. He scraped his claws over the hull, ripping apart screeching metal in thick furrows.

The laughter stopped.

With great heaves of his wings, Nihan leaped off the edge of the ship and soared upward. Kirehe checked the ground.

Her maras streamed into the clearing and mauled hevits.

Again, she wished for her spear. Kirehe held on to one of Nihan's bone spikes, waiting for the right time to leap off his back.

Laser blasts fired into the air. Nihan swung in an arc to avoid them. One shot past Kirehe close enough to feel the ripple of heat in the air.

Kirehe flung Skila to the side. The kukiri didn't belong in battle.

Nihan roared his anger at the ship and the gun shooting at him.

As they plummeted to the ground, Kirehe caught sight of the person with the gun. She had no name for their kind, having discovered neither a hevit nor a pharedim. The being had a large, blocky body with thick muscles and bright blue flesh.

Kirehe leaped off Nihan's back when he scraped his claws over the ship again. She ran to the side and flung herself at the shooter.

Her body collided with his before he could aim his rifle at her. They hit the ground together.

The bulky being failed to cushion her fall. She'd hit a solid wall of muscle. This creature seemed to have lost their balance rather than take any kind of harm from her impact.

Kirehe rolled to the side rubbing her arm, uncertain how to injure a person who suffered no ill effect from such a blow. Even Viriok had reacted to her strikes.

Shooting them with their own guns seemed plausible. At worst, she might need to have the dragons retreat so Madison could devise a plan for the situation.

Madison could plan for anything.

The creature retained their grip on their rifle with one hand. Kirehe leaped at the weapon. Her enemy sat up. She flipped over him, wrapping her hands around the rifle.

When she finished her flip, her feet hit the ground. The rest of her arched over because the being still held the rifle. So did Kirehe.

"Rila!" Kirehe twisted to gain leverage. She yanked at the rifle.

Her enemy did nothing other than hold the weapon and stare like they had no way to comprehend the situation.

"Fine," Kirehe snarled.

She stepped close, with her back to the enemy. The moment she released the weapon, she moved her hands to the being's arm. They had a wrist like anyone else with hands. With her thumbs on the back of their hand and her fingers gripping underneath, she twisted their arm.

The being grunted and turned. Kirehe applied more pressure and lifted their hand while pressing down on their elbow. They dropped to one knee.

They made a low, confused noise. They also dropped the rifle.

Kirehe shoved. She rolled in a backward somersault over the rifle, picking it up. When she landed on her feet, she pointed the weapon and fired at her enemy.

The bolts jolted their body. They collapsed to the ground, twitching.

For good measure, Kirehe shot them again.

She spun to survey the situation.

Several hevit corpses littered the area. The stench of blood and death hung thick in the air. Her maras licked blood off each other's bodies. Even these impaired maras would never stop to do that while enemies lurked nearby.

With the rush of battle passing, Kirehe wondered what purpose the hevits had served on this world.

"Skila!" Kirehe carried the rifle to the open cargo bay door, intending to check for anyone hiding inside.

Nihan plunged his claws into the ship as deeply as he could from the top. Metal screamed under his onslaught.

Skila fluttered to land on Kirehe's shoulder. "Excite!" She danced from hind claw to hind claw.

"Find Madison, then come back. I need to know if she's in trouble and where to find her. Very important."

"Find Madad! Find Kiki!" Skila leaped off Kirehe's shoulder and shot into the air.

"Nihan, enough," Kirehe said. "It's disabled."

Her krata stopped destroying the craft and remained sitting atop it. He would make sure the maras stayed close.

Kirehe stalked inside, yet again wishing she had a spear. If the rifle failed for any reason, she knew nothing about how to fix it. Later, she would ask Madison to show her how these shooting weapons functioned. The knowledge seemed important.

Especially if she kept encountering enemies using them while she had no spear.

She also missed her machete. The blade, left behind on Rikor Six, had served her well.

Maybe Madison's uncle could get her a new one. Madison clearly considered him capable.

This ship boasted less ornament than their stolen yacht. Blank metal walls formed a room wide enough for six people to stand shoulder-to-shoulder. A forest of black straps hung from the ceiling, each with a loop on the end. They reached to her armpits. Likely, the hevits traveled in this craft while standing with the loops around their arms to hold them steady.

A door in the back of this section, which took Kirehe twenty shallow paces to cross, opened into a short, narrow hall. The hall had one open doorway on each side, halfway down, and ended at an open doorway to a place like the control area on their yacht.

"If any inside," she said in the foreign language, "show and no die. I find, you die." Probably, she lied.

Madison would decide what to do with a prisoner. She might choose execution for a variety of reasons. Kirehe wouldn't argue with her.

"Please don't kill me," a smooth, pretty voice wailed. Something metal clunked against something else metal from the left side. Boots clomped in a hurry.

Kirehe's new prisoner stumbled through the doorway to the left with their hands high.

"Pharedim," she spat.

Every line of the woman's body from head to toe had flawless symmetry inside her maroon and black jumpsuit. The effect of such perfection set Kirehe's teeth on edge. Her recent experience with frustrating and cruel specimens of the race made her want to recant her offer of at least temporary amnesty.

The pharedim woman gulped and held her hands in front of her, raised and empty. "I'm just a pilot."

A pilot who unflinchingly and unfailingly followed orders from a lakhan.

"Why fly here?"

The pharedim's gaze flicked to the gun and back to Kirehe's face. "Orders. I don't ask why. They don't tell me. I just fly the ship."

Kirehe needed someone else to question this pharedim. She had no good questions to ask. Since she had no intention of using the gun, she lowered it to point at the floor.

"You trouble, I snap neck. Yes?"

"I understand." The pharedim nodded.

"Go. Out ship." Kirehe backed into the strap compartment.

"Message received," a strange man said. His voice had that same distant, machine quality as Madison's over the intercom. "Evaluating."

The pharedim froze, then she leaped at Kirehe.

Kirehe stepped aside. As the pharedim passed, Kirehe used the gun as a club to hit the pharedim's gut. She took the woman's arm and twisted it. The pharedim's arm snapped with a wet crack.

No noise came from the pharedim's open mouth as she stumbled and fell to the floor face-first.

"I warn." Kirehe tossed aside the gun. She planted her knee on the woman's back to hold her down. "Who talk?"

Though the pharedim's mouth opened and shut, she said nothing. Tears streamed from her eyes.

Breaking her arm had rendered her useless. Madison might regret the lost opportunity to interrogate the pharedim, but Kirehe knew a problem when she saw one.

She snapped the pharedim's neck and hoped the group could manage without the information source she'd just killed.

CHAPTER 7

MADISON

Madison crouched inside a building, trying with all her might not to throw up. The overpowering stench of messy death and stale alcohol made her eyes water and her stomach roil.

Several corpses lay strewn across the floor, all thick with a cloud of buzzing flies. Near the bar in the back, ooze covered the floor in a sticky layer.

She breathed through the lower hem of her shirt held over her mouth and nose.

Gordy fired at random intervals at the hevit troopers who'd chased them into the first open door they'd found. He grimaced at the heavy, disgusting smell but otherwise showed no sign of distress.

Laser rifle blasts zapped through the partially open doorway to hit the floor, wall, and liquor bottles.

At least they'd had a few seconds to run. The invisible hevits had announced themselves with the gate before opening fire. Madison had the feeling they'd expected the group to rush the gate in a vain effort to escape.

"Maddie, you have a plan, right?" Jaco asked. He crouched beside her, also breathing through his shirt.

Like Madison, he had no weapons. They hadn't found any on the yacht, and had only brought three from Rikor Six. Gordy had one. Shmar had the other. The third had stayed at the ship with Rho.

"You better," Shmar grumbled on her other side. "This is a deathtrap."

"Obviously." Madison had no such plan. These guys didn't need to know that.

They sheltered inside Captain Wayward's most favorite bar in the entire galaxy. Part of the wooden door hung from the lower hinge. The rest covered the floor in the form of jagged pieces of wood. Broken tables and chairs, some made of plastic and others wood, littered the room. Smashed bottles and barrels had sprayed their alcohol until it had congealed and partially evaporated.

The poor souls on the floor had put up a fight, at least.

If she wanted to venture deeper into the room or touch anything, Madison thought she'd find a pistol or two. People on worlds like this rarely left home without at least a sidearm.

"Skila!" Shmar shouted.

Madison sighed with relief. Kirehe would save them.

The tiny dragon streaked into the room, chirped in distress, and flew out again.

"Yeah, we think it's gross too," Madison muttered. "The plan is we wait for Kirehe to rescue us."

Gordy fired through the door. "That plan sounds like it has some flaws. The biggest one is the part where we can't see these pokkentoffs to know if I'm shooting anywhere near them."

Shmar raised his rifle and fired three shots in three different directions. "I'm with Gordy. Come up with a better plan."

Although Madison agreed with them, she had nothing. "We could all run through the flies and corpses to reach the back room and see if there's anything useful."

"I've heard worse ideas." Gordy fired again. "Go. I'll cover you. Maybe I can get one before I join you."

"Great," Jaco said as he straightened enough to move. "On the bright side, maybe there are no corpses?"

Madison hated this idea, but she launched herself into a run. She stayed doubled-over to keep her head down and wound her way through the debris and corpses. The sludge at the back of the room stuck to her boots. Each step made a ripping noise like her boots tore in half, and she had to slow down or fall on her face.

She shoved open the back door with her shoulder and stumbled inside. Jaco and Shmar followed her.

They found a dark room with no flies and no stench, which counted as an improvement.

"Shmar, wait for Gordy. Jaco, help me look for the back door." Madison shuffled as fast as she dared, her boots still making sticky contact with the floor. She held out her hands to avoid walking into anything.

"What? Why do we want to leave?" Jaco's boots made the same sticking noises as Madison's. "The hevits are outside."

"Do you really think half a wooden door is going to keep them out for long? We need to keep moving so they don't pin us down." Madison's hip hit something. She grunted.

"We're already pinned down," Shmar snapped. "For all we know, they're waiting by the back door already."

Madison patted the thing she'd walked into. "I found a table and a tablet." She picked up the handheld screen and ran her fingers along the edges. When she found the power button, she tapped it.

Blue light glowed from the screen, blasting her in the face and blinding her real eye. The cybereye compensated. She turned the screen and blinked while her real eye adjusted, using it as a flashlight to scan the walls.

The tablet pointed at Jaco first. He cringed and held up an arm to protect his face. "Kut on a cog, warn a guy when you do that."

Gordy ran into the room. Shmar slammed shut the door.

"I got one," Gordy said as he leaned against the door and caught his breath. "But there are plenty more where that came from."

The screen's light shone on a door. "Everybody ready to run?" Madison pointed the screen at the floor.

"Wait," Jaco said. He touched her arm and prodded it up again. "What's that?"

With Jaco's guidance, the light pointed at a metal panel on the wall with a bar handle.

"That," Gordy said as he hurried to the panel, "is a small weapons locker. The kind a veiligbaas might put in a central location for anyone to use when a settlement is assaulted." He smacked the handle and opened the panel.

Inside, the screen's light revealed four kinds of objects they'd all seen and used before. The stash held five small grenades, two pistols, three rifle recharge packs, and three smoke bombs.

"It's not much," Gordy said as he passed the pistols to Madison and Jaco, "but every little bit helps."

"Only three smoke, that's a shame." Madison checked the pistol and found it fully charged. "I think we should open the door, pop a smoke, run like hell, turn right, run some more, and find another hole."

"I'll take the lead," Gordy said.

"I'll drop the smoke," Madison said. "Shmar, take rearguard." She handed him two grenades. He didn't need instructions for those. They all knew better than to waste what few resources they had.

Jaco took another two grenades, and Madison tucked the last one in her pocket. She used a different pocket for the other two smoke bombs and tucked the tablet under her arm.

Later, they'd check the tablet's contents. She doubted they'd find any final messages, but they might find some useful information. For example, the date of Captain Wayward's most recent visit.

Gordy opened the door. Madison popped the smoke bomb and rolled it through. Gordy shut the door.

After a count of five, Gordy opened the door again.

They ran like hell. At least the acrid tang of the smoke smelled better than a pile of death.

The four of them burst through their thick cloud and kept running. Gordy ducked around a building to the right, then another to the left. Madison huffed and puffed to keep up with him.

At the first open door he saw, Gordy ducked inside.

Their new hole thankfully had few bugs and no corpses. It smelled like rotting vegetables, but not even close to how bad the tavern had stank.

Outside light streamed through two windows. They'd slipped into someone's dining room. An abandoned meal remained on the table, a few flies buzzing lazily among the plates. One chair lay on the floor, overturned. The rest had been pushed back from the table but not knocked over.

Madison's least favorite part of the room was a small chair designed for an infant. On the floor beside it, she spied a spoon designed for a toddler's small grip.

Oligarchy stooges had no sense of honor or decency. They killed or enslaved anyone in their way. No remorse. No mercy.

No soul.

She tore her gaze from the evidence they'd find the corpses of kids if they looked hard enough.

Without coordinating, the four of them flanked the door and waited.

A dark thought about Uncle Chris flickered in Madison's head. They hadn't checked the corpses in the tavern. If Christopher Wayward had sat in that tavern drunk off his ass when the hevits showed up, no question his corpse fed the flies.

No, he'd gone to Dridi Prime. Or maybe someplace else. The Oligarchy had made calculations based upon the yacht's jump trajectory. Even though they hadn't had time to tag the yacht and follow, the yacht had a small FTL drive. Oligarchy ships could've easily outrun them here.

Even if they hadn't known about Veriscova Four, they could've found it and murdered everyone before the yacht arrived. She had a lot less experience with planetary corpses than ship-side ones. On a ship, she'd guess those people had all died a few days earlier. On a planet with plenty of wilderness around, maybe this kind of thing only took a few hours.

Of course, she had someone with a lot more expertise handy. With the hevits out looking for them instead of firing at them, they had a little time to talk.

"Gordy, how old would you guess those tavern corpses were?" she asked.

He frowned at the floor. "Between the smell and the bug activity, I'd guess a few days. But those people were cut up, not blasted. The hevits killed them with blades. Innards bring the bugs fast. If we could find some intact bodies, that would help narrow it down. Not that I want to find more bodies, but I think it's clear everyone here is dead."

Madison took a deep breath, trying not to think about the toddler she knew someone had carried out of this house when the attack happened. "Do you think it could've happened only a few hours ago?"

Gordy grimaced. She had a feeling he got the point of her question. "It's possible, yes. The hevits did set a trap for us, after all."

Jaco blinked at her, his mouth falling open in horror. He said nothing.

"What do you mean?" Shmar asked.

Good ol' Shmar, always there to make sure Madison had to spell out and acknowledge the terrible things in simple detail.

"I think the Oligarchy guessed our destination from the orientation of our jump and sent these hevits ahead."

Shmar grimaced like he might throw up. "You mean we did what Orsino did."

"We didn't let them tag us," Jaco whispered. "How could they have known?"

Gordy sighed and closed his eyes. "I don't want to be the one to think of this, but this settlement may not be the only one. They could have sent ships to every planet they think might have a settlement within a particular range of our last jump location and slaughtered everyone. Their FTL drives are faster than that piece of kut we took."

Madison felt like Gordy read the worst things clicking through her brain. "Yeah, that's what I think they did. We're an excuse. The reason they decided to do something they could've done anytime but never bothered to. If they jumped a cruiser to a central location and sent out assault or troop ships, they could've gotten here six or seven hours ago."

Shmar swore under his breath. He hopped to his feet like he needed to pace.

A long blade slammed through the wall where Shmar had sat a moment earlier.

Madison leaped to her feet with a terrified, surprised screech and popped a smoke bomb.

They ran deeper into the house.

Jaco tossed a grenade.

CHAPTER 8

KIREHE

Though she examined the ship's interior, Kirehe needed someone else to come and determine if they wanted any of it.

She found silvery packages in bins and had no idea what to make of them.

The ship curiously lacked any places designed for sleeping. Hevits, so it seemed, did not get beds. Not even hammocks.

She stepped outside again to find Nihan eating the blocky being who'd shot at him. Better that than to leave behind a witness, she supposed. At least the creature hadn't suffered.

Skila plowed into Kirehe's back, hitting hard enough to knock her forward a step. Kirehe spun and caught the tiny dragon before she fell.

Lying in her hands, the stunned kukiri chirped drunken nonsense.

Kirehe could think of no reason for Skila to fly so fast other than danger. "Skila. Where is Madison?"

"Madad," Skila chirped.

"Yes. Madad. Where?"

Skila whistled long and low like she had no sense. "Dead."

Her blood turned to ice, Kirehe blinked at her kukiri. No. They had not escaped that horrible pit on Rikor Six to die on this stupid dirt planet. "What?"

"Huts."

"Nihan!" If something had happened to Madison, Kirehe needed to see it. And if anyone had harmed Madison, they would die. "Rila, bring the pack. Follow. More bad feather machines to kill."

Nihan shoved a forelimb at her. Kirehe climbed onto his back. The big dragon slammed his claws into the hevit ship and leaped off the top.

"Climb," Kirehe told him. "Find the town."

They streaked into the sky, flying higher and higher.

Kirehe watched below, looking for the town. She saw the hevit ship and the yacht, each a fair distance from the other. Between them and to one side, a puff of white smoke clung to a few trees. She saw no other evidence of a town.

Like her own people, they used the trees to camouflage their settlement.

"The smoke. That must be it."

As she offered the prompting, Nihan dove under the canopy again so the maras could follow him. He trumpeted his presence, also giving them noise to chase.

Gripping her kukiri and her rifle, Kirehe hoped Skila had made a mistake. She hoped they arrived in time.

"Expect shooting!" she told her krata.

They soared over a wall made from logs lined between trees and packed together with dirt and stone. The stench of death and the hum of hevits both hung thick inside the wall.

More than before, Kirehe wanted her spear. She tucked Skila down the front of her shirt and raised the rifle. As Nihan streaked over the town, Kirehe fired in a wavering line. Puffs of dust rose from the impacts of her shots.

Nihan had to slice through narrow passages between buildings while staying under the canopy. He aimed for the hevits. Kirehe fired in their area.

They found dissipating smoke in three places, all near building doors. Outside one, they discovered two hevit corpses.

Something boomed behind them. Nihan turned to go back and find it. Kirehe's rifle clicked without firing.

The stupid gun had a limit to the number of times it could shoot.

"Madison!" Kirehe roared.

She saw blood trailing from an indistinct shimmer on the ground. Kirehe threw her useless rifle at it.

Nihan swooped low and snatched two hevits off the ground. Kirehe's rifle hit the bleeding hevit and knocked it to the ground. Its feathers shifted.

Someone shot the downed hevit.

The maras streamed into the area, tearing through hevits.

After climbing a few dozen meters, Nihan smashed together the hevits in his claws and tossed them aside.

"Land. We fight."

Nihan obliged. They dove at the ground. He backwinged, driving dirt and debris into the air.

Kirehe jumped off his back and sprinted at a hevit. Nihan snatched another in his jaws and crunched it. The maras kept moving, seeking more hevits to maul.

"Madison!" Kirehe heard another hevit behind her. She grabbed handfuls of the one in front of her and spun. One hevit impaled the other.

"Kirehe!" Madison called.

"Madad!" Skila chirped.

"You said she was dead," Kirehe grumbled as she threw the dead hevit at the live one. Nihan slapped both into a wall.

"Saw bodies," Skila whistled. "Many dead. Head funny."

Nihan crushed the last hevit.

Kirehe put a hand on her hip and scolded the kukiri peeking her head out of Kirehe's shirt. "You should know better than to stop by hitting me."

"Is it safe yet?" Madison called.

"Yes, it's safe." Kirehe rubbed under Skila's chin so the kukiri would know she hadn't messed up too much.

Madison led Gordy, Shmar, and Jaco out of a nearby building. They hurried to her.

Gordy had the spear. He could keep it. They had another one, and she should've thought to take it. Her fault, not his.

"I am so glad you showed up when you did," Madison said as she approached. "Can I hug you?"

For once, Madison asked first. Kirehe preferred that to the random displays of affection Madison tended to inflict.

"Yes."

With a sigh of relief, Madison wrapped her arms around Kirehe. The embrace released tension Kirehe had held from the moment Skila had suggested Madison's death.

Seeing Madison had dispelled that concern.

Touching Madison made things real.

When Madison let go, Kirehe said, "We found a ship with hevits and a pharedim. And another person." She offered a description of the being Nihan had eaten.

"A tolo," Madison said. "Not too bright, pretty slow, but strong, tough, and able to follow directions. The Oligarchy uses them for grunt work. Tell me about this pharedim, though."

While they spoke using Kirehe's language, the three men stood in a loose arc and kept watch. Kirehe found this charming. As if they would see anything coming before Nihan noticed it.

"She said she was just the pilot. While I spoke to her, the ship talked and said it had received her report." Kirehe tried to remember the other word. She wasn't sure she knew what it meant. "I think it said 'availabitating'? Something like that."

Madison moved her lips and squinted at the ground. "Evaluating?"

"This sounds right, yes."

She nodded. "Okay. That means they needed to pass on whatever the pharedim reported for someone else to make a decision about how to proceed. Where's the pharedim? Did you tie her up so we could question her?"

Kirehe grimaced. "She tried to fight me."

"Ah. She's dead because you're amazing and wouldn't hold back against a pharedim." Madison shrugged with a smile around the edges of her mouth. "That's okay. Where's the ship? Is it big enough to hold us all? That would save us the time to repair the yacht."

"The ship is..." Kirehe sighed. She should've considered that option. "Not able to fly anymore."

Madison stared at her.

Kirehe pointed at Nihan.

Nihan twitched his tail.

"Okay." Madison raised her brow at Nihan, who continued to twitch his tail. "Did he rip it apart? Are there still supplies and maybe parts to salvage?"

"He damaged the outside. The inside remains intact."

"That's something." Madison tapped her chin in thought.

The gesture made Kirehe smile.

"Guys, we might have company coming," Madison told the men. "Jaco, check the bodies in the tavern to make sure none of them is Captain Wayward."

Jaco paled. Shmar scowled at the ground and muttered something to Jaco, who nodded.

"Gordy and Shmar," Madison continued, "our ship still needs repairs. Find whatever you can to fill that plasma scar and get it back to the ship. Take other supplies if you guys can carry it all in one trip. Don't leave Jaco in town by himself. I'll be with Kirehe, checking the enemy ship."

Kirehe whistled for the maras. As the men jogged to handle their tasks, Rila led her pack to Nihan.

"Guard that one." She pointed to Gordy. "When he returns to our big machine, guard it instead."

He could take care of himself, but of the three men, she liked him the best. They would need an escort while transporting the mysterious supplies to avoid problems with local creatures.

Rila nodded and whistled her understanding. The pack turned and followed Gordy and Shmar.

"Nihan, we fly back to the enemy big machine." Kirehe helped Madison climb onto Nihan's back to experience her first krata flight.

Oolaang had not enjoyed his experience on Nihan's back. Pharedim and hevits had shot at them, though. This flight would not involve battle.

Madison sat in front of Kirehe and gripped bone spikes without being told. She settled with her back against Kirehe. Her entire body stiffened with tension.

"This will be fun, right? It's exciting, not terrifying?"

Kirehe clamped her knees in place and pushed Madison forward so they leaned over Nihan's broad shoulders. She tucked Skila safely between them.

"Of course," Kirehe said.

To Nihan, she whistled, "Slow. Easy. She is scared and we are not in danger."

Nihan turned his head to see her with one large, yellow-green eyes. His slitted pupil widened and narrowed.

She resigned herself to his mischief.

The krata bounded across the ground, his body rising and falling in bone-jarring waves. He leaped onto a building, jumped to a tree, bounced off a roof, and flapped into the air.

Through this, Madison pressed against Kirehe and tightened more and more until Kirehe thought Madison might explode. She shivered. Her eyes stayed screwed shut, even the machine one.

Nihan burst through the canopy and flipped in the air.

Kirehe held them in place. She put her mouth next to Madison's ear. "You are safe. I won't let you fall."

Her krata swished from side to side like a pendulum slicing through the sky.

"I promise," she murmured to Madison.

Madison said nothing and remained taut.

If she chided Nihan, Kirehe had a feeling he would do worse. She needed to distract Madison. All that tension would give her a headache, and they needed their pilot to make the yacht go. Kirehe doubted a headache helped.

The one time Madison had kissed her, Kirehe had found it exceptionally distracting. She'd liked the hug. Even this closeness, despite the cause, felt good.

But she refused to do such a thing without asking first. Kirehe wanted that simple courtesy. Madison deserved it also.

"May I kiss you?"

"What?" Madison blinked and jerked her head aside. Her body remained tight and tense. She stared at Kirehe despite the wind whipping past.

Kirehe assumed she'd asked at the wrong time. "Nothing."

"Wait. You said—" Madison pressed a palm to Kirehe's cheek and kissed her.

Heat rushed around Kirehe's body in strange places. She wanted to let go of Nihan's spikes and squeeze Madison close.

Madison's body relaxed. The tension drifted out of her.

When they broke apart, Nihan stood on the ground beside the hevit ship. He'd stopped swerving and landed gently to avoid dislodging them.

Kirehe met Madison's surprised gaze with only a few inches between their noses.

They stared at each other. Kirehe had no idea what to say. She wondered why she had to gasp for breath.

Madison blinked first. She turned her head. "Um. Thank you. That was…nice."

"Yes. Nice." The spell over Kirehe broke. She took Madison's hand and helped her climb off Nihan's back.

With their feet on solid ground, the two women stood side-by-side, not looking at each other.

"Nihan certainly did tear up the ship," Madison said. Her voice seemed higher than normal.

Kirehe crossed her arms over her chest to avoid rubbing her lips. "I told him to disable it. I thought it might try to leave while we killed the hevits."

"Makes sense." Madison coughed and strode to the open bay door.

Kirehe smacked Nihan's forelimb. "That was mean."

"Fun," Nihan whistled with laughter.

"Kiki likes Madad!" Skila chirped. She climbed up Kirehe's chest to perch on her shoulder. "Kiki likes Madad!" The kukiri repeated this several times while Kirehe rolled her eyes.

When Kirehe reached the ship door, she found Madison crouched over the dead pharedim.

"Subjugator Cradok is absolutely after us," she said. "These are his colors."

CHAPTER 9

MADISON

With no way to know what message the pharedim had sent, Madison wanted to get away from the planet as soon as possible. She considered trying to check the message log. If she had a small army of Stardrifters to haul out booty, she'd do it.

She instead moved swiftly to check the contents of the ship. They carried sealed rations, rifle recharge packs, medical supplies, stim packs, and basic ship repair material. Oolaang would appreciate the tools.

As she moved, she stuffed down her glee that Kirehe had asked to kiss her. Sure, she'd done it because Madison had found flying on Nihan's back completely terrifying. Not the point.

They'd kissed. On purpose. For several seconds.

That kiss had inspired all kinds of excellent plans in her head. Most required prying Kirehe out of her dragon nest for an hour or two during their next FTL jump. She'd come up with a way.

And ask permission for everything. Every single thing.

"Kirehe?" She returned to the hevit holding bay struggling under the weight of a box for Oolaang. "Can you take this to Oolaang? Ask him if he wants to come inspect this ship or trust me to dismantle whatever he needs. If he wants to come, bring him."

Kirehe nodded and took the box. She held it with one arm like it weighed nothing. "Back soon." She turned and whistled.

The big dragon thumped the ground with his claws.

Madison watched the awesome sight of her warrior princess climbing onto Nihan's back while holding a heavy box. The woman's whole body rippled with muscle.

As soon as the dragon loped to gain some speed, Madison ducked inside the ship again. She needed to focus.

On something besides how Kirehe tasted. No other girl Madison had kissed had ever tasted like that. They all faded into a blur of mundane sameness compared to Kirehe.

Yes, time to focus on these rations. She almost wanted to open one to discover what hevits ate.

The ship's radio activated. "Assault Cradok alpha twelve, your request for reinforcements has been accepted and confirmed. Estimated arrival time is one hour three minutes."

If she had any question of whose forces they faced, that message dispelled them.

They had an hour to get out of the system. Had anything they'd done in town left enough evidence to suggest their presence? She thought they might scan the site and assume the local fauna had attacked.

She preferred for Cradok not to track them well enough to realize they'd killed this many hevits with this much relative ease.

Heavy thumps on the ground announced Nihan's return. Madison carried a second box out of the ship.

Kirehe helped Oolaang off the dragon's back. The small man took a deep breath when he put his boots on the ground.

"I've got another box," Madison handed it to Kirehe with a smile. "The ship just received another message. We have forty-five minutes."

Better to give them a shorter deadline to make everyone move faster than to risk detection.

"Kirehe, take this box to our ship then check on the guys and let them know we have a time limit. Oolaang, whatever you want, we have to get it fast."

Oolaang clapped two hands and rubbed them together. His other two hands held up a crowbar and a power screwdriver. "Let's loot this thing."

Nihan took Kirehe from the site again.

Madison let Oolaang do his thing. When he asked for her help, she gave it. Otherwise, she packed the supplies in boxes for Kirehe to ferry to their ship.

Twenty minutes later, Oolaang gave Madison directions for what else to loot and returned to the yacht to complete the critical repairs. Kirehe ferried Gordy to the ship and they worked together to take as much as possible in as few trips as possible.

When Madison and Gordy returned to the yacht for the final time, Oolaang had finished patching the topside and worked on the underbelly instead. Shmar and Jaco needed one more minute to finish sealing the hole caused by the debris.

To her immense relief, Jaco had assured her he hadn't found Captain Wayward or anyone else they knew among the corpses.

"I just need ten more minutes," Oolaang said before Madison opened her mouth to gripe about the time again.

"You've already had ten more minutes."

"But I can seal it." He kept working. The flame from the blowtorch in his hand glinted off his goggles. "I have what I need. If I can finish sealing it, we can handle at least ten more atmosphere crossings. Maybe a full dozen."

Ten more crossings meant the ability to safely check four more settlements and leave fast if they needed to. "How many if you can't?"

"Three, maybe four."

She sighed and checked the time. "Fine. Ten minutes. The second you're done, you get your ass inside the ship."

"Yes, ma'am."

Leaving him behind, she hurried to where Kirehe and the dragons lounged in the trees beside the ship. "As soon as Oolaang is done, we're leaving." She considered Kirehe might not grasp the full meaning and added, "That means get on the ship and get settled now. We account for everyone now and prepare to lift off so there's no waiting when he's ready."

Kirehe nodded. She stood and planted the butt of her spear on the ground like a goddess in need of worship. "I understand."

Given more time, Madison had every intention of piling that adoration at Kirehe's bare feet. And as many of her other parts as Kirehe allowed.

"Good." Madison turned her back on whistles and chirping. She sent Lylla to strap herself into the navigator seat. Rho took a seat in her new impromptu medical bay, where she could strap in.

"Gordy," she called to her lone man standing watch over the perimeter. "Get those two men off the ship and into it. Now. As soon as Oolaang is inside, you do a headcount and shut the door. We're taking off immediately."

"Aye," Gordy called back.

Feeling more like a captain than usual, Madison marched into the ship and strapped herself into the cockpit. She plugged the cable into her eye socket to connect to the ship. The systems whirred to life.

Everything would be fine.

They'd find Captain Wayward and his ship.

After that, Uncle Chris would take charge. Madison could stop commanding everything and take five minutes to breathe once in a while. With Kirehe.

This plan had no reason to fail.

"Where are we going?" Lylla asked.

"Dridi Prime," Madison said. "But let's be smart about it. Find a point between here and there and take us to that. Keep doing that until we land someplace without Oligarchy ships in range. I don't want them to figure anything out from our trajectory, so keep that in mind when you pick points."

Lylla nodded. "I can do that. I like these maps. They feel right. Like something I learned when I was little but can't quite remember."

"Like a lullaby your mom used to sing but you can't remember the words?"

A profound silence following this question made Madison check Lylla.

The girl faced the map screen with her eyes closed. "Yes," Lylla murmured, "exactly like that."

Madison sighed at herself. "Sorry. It's easy to forget how raw that is for you when it's been such a long time for me."

"Yeah," Lylla said, her voice staying soft. "I'm okay. We're gonna outjump the Oligarchy."

"We sure are, thanks to you." Madison reached as far as she could toward Lylla. "Best navigator in the galaxy."

The girl rewarded her reach with a slap on her palm. "Let's do this."

Jaco stepped into the control pod. "Who do you want in the second seat here?"

Madison considered telling him to go hide from Kirehe someplace else. They'd have plenty of hours to grate against each other's nerves, though. "I think Lylla's fine now, so anyone can sit there. Sit your ass down if you want."

He sat and strapped on the harness.

Shmar poked his head into the control pod. "All dragons inside the ship. Gordy is watching Oolaang and prodding him to go faster. Rho is strapped in. I'm going to go do that. Kirehe says she doesn't need any straps, so I guess she didn't learn anything from our Rikor Six departure. But I'm not going to argue with her. That's your department."

"Thank you, Shmar." Madison flipped a few switches to try to entice Oolaang to hurry. The fuel gauges reported what she expected. She'd seen how much the guys had brought from the town.

"We…" Shmar sighed. "Did Gordy tell you about the rest of the bodies?"

Madison almost said yes to avoid hearing confirmation of what she already knew. "No."

"They killed everyone. I'm going to have nightmares in my next sleep cycle."

"I'm pretty sure I will too," Madison said.

"Yeah," Jaco said. "A few stiff drinks sound good right about now, except I don't think I want to taste or smell alcohol again anytime soon."

Shmar and Madison both murmured their agreement.

Madison huffed her annoyance. "Good thing we'll find the captain in a bar."

"I'm going to strap in. Don't get us killed." Shmar left the pod.

"I'm almost offended he said that." Madison ran another routine check of all systems to keep herself occupied while they waited. "Almost."

Jaco snorted.

The cargo bay door hydraulic system activated.

"Yes." Madison wiggled in her seat to make sure her butt wouldn't go numb if she had to stay for a while. "Time to go."

A nanosecond after the cargo bay door reported itself shut and sealed, Madison engaged the thrusters for takeoff.

"I have three waypoints scheduled," Lylla said. "The first one is programmed already. We can jump as soon as we clear the atmosphere."

"You can't set that up in advance like that," Jaco said. "Can you?"

"You can't," Lylla said with a healthy dose of smug. "I can."

Madison laughed.

The scanners picked up two scout-sized ships arriving in the system near the planet.

She stopped laughing and swore instead. "So much for a clean getaway," she grumbled. With a thought, she activated the intercom. "Brace for fancy flying."

Anyone Cradok sent would have the scanner signature of this stupid yacht. Long-range scanners had trouble penetrating atmosphere thick enough to support most life forms, at least. Until they passed through, those two ships had a minimal chance of detecting the yacht.

"Ten more minutes," she groused as she shifted their angle of ascent.

"What?" Jaco asked. "We don't have ten minutes."

"Shut up. I'm concentrating."

FTL engines could activate in atmosphere. Doing so caused intense meteorological disturbances and blasted the ground. Everyone knew better than to do it.

No one on Veriscova Four cared anymore. Maybe some crew of Stardrifters could return and give those people proper burials, and maybe they could try setting up a new settlement.

More likely, no one would set foot on the planet again for a century.

The Oligarchy had discovered the planet. They'd noted it had livable atmosphere and plenty of indigenous life. Humans had run a successful colony, which meant it could support them.

No Stardrifter captain in their right mind would chance Veriscova Four again anytime soon, not even to identify the dead.

Granted, Captain Wayward might do it, but no one else would even think about it for more than a nanosecond.

"Jump us," Madison said.

"Wait," Jaco barked. "We're still in—"

The ship jumped.

Lylla took orders from Madison, not Jaco. As it should be.

CHAPTER 10

KIREHE

Three jumps later, the ship landed on another planet. Kirehe stayed onboard with the dragons while Madison, Jaco, and Gordy checked the settlement. They returned in short order and left the planet without explanation.

Kirehe assumed this meant they had not located the elusive Captain Wayward.

The jumps took a long time. Kirehe remained in the cargo bay for the many long hours between bouts of near-nausea. She wanted to seek out Madison. The dragons had other plans.

Skila fluttered everywhere, all the time. The maras paced. Nihan stretched his wings over and over, one at a time. Their disquieted chirps and whistles echoed off the walls.

Despite having spent hours lying still in the sunshine at home, he squirmed endlessly inside the ship. The maras had likewise slept and huddled in their misery for most of their lives yet wanted to roam. She wondered if the respite on Veriscova Four had done more harm than good. They certainly acted like it.

Those few times when Madison stepped into the cargo bay, she scanned the chaotic space and retreated.

Restless dragons chased away everyone. They all had other places to go while Kirehe managed the animals.

Lylla poked her head into the cargo bay after several long, empty hours. "Kirehe?"

"Yes?" She looked up from trying to convince Wooni to stop smacking heads with Heetay. The two males wanted to fight for mating dominance yet had no females suitable for mating.

"We've got about an hour until we reach the next planet. Can I ask you something?"

The girl sounded young and uncertain. Kirehe could make time for her. She bore the blame for the girl's presence among them, after all.

Kirehe cracked the two males' heads together herself. "Stop it," she grumbled in chirps too low for human hearing. "No fighting."

Turning her back on them, she wondered how much blood she could expect to find on the walls when she returned.

"Why did you do that?" Lylla said with a furrowed brow as Kirehe approached.

"Dumb boys." Kirehe shrugged and led Lylla through the door. She stopped on the other side to avoid the noise of the squabbling maras.

In this part of the ship, the engine hummed quieter. Voices murmured too distant for her to interpret.

"Boys are pretty dumb," Lylla said with a nod.

"Yes. What question?"

Lylla wrung her hands. "You can understand the dragons, right? Is that…common for your people?"

Hopefully, this conversation would not include the kind of stupidity she'd suffered among her people. "No. Not unique, but not common."

"What did they…" Lylla bit her lip. "What did they call it? A gift? A curse? Ability? Magic power?"

Kirehe raised her brow and tried to come up with the words to explain in the infernal language they all spoke. "I not know words. Madison?"

The girl took her hand and led her deeper into the ship.

Kirehe followed. She'd explored enough of the ship to use their toilet facilities and clean her body as needed. No more than that. The longer she left the dragons, the more trouble they caused.

Nihan, at least, would keep them from destroying anything or killing each other. He had enough sense for that.

They found Madison in a room with Oolaang, talking. The pair sat in white chairs facing each other in a small metal room, and the conversation carried the weight of serious intent. Oolaang, Kirehe knew, had spent time wriggling through the ship's innards. He may have discovered some serious problem in need of correction without the means to do it while they traveled through space.

She hoped not.

"I need you to translate for me," Kirehe said in her native tongue as both Madison and Oolaang looked up. "But it can wait. It's not time-important."

"It's fine." Madison waved off any concerns about disturbing them.

Kirehe's belly fluttered as she became the focus of Madison's attention.

That made no sense. She'd interacted with Madison before. They were friends. Every day, they exchanged many words. Most floated on the surface of life, irrelevant and routine.

She thought of that kiss on Nihan's back and had to restrain herself from touching her mouth.

"What's wrong?" Madison asked.

"Nothing." For a moment, no other words popped into Kirehe's head. Fortunately, Lylla shifted her feet, reminding her of the reason why they'd come. "She wants to know about dragoncalling." She pointed to Lylla. "Tell her it's hereditary. Our elders call it a two-gene recessive trait."

Madison opened her mouth, squinted at her, and shut it. After a moment of obvious thought, she said, "I'm still kind of confused by your people. They wear feathers and scales and stuff but have plastics and know about recessive traits."

Kirehe raised her brow. "It's a jungle, not a vacuum of stupidity."

For a moment, Madison stared at her. Then she grinned. "Sorry."

To Lylla, she said, "It's genetic. They consider it a trait. Is this about your amazing navigation skill?"

Lylla blushed and nodded.

"Navigation skill?" Oolaang asked.

"Lylla can plot navigation courses in her head. Faster than a computer can do it." Madison gestured to Lylla with a flourish. "Like magic."

The girl blushed harder.

Kirehe set a hand on Lylla's shoulder to steady her. She wished someone would do the same for her.

No, not someone. Madison. Except Madison's hand on her shoulder would make the problem worse, not better.

"Oh!" Oolaang smiled. "I know of a few recorded instances of humans with extraordinary gifts, but not that one. There's the woman who could detect toxins by smell, like some animals. She helped turn a number of Stardrifter colonies self-sufficient by identifying which plants and animals were safe to eat and use. They otherwise had to bring in testing equipment, and some of the materials necessary were, at the time, difficult to obtain.

"And then there was a man who could subtly alter his appearance and smell to disguise himself. He was a spy for the Stardrifters in a time when we had violently clashing factions. Not a lot of recorded history about him, but he left behind a journal. And then there's the lost colony of Seris Five, allegedly full of telepaths."

Kirehe asked Madison to clarify a few of the words. When she did, the information didn't surprise her. Her dragoncalling gift allowed her to hear and communicate at frequencies beyond human hearing. Among her people, they considered it somewhat magical and strange.

Another time, when she had no bored dragons to entertain, she thought Oolaang might like to hear what she knew about the history of her people.

"Why didn't my mom have it?" Lylla asked.

"Maybe she did," Kirehe said with a shrug.

Lylla frowned at the floor. "Thank you, Madison." She tugged on Kirehe's hand and pulled her back to the cargo bay.

Kirehe waved to Madison and Oolaang as they left, wishing the dragons would settle and let her spend time with anyone other than themselves. Bratty things.

At the door, Lylla scuffed her boot as if she had something to say. Yet she said nothing.

"Gift is hard." Kirehe squeezed Lylla's hand. "Different. Apart. Scary sometimes. To you and to others. Never scary to me. Always friend. Come when sad, yes?"

Lylla hugged Kirehe. The girl wrapped her arms around Kirehe and clung like she expected a harsh wind to pry her into oblivion. "Come when sad, yes."

"Good." Kirehe ruffled Lylla's hair and held on until the girl decided to let go. "But dragons act dumb in ship. Danger of hurt. Accident but still hurt."

"Okay. I won't come in, I'll ask you to come out."

"Yes, good."

"Thank you, Kirehe."

Lylla let go. Behind her, Kirehe noticed Madison leaning against the wall. She seemed casual.

As soon as Lylla ran off, Madison moved closer.

"Are things okay in there?" Madison pointed to the cargo bay. She stopped a few meters away and leaned against the wall again.

"It's fine." Kirehe wanted to close the distance yet remained rooted to the spot. "They're bored."

Madison nodded. "Space is like that."

Kirehe groped for something to say. "Did anything bad happen on the last planet? We barely stayed long enough to do anything."

"Ugh." Madison rubbed her face and grimaced. "The security guys wouldn't let us walk around. They told us Captain Wayward wasn't there and gave us someplace else to check. I got the feeling there's a lot of concern we'll bring the Oligarchy wherever we go. I don't think they care that Cradok is just going to burn down everything he can find whether I'm there or not."

"Is this worth it? Do we have other options?"

All of this frustrated her and the dragons. They wanted to roam.

"Our choices are pretty minimal. Changing the ship signature would give us freedom from all this. It would take parts and tools we don't have. There are places we could buy or borrow them, but if they won't let us land long enough to do it, that's not helpful.

"We have to stop for food, water, and fuel. While we could get food and water on our own, fuel is harder. We need to find safe places to dock. Captain Wayward's ship is a great place to dock. We can change the signature, retrofit, add weapons, and all kinds of stuff. But we have to find him first. Another captain could help us. The problem is that I don't trust anyone like I trust my uncle."

Kirehe failed to grasp the significance of familial ties as hers had done her no good. She recognized Madison's affection for her uncle, though. Every time she said the man's name, she revealed an unshakable bond.

"What do you think these other captains might do?"

Madison twitched her mouth, leading Kirehe to believe she had to consider the question and found that distasteful. "I just don't know. At least with my uncle, I know he'll do what he can to keep us safe without asking for payment."

Payment. Kirehe remembered someone mentioning that Stardrifters liked to steal things. Their scruples had different boundaries than Kirehe's people.

She felt the Oligarchy deserved this theft performed by the Stardrifters, at least. The lakhans seemed to thrive on destroying their enemies without prejudice. In return, taking money and goods seemed the least anyone could do to them.

But payment between Stardrifters was a different matter.

Oolaang had mentioned violent infighting in the past. They had no assurance such a thing could never happen again.

Kirehe wanted to prod this subject. She wanted to understand. Among her people, they had few personal possessions. Useful items belonged to the tribe. Ornaments with sentimental value belonged to people. Everyone worked, everyone ate, everyone thrived.

Stardrifters used a different paradigm.

"Anyway." Madison glanced up and down the hallway. She took a few steps closer and lowered her voice. "We should maybe talk about that kiss?"

"Ah." Kirehe touched her lips before she could stop herself. "It was…" No particular words filled the empty, buzzing space in her head.

"It was nice." Madison grinned at her. "Thank you for distracting me from the sheer terror of Nihan's flight. And also for asking first. That was pretty distracting in its own right."

"Asking. Yes. This is important. To ask first." Kirehe tore her gaze from Madison's mouth to scowl at the floor.

"Did you know you get little lines here when you glare at the floor?" Madison touched a single fingertip to Kirehe's cheek next to the corner of her mouth. "It's cute."

"Cute." Kirehe rolled her eyes and turned to listen at the door.

At that moment, a mara chose to screech outside of human hearing range. The shout spoke of pain and frustration.

"I have to tend the dragons," Kirehe said, relieved and annoyed at the same time. "They're acting stupid again."

"Okay." Madison took a step backward, leaving Kirehe's personal space. "Come find me later. We can talk more."

Kirehe wanted to take a fistful of Madison's shirt and haul the woman into the cargo bay with her. She also wanted Madison to leave. The conflicting impulses confused her.

What would she even do with Madison in the cargo bay? Kiss her until the dragons sat down and shut up? Dragons didn't work that way.

Kirehe fled for the safety of dragon wrangling. At least she knew how to handle them.

CHAPTER 11

MADISON

The second planet they tried had a cold climate. Snow and ice covered most of the surface, and it had minimal atmosphere. Stardrifters had built an enclosed mining settlement near the equator.

This time, Madison left Kirehe on the ship both to protect it and keep her dragons from organizing into a mutiny. Bedi Two had no options for running or flying. Dragons roaming even within ten meters of the ship had a lot of potential to cause mass panic or get them spaced.

She led Gordy, Jaco, and Shmar through the docking bay. Their boots clanged on the metal floor, echoing in the wide space. They carried no weapons, as the settlement required of visitors.

Several other ships, all scouts or transports, sat in the huge, chilly bay. People worked at refueling or repairs. Tools clanked. Grease clung to the air. Madison saw no ships with her uncle's markings, so she doubted they'd find Captain Wayward on the planet. At least they could refuel and ask if he'd showed himself recently.

At the door to the rest of the settlement, Madison pushed the green button on the wall. The wide door separated in the center and slid open.

A different kind of noise rolled over them. People shouted. Animals called. Metal scraped and shrieked. Boots clomped. Fans whirred. All kinds of things creaked and groaned.

Madison marched through the doorway and into the sweaty, metallic air.

Four guards flanked the door. The big, beefy men in matching body armor casually held rifles. In a place like this, they used stun weapons to avoid causing inadvertent wall breaches or damage to the environmental system. Just like on a ship.

Unlike the previous settlement, security let them through without a challenge. They watched, though. They watched with suspicion and wariness.

Beyond the door, metal walls from floor to ceiling dotted with metal doors at regular intervals created straight paths wide enough for cargo platforms to pass. This underground settlement housed about ten thousand people, making it the largest human population cluster in the galaxy, as far as Madison knew.

Everyone except Gordy knew the way to Captain Wayward's preferred tavern.

Knowing she had a distinctive cybereye, Madison urged Shmar to take the lead as they headed to the bar under the yellow-orange glow of day-cycle lights. She kept her head down and wished she had a hood.

People passing them glanced at Shmar and ignored the group.

At least three times during the walk, Jaco opened his mouth to say something yet never spoke. Madison assumed he itched to point out the obvious futility of their visit.

The bar had a plain door in the wall like every other place here. Like every other door, a screen beside it announced the name and type of the location. Biscuits and Gravy declared itself a "public nourishment establishment." Every bar and restaurant on Bedi Two used the same phrase as mandated by their regulations.

Shmar hit the green button to open the door and led the group inside.

As expected, Madison saw no one from *Wayward Star*. She did, however, pick out the first mate from *Zanmi's Revenge*.

"Tovar!" Madison strode to the swarthy man at the bar.

The rest of the patrons, at least twenty people in all, turned to see her. They fell to muttering among themselves.

Tovar had a long brown beard and a paunch caused by too much beer. When he looked up, he lacked the infectious smile he usually grew when he saw her. Instead, he sighed and frowned into his beer.

"Madison." He shook her hand, at least. "You shouldn't have come here."

Madison leaned against the bar next to him. "Why not? I'm looking for Captain Wayward."

He snorted. "Like I couldn't have guessed that. You shouldn't have come here because the Oligarchy upped the bounty on your head. Which you should've expected."

"Yeah, and? Do you know where we can find him?"

"I'm going to guess you haven't tried to imagine how much the Oligarchy now wants your head." Tovar summoned the bartender with a flick of his hand. "She wants a kiddie drink."

"No, I don't." Madison waved off the man before he reached them. "I won't stay long enough to bother."

"Good plan. Because some of these assholes are, right now, trying to decide if they can take you. Your bounty is so high, I'm almost thinking about it." He grinned. "Almost. They're offering amnesty to whoever turns you in, Maddie. Citizenship. A free pass to conduct legal trade and own slaves. You know, like a ship crew. Plus that fat finder's fee."

She blinked at him. "But no one would want that. It would mean living under Oligarchy rules." Even as the words tumbled out of her mouth, she knew the lie she spoke. Plenty of Stardrifters would jump at the chance to sacrifice one person for a guarantee of safety and comfort.

Jaco had.

Only a few would hesitate because they knew Madison personally. Like Tovar and his captain, Zanmi. Uncle Chris. Maybe others.

Maybe.

"I know you're not that naïve, Maddie." He nodded to the door. "There are rewards for information on your whereabouts too. Get out of here and stick to the smaller settlements. They'll give up and lower the reward eventually. Check Ghati Prime."

"Thanks for the warning." Madison patted his arm in gratitude. "By the way, tell Captain Zanmi I said hi. Also tell her we may have some options for fighting Oligarchy ships instead of just running from them."

He snorted again. "Nobody has that."

"I do." Madison straightened and left him. The guys followed as she hurried out of the bar and back to the ship.

Shmar took the lead again once he caught the pace.

No one spoke until they entered the cargo bay.

"Why are we in such a big hurry?" Shmar asked as they rushed to the yacht.

"The bounty is higher than I thought," Madison said.

The three men glanced at each other. She wondered if any of them considered the option of collecting that bounty.

As they reached the ship, Madison saw two men and a woman backing out of the yacht with their hands raised in surrender. Kirehe stepped into view. She held her spear ready for violence against the trio.

"Just a misunderstanding," one of the men said. "No big deal."

"Go now or die," Kirehe growled.

The woman turned and saw Shmar then Madison. She elbowed one of her companions in the side.

Still backing away from Kirehe, the man turned his head. He grinned and patted the second man's arm. "No harm done, right?"

"Let's get out of here," Gordy muttered. "Fast."

"Yes." Madison kept her three men between her and the trio.

"Well hello there, Madison Wayward," the woman said. Too loud. Too clear. "Nice to see you."

"Pike off," Jaco snapped.

Kirehe reached the bottom of the cargo ramp and continued stalking toward the trio. "I warn you," she snarled.

Madison rushed to Kirehe and blocked her path. "No, we're not going to kill anyone here. They left the ship, and now we're going to strap in and get off the planet. Please get back into the ship?"

Her magnificent warrior princess bared her teeth as she glared over Madison's shoulder. "You come again, you die." She pushed Madison inside the ship and pointed at them with her spear. "No warn. Only stab."

Once they jumped, Madison knew she'd have time to explain. They'd use stricter security on Ghati Prime and go in expecting a fight.

She rushed to the cockpit and strapped herself down. "Lylla! I need my navigator! Jump as soon as we cross!"

Instead of relying upon the control tower, she fired up the engines and scanned for incoming and outgoing craft. She had no intention of allowing them to delay their takeoff long enough to earn amnesty for the whole planet by holding her.

They wouldn't contact the Oligarchy without absolute certainty they had Madison, of course. Otherwise, they risked the entire settlement. Given that the guards hadn't tried to stop them, she doubted they'd take this approach.

Better to expect it than to wind up dead.

"Craft designation victor zulu seven seven three, you are not cleared for exit. Land and request clearance."

"Nope. Not today." Madison flew the ship through the force field. She angled the ship straight up and pushed it to full speed. The sooner they left this planet, the better.

"Craft designation victor zulu seven seven three, you have violated our bay protocols and caused a serious safety concern. The standard penalty has been assessed against your craft. You are hereby banned from Bedi Two for a period of—"

The ship hit space and jumped, cutting off the rest of the transmission.

"Fortunately," Madison muttered, "we'll never return on this ship."

"What happened?" Lylla asked. "We didn't leave that other planet like this. We left fast, but not like this."

Madison wanted to explain to everyone at once. She also wanted to think about it first. "What's our jump time?"

"I did a short one. Forty-five minutes. Where are we going after that?"

"Ghati Prime. I'll talk to everyone when we hit the second jump." Madison settled to stay in her seat for a while.

They all deserved to know. No one on this ship would think twice about turning her in for the bounty. Shmar or Gordy might think once, but not twice. They wouldn't do it.

Shmar trusted Captain Wayward like a father. Everyone on *Wayward Star* saw him that way, even the oldsters. No one who'd served on that ship would cut and run to the Oligarchy, no matter how big the bounty for Madison's head. They'd all refused the allure of the bounty on Uncle Chris's head for long enough to make her certain of that.

Gordy, she thought, respected Kirehe enough to stay loyal.

Even if Kirehe hated Madison, she had no interest in bounties. But she liked Madison. How much she liked Madison, they had yet to truly discover.

Jaco would never turn on Madison. He hadn't betrayed Madison, he'd betrayed Kirehe in an effort to protect Madison.

The Oligarchy had murdered Lylla's mother and Rho's entire family, so she doubted she needed to worry about either of them.

Oolaang might fall prey to temptation briefly, much like Shmar or Gordy. Then he'd shake it off in favor of all the reasons he'd remained loyal through the trials on Rikor Six.

No, she had nothing to fear among her current little crew. Telling them the grand offer from the Oligarchy presented no particular danger.

Some of the crew on her uncle's ship might consider trying it. She'd have to get ahead of that as fast as possible. Uncle Chris needed to hear what she'd discovered about Oligarchy ships. He'd want to know more about their escape too.

In all likelihood, the video feed had cut off as soon as someone realized the execution had been botched a second time. People knew Madison had escaped because of the bounty. They hadn't watched it.

She sat and waited for the jump to end. No one joined them in the control pod.

As soon as the jump ended, Madison scanned the sector. "Nothing here," she told Lylla. "Jump straight to Ghati Prime."

The ship jumped.

"This one will take seventeen hours and twenty-three minutes."

Madison activated the intercom. "We've got a long jump ahead of us. Can everyone please join me in the cargo bay?"

She unplugged and unbuckled. Once she climbed out of her seat, she let out a long, slow breath. "It's time to explain the situation to everyone."

Lylla gulped. "That sounds bad. Do you have a plan?"

"Yes. It's not a great plan, but it's definitely a plan."

CHAPTER 12

KIREHE

The dragons grumbled as Kirehe left the ship with Shmar, Gordy, Jaco, and Madison. They wanted to leave the ship too. Her dragons grumbled through every jump the ship took. All of them sniped at each other.

At least they'd stopped fighting with their limbs. Mostly.

None had suffered serious injuries. They'd cut and scraped each other, and Skila had accidentally clawed Fobi's leg once in fright.

Oolaang shut the cargo bay door behind them. After people had boarded the ship uninvited to try to snatch Madison, they elected to take no chances.

Her dragons, Madison had assured her, would have a chance to roam. Maybe here, but not now. Safety first. Besides, they'd have to get used to staying inside relatively small spaces.

Kirehe would not consider finding a planet to leave them behind. They would stay with her or go home to Rikor Six. Anything else would be cruel.

Their ship sat in damp, chilly air under an enormous canopy of metal with branches and small-leafed vines hanging off the roof. They walked across a metal grate over stone or more metal angled to drain away from the settlement. Through curtains of vegetation on two sides, Kirehe could see more ships of similar size.

She wondered if everyone chose the same size of ship for a reason other than the size of the docking areas on all these planets.

Trees and shrubs lined a path of more grate-covered drainage from the dock to the settlement. Rain pattered on leaves much smaller than those on Kirehe's world. At the other end of the path, they passed between a pair of thick trees covered with green fur and draped with thin, small-leafed vines.

Tiny boxes with round lenses hung on the trees. They swiveled on mounts, following the group as they passed. Cameras, Kirehe thought, though she'd never seen ones like these before.

Low buildings clustered around trees with brown and green nets hanging between the canopies. They had brown and green roofs of dull materials. Everywhere they should have seen dirt, the town had grates over stone or metal tunnels. Considering that water burbled continuously through the tunnels, Kirehe supposed they needed it.

After a minute or so of walking through the town, thumping the butt of her staff on the grating, Kirehe realized it lacked color. No flowers bloomed anywhere. The locals wore brown, gray, and green, and everyone had a scarf, hood, and jacket or draping cloak.

People turned to watch them pass. Skila, sitting on Kirehe's shoulder, chirped at everyone and everything as she hopped and danced to catch bugs.

"Is that Pirro?" Jaco asked.

"Kind of looks like him," Shmar said, "but no. That guy hasn't broken his nose."

"You're right." Jaco sighed. "I just want it to be him."

"We're not expecting to find the captain here," Madison murmured. "If he is, great, but he's probably not."

Kirehe noticed people in clusters watching them. They chattered amongst themselves and stole sidelong glances. Madison had made clear her concerns about those motivated by greed. This made no real sense to Kirehe but she trusted Madison.

They reached a door with an etched metal sign on the wall. Along with words Kirehe couldn't read, it had an outline of a mug. Shmar opened the door and led the group inside.

"Stay here," Kirehe told Skila as she left the kukiri outside.

Skila flitted around the tree, chasing bugs and bouncing off strange green fur.

Inside, at least three dozen people sat on chairs around small tables or on stools at a long, high table. A man wearing a beige apron stood behind the high table. Three women, also wearing aprons, milled about the room carrying trays. Dim strips of lighting flickered on the ceiling. Flasks with dull labels lined the wall behind the high table. The floor felt spongy beneath Kirehe's feet, like walking on plants.

The room stank of alcohol, sweat, and damp wood.

Several patrons wore coats with shiny buttons similar to the ones Madison, Jaco, and Shmar had lost on Rikor Six. Theirs had been blue. These were muted red and brown. Many more wore the drab hooded cloaks of the locals. Even indoors, they kept their colors and selves hidden.

Fear had become routine for these people.

"Should we mix with Janssen's crew?" Jaco muttered.

Madison scanned the crowd.

A dozen people watched them. The room felt tense for some unknown reason. She had a feeling they stood a small chance of leaving the establishment without a fight.

"I'll talk to Famke," Madison told Shmar and Jaco. "Try not to look like bodyguards. Except you, Kirehe. Come with me like a bodyguard."

Shmar and Jaco approached the high table. Gordy followed them.

Madison wove through the room to reach a small table near the back. A man and woman, both in the brown and red coats, sat together with cups. The man had streaks of gray in his brown beard and small lines on his pale face. His companion seemed closer to Madison's age. Both watched Madison approach.

"Famke." Madison smiled at the woman and failed to acknowledge the man.

The man appeared uninterested in Madison's presence or conversation.

Famke smiled without letting it reach her eyes. "Nice to see you, Madison. What brings you way out here? Looking for a date?" She waggled her eyebrows.

For that tiny gesture, Kirehe wanted to punch Famke's face.

"Not today. I'm looking for Captain Wayward. Have you seen him here recently?"

Kirehe heard the scrape of a chair as someone stood. Voices murmured too quiet to understand. Shmar leaned over the high table and spoke to the man on the other side.

"Can't say that I have." Famke shrugged and gestured to include the room. "We've only been here for a few hours, though. And I haven't asked around for him. Captain Janssen might know where to find him."

The man stood with a smile Kirehe found unsettling. Like a mara watching something in the moments before a vicious pounce.

"You could come back to the ship with us." Famke also stood. "I'm sure he'd be happy to talk to you."

Behind Madison, two men stood without scraping their chairs.

"They're going to attack," Kirehe said in her language. "I can see it."

Madison nodded to her. "Don't do anything unless they start it. And don't kill these people. They aren't the enemy." To Famke, she said, "I'm not looking for Captain Janssen. Unless he has Captain Wayward held prisoner on his ship?"

Famke laughed. "As if anyone could catch him." She pointed at Madison with a smirk. "You, on the other hand, I've heard can be caught."

"Careful what you wish for, Famke." Madison crossed her arms. "Maybe you've also heard I'm hard to hold onto."

"Everyone likes a challenge."

Kirehe refused to allow the man behind Madison to hit her. She side-stepped and slammed her body against his as he threw a punch.

The entire room erupted into chaos. Everyone shouted and chairs scraped. The man behind the high table moaned in despair and ducked out of sight. All three of the women in aprons scurried to leave through the back door with tiny yips of fright.

Kirehe swept her spear to flip a brown-coat woman onto her back.

Madison shoved Famke.

The brown-coat people leaped to their feet.

Gordy launched himself at a knot of three men.

Shmar picked up his stool. He threw it across the room. It thudded into a brown-coat man.

Beside Shmar, Jaco kicked the back of a brown-coat woman's knee. She groaned.

As she whirled to avoid a blow aimed at her head, Kirehe counted combatants. Twenty-five brown-coats. Six locals backed against the walls. A cluster of seven more locals stayed at the high table, ignoring the brawl. Two drunk locals threw punches without targets.

The brown-coats had a good chance of taking Madison if they focused on that objective. Shmar, Madison, and Jaco each could handle one person at a time. Kirehe and Gordy could not keep over twenty people busy all at once. The enemy would not win this battle, but they could easily swipe Madison and flee.

Kirehe jabbed the blunt end of her spear at Famke's gut. Whatever happened, Kirehe would keep Madison in sight at all times. Anyone attempting to reach her had to get through Kirehe first.

Kick. Block. Punch. Dodge. Dodge. Punch.

She shoved the man with Famke and slapped her spear's shaft against his back. Famke lunged at Madison. Kirehe kicked Famke in the face. She landed and swept her spear to thwack against the back of the man's knee. He grunted and fell forward.

Wood shards flew as Gordy hit someone across the back with a chair. He took fistfuls of two men's shirts and smashed the two men together. They collapsed.

Madison punched a brown-coat in the gut. The man grunted and swept Madison's legs. She hit the floor with a squeal of surprise and pain.

Kirehe growled at the brown-coat and crashed into him. He staggered into Shmar. Someone else jumped on Kirehe's back and wrapped an arm around her neck.

She swung her spear over her head and cracked it into their skull. They let go.

"Famke, that's not sporting!" the clear, commanding voice rang out above the din.

Kirehe snapped her head to see Famke raising a pistol to shoot Madison. She leaped into the path of the shot and charged Famke.

Famke's eyes widened. She tossed a table at Kirehe.

Kirehe leaped over the table before it landed and slammed Famke into the wall. She punched her forearm against Famke's hand, thumping it against the wall. Famke dropped the gun.

To keep her out of trouble, Kirehe punched Famke in the face. The brown-coat's head hit the wall and she crumpled to the floor, groaning. This woman would stay down, at least long enough to deal with the rest of these people or to escape.

With that problem dispatched, Kirehe whirled to find Madison.

Seven new people in blue coats joined the fight. One of them held off the older brown-coat, dodging his opponent with the skill of a seasoned fighter. He had light red hair thick with curls and a sword on his belt.

"Really, Emilio, is this necessary?" the man asked as he evaded blow after blow by twisting his body and slapping punches aside. "If I'd known you were only waiting for her, we would've trounced you before they got here."

The older brown-coat shouted at him in wordless frustration.

"No, I will not stand still," the blue-coat man said. "I have better things to do than getting hit by you today."

The rest of the blue-coats had at least as much skill as the talkative man. One in particular, a thick, muscular man, waded through brown-coats with ease. He tossed them aside like toys. One, he batted at Gordy, who took the victim and threw them to the ground.

Madison sat on the floor behind the redheaded blue-coat, rubbing her head in a mild daze. Jaco crouched beside her with a mad little grin.

A blue-coat woman straddled a brown-coat on the floor near Madison, punching him in the face with alternating fists.

Shmar sat on a stool, watching. Under his stool, a brown-coat wriggled against the crosspieces holding him down.

With the entry of the blue-coats, the fight had ended. A few of the brown-coats had yet to admit this fact.

For example, this Emilio man.

Kirehe slipped behind Emilio and kicked him in the back. He squawked and stumbled into the redheaded blue-coat's fist.

Emilio wavered. Kirehe kicked the back of his knee. At the same time, the redheaded man shoved his shoulders. Emilio fell on his face with a groan.

The redheaded man watched Emilio fall with a small sympathetic wince. "Thank you." He flashed Kirehe a bright, cheerful grin. "A timely addition to the situation."

Not sure what to make of the blue-coats, Kirehe raised her fist and held her spear ready to fight the one man between herself and Madison. She narrowed her eyes and saw him as one more gladiator she needed to beat.

"You no take Madison," Kirehe growled at him.

He chuckled. "On the contrary, I most certainly will." He offered Kirehe a hand to shake despite the last gasps of the fight continuing around them and her tense pose. "Christopher Wayward, at your service."

CHAPTER 13

MADISON

Madison took Jaco's help to stand. She needed it. One of Janssen's jerks had clocked her across the jaw when Kirehe turned her back.

"Captain?" she mumbled, still halfway in a daze.

Captain Wayward shook hands with Kirehe. He ignored Madison completely as he turned to the bar. "Sorry, Kev. Blame Janssen. His people started it."

The bartender peeped his head over the bar. "It's her fault," he groused as he pointed at Madison.

Madison opened her mouth to object.

Her uncle didn't let her. "Yes, well, we won, didn't we? Winners walk out, losers pay the tab. Janssen can pay for it." The captain gestured toward the door. "We should get scarce."

Captain Wayward's crew followed orders.

Kirehe moved to Madison's side and stayed there as they all trooped out of the bar. She whistled outside the door. Skila fluttered to her shoulder and chirped up a storm.

"What's that?" Captain Wayward asked Kirehe.

"Skila."

"It's a dragon," Madison added as her wits settled. "A teeny-tiny dragon."

They'd found Captain Wayward. She grinned like an idiot.

The captain nodded like he accepted the answer. Ahead, Jaco and Shmar greeted their superiors. Bosun Pirro, the biggest, baddest badass Madison had ever met other than Kirehe, smacked Jaco upside the head. Gordy shook hands and walked with Navigator Naomi. Shmar walked with more bounce in his step than he'd had since their capture.

"This is Kirehe," Madison said, trying to engage her uncle in whatever way possible. Her grin faded.

The captain flashed Kirehe a polite smile. "Get your ship into space and dock. We'll talk on the *Star*."

"Yes, sir."

Madison hurried ahead, worrying about what he'd say later. Until this moment, she'd expected him to be happy to see her. She'd thought he would hug her, or at least smile at her.

Her uncle had always made a point to show he cared. He had, of course, by stepping in when the fight turned sour. But she'd expected some sort of relief to find her whole. Or something.

Anything.

"Jaco, Shmar," the captain said, "you're coming back with us."

"Yes, sir," both men intoned.

Kirehe trotted after Madison. "You're in trouble," she said.

"I figured that out for myself, thanks," she snapped.

Kirehe said nothing else. They reached the yacht with Gordy.

The cargo bay door opened for them.

Oolaang stood at the top of the ramp. "Where are Jaco and Shmar?"

"With the captain." Madison bustled through, disengaging her cybereye as she headed for the cockpit. "Get ready to lift off."

"We found him?" Oolaang sounded happy. As well he should. He considered the *Star* home too. "He's probably pissed, though?"

"Understatement," Gordy said. "I don't even know him and I could tell."

"Hooboy." Oolaang sighed.

The cargo bay door shut.

Madison slipped into the cockpit and plugged in. Some stupid tears rolled down her cheek. He might've at least tousled her hair. Said something welcoming. Acknowledged her presence as someone other than any random crew member he'd rescued from the brig after a night of forgetting how to exercise judgment.

"Where are we jumping?" Lylla asked.

"We're not." Madison wiped her face on her sleeve and asked for clearance to leave over the radio.

"Oh. Do you need my help, then?"

"No."

"Do you want me to go sit with Rho instead?"

Did she? Madison shrugged. "You can if you want. This won't take long."

The local tower gave her clearance. She nudged the ship out of the dock and into the sky.

"Craft victor zulu seven seven three," a familiar voice said into her ear, "hold for clearance to enter the *Star*."

"Hi, Violine," Madison said.

"Hi, Madison," Violine said. "It'll just be a few minutes while we get the *Freight* stowed."

The yacht's scanners picked up the *Wayward Freight* zipping past. The captain's ship took priority.

"Yeah. Thanks."

"Who's Violine?" Lylla asked.

"Chief Communications Officer of the *Wayward Star*." A friend, though Madison had no idea what kind of welcome to expect from anyone anymore.

Dani had worked for Violine.

The bulky, bulbous *Wayward Star* resolved from an anomaly near the planet into a ship. Her home swallowed the captain's ship.

"Okay, Madison. You're clear. Use bay four."

Instead of responding to Violine, Madison turned the ship and followed orders. They slid into cargo bay four, a space usually reserved for the lost *Scout*. As the landing struts touched the deck, the bay door slid shut.

She felt the expected gut-churn of an FTL jump. Where would Captain Wayward take them? Somewhere else. Beyond that, she had no guesses.

Lylla unbuckled and left the control pod.

Madison remained in her seat. She opened the bay door for everyone to leave and powered down the ship.

"Madison?" Oolaang asked after a few minutes. "He's not going to get less angry for being kept waiting. Also, Kirehe has Bijou in a headlock because she started yelling about the dragons."

With that news, Madison unplugged and scrambled out of her seat. She sprinted through the ship to find Kirehe holding down one member of the crew and pointing her spear at another two.

Gordy stood to the side with his hands up, staying out of the situation.

The maras surrounded Kirehe like a loyal crew, hissing at the cargo bay crew.

"Whoa! Whoa," Madison said as she reached the bottom of the ramp. "Kirehe, these people aren't the enemy."

Captain Wayward stepped into view with his arms crossed over his chest. He glared at Madison like a stern father disappointed in his disobedient child. "Oolaang, you can go."

Oolaang shuffled down the ramp with his head down. "Yes, sir. I'll get right to work."

"Kirehe, let her go," Madison murmured. She would not cry in front of her uncle, dammit. "She was just doing her job."

Kirehe growled. "Her job is yelling?"

"Her job is keeping the cargo bay in order."

With an irritated huff, Kirehe released her prisoner.

Bijou, a dusky, doughty woman, stumbled forward and gasped for breath. Captain Wayward caught her.

"Dragons not monsters," Kirehe snapped at both Bijou and the captain. "Trained. No eat people."

"Glad to hear it. Keep them on a tight leash anyway." Captain Wayward kept a grip on Bijou while she recovered. "Are there any other surprises inside this thing?"

Madison wiped her cheek again as she turned to see the others. Gordy stood out of the captain's sight with Rho. Lylla clung to Rho's side with her face buried in their short, tawny fur.

"There are three more people."

"I assume you can get them to the right places before you come see me in my cabin?"

"Yes, sir," Madison mumbled.

"Good." The captain turned on his heel and left.

"What does 'leash' mean?" Kirehe asked.

Madison shook her head and shuffled down the ramp to her side. "Restraint. He doesn't want them to scare anybody or cause damage."

Kirehe took her chin in hand and peered at her face. "I thought finding him was supposed to make you happy."

At least Kirehe touched her. "It was supposed to make us safe." Madison huffed. "I'm fine. I need to get everyone settled. Would you apologize to Bijou, please? And also stay here to keep an eye on the dragons while they get some small amount of exercise?"

Bijou stood with one hand on her hip and the other rubbing her neck. Two other crewmates waited with her, both ready to protect her.

"Apologize?" Kirehe let go and crossed her arms. "What for? They're acting like we're the enemy! Why did we come here?"

For all her wonder and magnificence, Kirehe had little experience dealing with people. She'd served her people as a protector from afar, not as a leader or part of a team.

"Never mind. Just keep the dragons in the cargo bay for now and ask them not to go near any of the people. I'll be back later." She gestured for Gordy, Rho, and Lylla to come with her and approached Bijou.

Behind her, Kirehe grumbled under her breath. Her bare feet crossed the small ship's ramp.

"Hey Bijou." Madison forced herself to offer Bijou a friendly smile. "She doesn't speak the language well and misunderstood you as a threat. I've asked her to keep the dragons away from people and confined to the cargo bay. As long as you don't yell at her, she won't attack you again."

Bijou huffed and waved a hand at the yacht. "So we're stuck with this piece of crap? Captain said to dismantle it."

"You can try while it's full of dragons." Madison shrugged and walked away.

Of course he wanted to rip it up for spare parts. A ship like that had no actual value. Even if Oolaang thought he could retrofit it to make a new *Scout*.

Plodding all the way, she handed off the trio following her to someone who could assign them quarters and help them figure out what teams to join.

As she shuffled down hallways, others noticed her. No one seemed to know what to say or do. They let her pass without interruption.

Long before she wanted to see it, she reached her uncle's cabin door. She stood and stared at it. As a child, she'd gotten into trouble all the time. Visits to the captain's cabin, often with Jaco, had frequently involved disappointment, frustration, and annoyance.

Despite that, never in her life on the *Star* had her uncle made her feel like an unwanted piece of trash.

Not until today.

She tried and failed to remember her uncle's smile.

Then she opened the door.

Captain Wayward sat in his cushioned armchair. The chair faced a screen displaying a variety of information about the ship's status. At other times, he liked to watch outside the ship. Madison and he both found that soothing.

Two other chairs sat to the side. Madison and Jaco had sat in those metal butt cups many, many times.

Not all of her memories in this room full of paper books, potted plants, and plush rugs were bad. Less than half had ever involved discipline. For the moment, she forgot all of them.

"Reporting as ordered, Captain." She stood with her arms at her sides, trying not to fidget with her frayed pants.

Several long, quiet moments passed while he continued to read the screen.

Madison shifted her weight and thought about which other captains she could appeal to for a spot on their ships. With the ridiculous bounty on her head, probably none.

"You stole my scout ship and an eighth of my crew," Captain Wayward said without taking his gaze from his tablet, "including my best pilot, a gifted engineer, and several critical members of their teams." The disappointment ran thick in his quiet words. She heard the thread of anger in them too.

"Nine are dead, and we all got to watch eight of them die. The Oligarchy wants your head so badly they're offering citizenship to humans. Which, of course, means the circle of people I can actively trust has shrunk significantly. You've replaced my scout ship with a near-useless luxury yacht full of oversized lizards which probably have odd diets."

He paused and finally looked at Madison. Instead of the anger and frustration she expected, he seemed tired.

She dropped her gaze to the floor. "I only wanted—"

"You wanted." Captain Wayward had the curious ability to come off as snapping and snarling despite doing neither. "Did you stop for one moment to think about the rest of the crew as you formed your mutinous little plan?"

"It wasn't a mutiny," she rushed to say before he cut her off again.

"You stole my scout."

She wiped her face again. The stupid real eye wouldn't stop leaking. "I borrowed it."

"Borrowing something without returning it is stealing, Madison."

"I meant to return it. We got interrupted."

His nose twitched, the only visible sign of his frustration. "Do you have any idea what watching those eight people die was like?"

"Yes, I do." She tried to keep herself calm like he did. Her body shook with the effort, and so did her voice. "I was there. I saw it, I heard it, and I smelled it. I watched them lie on the ground, beyond hope, calling for help I couldn't give. Without Kirehe, none of us would've survived that at all."

"And without you, none of them would've been captured in the first place."

He had an answer for everything, of course. The captain always did.

Madison scuffed her boot on the rug. "The mission was successful."

"If that's what you call success, I'd rather have failure." He returned his attention to the screen.

"I don't mean that. I mean—"

"I'm not interested." He waved to dismiss her. "Go to your quarters. Stay there. Get some rest."

"But I was right!"

"Being right won't bring them back. Go."

She sniffled. He wanted to treat her like a member of his crew instead of his niece. But she needed him to welcome her home. "I'm sorry, Uncle Chris."

He sighed.

The room felt empty and also thick with unspoken pain at the same time.

Christopher looked at his hands in his lap. "You're the only family I have left, Madison. I wish you would remember that when you come up with your plans."

"I do. That's why I did it. I was right, Uncle."

He shook his head as he stood. "I wonder if you have any idea what it felt like to hear the announcement that your execution would be broadcast live from Rikor Six?"

"Probably not a whole lot better than hearing it said to my face."

With two steps, Uncle Chris wrapped his arms around her.

Tears spilled down her cheeks.

"Welcome home, Madison."

CHAPTER 14

KIREHE

With three blue-coats poking inside the ship, Kirehe brought the dragons into the larger cargo bay. The cubical area had almost twice the space needed to house the yacht. Several thick ropes or tubes hung from various parts of the metal ceiling. Rungs mounted to the wall offered a method to climb to the top.

Tall, round containers painted dull blue stood in a cluster on one side. A wheeled vehicle with prongs sticking from the front rested on the other side. Three of the four walls had small, person-sized doors.

Kirehe had no idea how the small ship had entered the big ship. She assumed one of the sides of the bay opened in some fashion.

The maras, she allowed to race around the yacht, jumping over cables and grate-covered gaps in the floor. Nihan tried and failed to find anything he could climb without using his claws. He'd opted to sit on top of the ship and stretch his wings. A small part of one wingtip dangled over the side. His tail reached halfway to the floor.

Skila had disappeared to explore the ship. Anyone afraid of the kukiri could complain to Kirehe's fist.

Using her spear, Kirehe stretched and ran herself through weapons drills. She jogged with the maras in a maddening circle. Everything she could put her weight on, she climbed.

Half an hour after she started, she needed something new to do. Her dragons felt the same way.

Nihan rolled and flapped. The maras practiced mock fighting. Kirehe whacked her spear against the containers.

Well before she wanted to stop, Kirehe had nothing left to do. Though they'd suffered this ridiculous boredom on the small ship, the walls had felt different.

Closer and yet more welcoming.

Kirehe wanted to see Madison.

She wanted someone to say they wanted her on the ship.

These people were supposed to be their salvation. Madison had talked about the warm, caring family on her uncle's ship. Everyone in that pit, before most of the deaths, had acted like a pack.

The reality underwhelmed Kirehe. They yelled, growled, sneered, and snarled.

Everyone had abandoned the yacht and Kirehe, even Madison. While they all remained on the smaller ship, she hadn't needed them nearby. Knowing they slept close at hand or did their jobs had kept her confinement from feeling like a prison.

This cargo bay felt like more of a prison than the gladiator pit ever had.

"Stay here," she told the maras. "Avoid people." She knew better than to leave the area without reminding them.

"Eat soon?" Rila asked.

Food would occupy them. On this bigger ship, they undoubtedly had a great deal of food. "Yes."

She boarded the small ship and discovered several boxes of supplies already moved into the bay. One had the yacht's remaining original meal packets on the top of a pile.

"Hey," the blue-coat called Bijou said. She pointed an accusing finger at Kirehe. "Don't touch that."

Kirehe raised her brow and took a third packet. "Dragons eat."

"We've already counted them. You can't just take whatever you want." Bijou planted both fists on her hips.

"Dragons eat," Kirehe repeated as she took a fourth packet. "Not know if eat other strange food. Know eat this food."

"I've already reported the inventory. That's Captain Wayward's property now!" Bijou strode toward her like an angry mara.

"No yell. I hear." Kirehe turned her back on Bijou and walked down the ramp. "You wrong. Kirehe take for dragons. Dragons hungry. Need eat."

"That's not how things work on this ship, missy." Bijou followed her. At least she'd stopped yelling.

"Kirehe not part of big ship. Dragons not part of big ship. Still need eat." She tore open the first packet and dumped the contents on the floor. "Use food not make sick."

Her maras had learned to let their alpha eat first. Rila slipped close and took her time sniffing and tasting the food.

"What are you talking about?" Bijou squawked. "Of course you're part of the crew."

Kirehe snorted and opened another meal packet. "Not know this word. No place here for Kirehe and dragons."

Bijou harrumphed and returned inside the yacht, leaving Kirehe alone.

She finished opening the packets and pouring them on the floor for her maras. "Nihan can eat later," she whistled to the krata.

"Stay here," Nihan said. "Bad choice?"

From flavors of his tone, she knew Nihan meant the choice to come with her on the yacht. To leave their homeworld.

She'd made that choice too.

"Maybe." Kirehe picked one of the doors and used it. The metal portal slid to the side when she approached.

The big ship, she discovered, had a lot of corridors. She lost herself in a maze of gray passages, each big enough for four people to walk abreast. Every door she passed had a screen beside it. Some flickered at her, others did not. All had squiggly lines of writing Kirehe couldn't read.

At a dead end, she found a small bank of four red numbers

mounted on the wall. Her people had a clock much like this one. They used the sun for actual time, of course. The Founders had used the clock to maintain a tenuous connection with their homeworld and history.

She touched the clock, wondering what time the one on Rikor Six showed. Her fingers traced the number eight displayed on the smooth surface.

"Can I help you?" a man asked.

Kirehe turned to find a man in a blue coat, like everyone else. A sparse film of gray hair failed to cover any of the beige skin on his head. Tall and thin, he had an officious manner about him. The man reminded Kirehe of the head cook in her village.

Except not friendly.

"Where find Madison?"

"Probably in her quarters." He tapped a section of the wall.

To Kirehe, that section seemed blank like the rest of the metal walls. When he touched it, though, the surface shifted to a map of a long object. Small word-squiggles lived inside boxes of various sizes. Strange symbols marked several different spots. A tiny red dot pulsed on one end.

He gestured to the map as if it held answers to all her questions.

Kirehe blinked at it, then at the man. She thought she'd used the correct words in the offworld language. Maybe she'd pronounced it wrong. Why else would he tell her about something in four pieces? "Madison. Want Madison."

The man pursed his lips and furrowed his brow. "Are you not familiar with how to use a ship map?"

She frowned at him. He spoke too fast and used too many words she didn't know. In the gladiator pit, she'd dealt with this kind of thing too. Except they'd always brought Madison when she asked. "No understand. Madison. Go Madison."

"I suggest you ask her to show you how to use the ship maps." With a swipe of his hand over the wall, the map disappeared. He swiped his hand beside the nearest door to make it open and gestured for her to go inside. "Up four floors."

Kirehe held up four fingers to make sure she remembered the number right. When he nodded and pointed upward, she stepped into a small room with two ladders on the walls opposite each other. They ran both up and down in an oval hole wide enough for two people.

As instructed, she climbed up the ladder. One, two, three… Did he mean for her to count the floor where she started, or start counting at the one above it?

She decided not to count the one where she started. On the fourth floor up, she used the door in the small ladder room and stepped into another corridor.

Aside from the soft machine hum everywhere, the ship sounded dead and empty. It smelled like old, grimy metal. The floor chilled her feet.

These people wore boots because they lived in places like this.

Not sure if Skila would hear her, she whistled for the kukiri. If anyone could find Madison, Skila could.

Taking her time, Kirehe paced up this corridor just like the one four floors down. She sniffed the air often, hoping for a whiff of something different to follow.

Ahead, she heard a sudden surge of voices. The noise cut off swiftly. Boots tapped on the floor, heading toward her.

A portly blue-coat woman turned the corner ahead, intent on a brisk walk. She had a ponytail of frothy dark hair and dark brown skin. When she saw Kirehe, she slowed to a stop.

"Who are you?"

"Kirehe. Find Madison?"

The corners of the woman's mouth turned down. "Sitting in the brig, hopefully," she sneered. "But probably in her quarters."

Again, this odd mention of four pieces. Kirehe decided that word meant something different than she thought. "Where?"

"Right, you're one of her strays. New to the ship." She seemed put-upon yet willing to help. The woman pointed back the way Kirehe had come. "That way, take the first left. It's got her name on it."

Before Kirehe could ask for better directions, the woman stalked in a different direction with swift purpose.

She turned down the indicated corridor and whistled for Skila again. The new hallway had five doors, four along the two sides and one at the end.

Kirehe had no idea which door to pick. She considered shouting Madison's name but thought it might disturb too many of these surly blue-coats. Either that or nothing would happen because no one would hear her.

With a shrug, she picked the door at the end of the hall. It opened as she reached it. Inside, she found the captain sitting in an armchair, his attention on a screen set into the wall to the side.

A faded blue rug covered the floor. More books than Kirehe had ever seen in her life sat on shelves against the walls. Several plants with small, bright green leaves grew from brown pots, some on shelves and some on the floor. Another closed door suggested a connected room. Soft white light glowed from the seams where the ceiling met the walls.

"Kirehe, wasn't it? Are you lost?" The redheaded man offered her a polite smile.

"Madison."

He used a vague pointing gesture at the door. "She's either in her quarters or running rampant across the ship as usual."

This man, as far as she understood, ran the ship. He was their leader. Madison adored him. Jaco, Shmar, and Oolaang spoke of him fondly.

No wonder no one answered her questions. They all took their cues from him.

She glared at him.

He raised an eyebrow. "Her quarters are not in my cabin."

Tired of this, she jabbed a finger at him. "I come here need place. You have place. Madison like place. No hello, no friend. No you, we stop fight and go. Bad place. Bad choice." She turned on her heel and stormed out of the room.

The door shut behind her.

She whistled for Skila again and retraced her steps to return to the cargo bay.

Without a pilot, they had no way to take the yacht back to Rikor Six. She should've let the Oligarchy ships shoot down the yacht on Rikor Six. Nihan and the maras could've helped the whole group escape into the jungle.

Madison could've convinced her people to rise against Irondoom. Kirehe couldn't have, but Madison had a better way with words. She made people do insane things. Her plans worked. When a plan fell apart, she picked up the pieces and stuck them together again with new parts.

But no, they'd left for this terrible place.

She should've listened to her gut and stayed on her homeworld.

At least she had dragons to keep her company.

CHAPTER 15

MADISON

Halfway to the cargo bay to check on Kirehe, Skila found Madison and settled on her shoulder. She rubbed under the kukiri's chin as she hurried along. Fortunately, most of the crew stayed in their cabins, at their duty stations, or in one of the three public areas. Walking the corridors rarely meant encountering people.

With her eye red and swollen, she had no desire to meet anyone who wanted to kick her or shout at her.

The maras jumped and played in the cargo bay. They had a crowbar and treated it like a stick. One mara flung it for distance. All of them chased it.

Nihan lounged on top of the yacht. Like any krata dragon would, she supposed.

"Madison!" Bijou screeched from the bottom of the yacht's ramp.

"What?" She crossed her arms and scowled, sure she'd hate whatever Bijou wanted to complain about.

Bijou wagged a finger at Madison. "That girl stole food and fed it to these monsters, then she left them unsupervised. I have no idea where she went."

Just what she needed. A fight. "That girl has a name. It's Kirehe. Those creatures are not monsters. They're dragons, and they don't require constant supervision. They're not stupid or feral." She stopped short of asking if Bijou thought she was dumb enough to bring feral monsters onto the *Star*. At the moment, almost every member of the crew, including Bijou, would say yes.

"Don't argue semantics with me," Bijou growled. "She stole food! Right under my nose."

"Since when is taking food called 'stealing' on this ship?" Madison crossed her arms over her chest.

Skila stood on her hind legs and crossed her forelimbs. She twittered a blistering scolding at high speed.

At least, it sounded like scolding to Madison.

Bijou jabbed a finger at Skila. "Don't you get all uppity at me, fancy-feathers."

Nihan lowered his head over the side of the ship and growled. With his large head upside-down, he seemed more ferocious, not less.

Bijou took a step back. "I don't care what pokken word you want to use for these things. They're monsters."

Madison liked having dragons on her team. She should've come down sooner. They made her feel welcome unlike every other person on the ship. Her uncle had hugged her but he still wanted her to sit in her quarters for a while.

Either that or the brig.

Stay out of sight. Let people get used to having her on the ship again. They'd resigned themselves to the loss of everyone on that mission. While Jaco, Shmar, and Oolaang had all earned some small amount of ire from the crew, everyone knew Madison had led the mission.

She'd convinced them to follow her. Her plan had failed.

They blamed her for those nine deaths, not anyone else.

If she'd had the grace to die with them, no one would hate her. Since she came back, they wished for her death. Or something along those lines. They absolutely wanted to trade her for those nine lost crewmates.

She would've done it in a heartbeat.

"Grow up," Madison snapped at a woman twice her age. She stomped up the ramp and saw the boxes. Pulling out one of the yacht's rations, she said, "Leave all these for the dragons. We know they can eat it and not get sick."

"The captain said to take it all."

"The captain wants the dragons fed. I think we all want that, don't we? They're meat-eaters, you know."

Bijou raised her hands in exasperation. "Fine. If he asks why I changed the inventory, I'm telling him."

"You do that." Madison dropped the ration pack into the box and patted Nihan's cheek as she left the ship again.

Nihan rumbled a sort of purring noise.

"Yeah, I like you too, Nihan."

The crowbar clanged against the wall again, then clattered to the floor. Maras chirped their delight.

Skila hopped off Madison's shoulder with no warning and chirped like she'd spotted or smelled her favorite thing in the galaxy.

Whistles and chirps echoed off all the metal surfaces.

"Madison?" Kirehe called.

Thank goodness she'd found her warrior princess. "Yeah?" Madison took a few more steps from the ship and saw Kirehe approaching with Skila on her palm.

"I just looked for you. I met a tall man who used too many words too fast and thought a map of the ship would help me find you. Then I met a woman who hates you and thinks her directions are good. Then I met the captain, who seems less angry and also thinks his directions are good."

Despite Kirehe's obvious frustrations, Madison grinned to see a friendly face.

"I don't like this ship." Kirehe crossed her arms and scowled at the floor.

"It's not great right now." Madison couldn't decide if she wanted a hug from angry, cranky Kirehe or not. "It'll get better."

"If I thought we could get back to Rikor Six, I would make you take me home."

Kirehe hated this. Why did she hate this?

Madison frowned. "No one would expect that, but no, it's not going to happen anytime soon. Maybe someday. When the Oligarchy is defeated."

Jabbing a finger at the floor like she delivered an ultimatum, Kirehe snapped, "Then I want the Oligarchy defeated."

"I'll get right on that." Madison sighed because she didn't know what else to say. Her amazing jungle warrior princess wanted to gripe.

The ship fell out of FTL. Madison felt it. She wondered where they'd gone. Uncle Chris hadn't told her. Not that she'd asked.

As Madison groped for the right question or statement to help, warning klaxons screamed to life. The accompanying red lights flashed.

All the dragons raised their heads.

"The ship is under attack," Madison said. "We have to fight them off until we can jump." No matter what he'd said, Uncle Chris needed his best pilot. She sprinted for the door closest to the bridge.

"What do we do?" Kirehe called after her.

As she hit the door, Madison tried to imagine anything Kirehe might contribute to the ship during an attack. Keeping the dragons calm stuck out as a high priority. "Stay!" She dashed to the nearest ladder and climbed.

Others used the ladders too. She had to wait for a gap to join the flood.

People climbed up one side and down the other, as always.

"Anyone know where we are?" she asked.

No one answered as they all climbed.

On the command deck, she hopped off the ladder and sprinted for the bridge. She plunged into a room full of quiet, furious activity.

Captain Wayward sat in his chair, hands on his control panels and gaze on the massive viewscreen dominating the far wall. The screen showed an Oligarchy flagship.

Plasma blasts flew across the gap to splash against shields protecting both ships. Those weapons functioned as a numbers game.

Whoever wore down the other side's shields first got to cause real damage.

Against a flagship, they only stood a chance of holding out long enough to program an FTL jump.

Arrayed on tiers beneath and around Captain Wayward, several members of his crew sat at their own consoles.

Violine, a tough, dark-skinned woman, sat at the communications console, her fingers flying over the controls. As usual in this kind of situation, she sent messages to other Stardrifter ships to request backup.

The head navigator, Naomi, tapped on a screen and ran calculations through the computer. They'd already begun evasive maneuvers, making her efforts worthless.

Lylla could get them a jump. Captain Wayward wouldn't let that happen until he had time to hear the explanation and see a demonstration.

The first mate, Xavier, stood on the captain's right side with a tablet. A tall, thin man with gray, failing hair and pale skin, he managed the crew in emergencies so the captain could focus on the ship.

A few steps into the bridge, Madison saw the pilot seat had an occupant. Hennrick, a decent flyer, had the controls. Five years Madison's senior and experienced, he could do what the captain wanted.

Doing what the captain needed, on the other hand, was Madison's specialty.

"Go back to your quarters, Madison," Xavier said.

She pointed. "But I can do better than Hennrick and you know it."

He snapped a hand to shoo her off the bridge. "Hennrick is already in the seat and your interface cable is in storage. Get out of the way and let me do my job. I can call Pirro if you won't leave."

"Let me help," she begged.

"Get her off my bridge," Captain Wayward snapped.

Part of the screen showed options the captain scrolled through and selected. The view of the Oligarchy flagship split into panes as the *Star* turned.

"Violine, do you have the identification for this ship?" Xavier asked.

"No. The translation algorithm is taking too long."

Madison hadn't seen the ship from the outside, but she had a strong feeling she knew who they faced. "It's Subjugator Cradok."

"We don't know that," Xavier said. "Two other flagships have also been spotted in the sector since your escape. Get out. The next time I tell you, I'm calling Pirro to remove you."

She wanted to know. How did they expect her to sit and wait through this, doing nothing? "Can I at least watch?"

"If you keep your mouth shut," Captain Wayward said. "Hennrick, head for that asteroid field."

Hennrick gulped and craned his neck to see the captain. "That sounds like a bad idea, sir?"

Madison could handle flying through an asteroid field. Captain Wayward knew it.

"It's a terrible idea," Captain Wayward said with a nod. "Do it anyway."

"Yes, sir."

"Shields holding steady at eighty percent," a low voice said. "The flagship is releasing fighters." Adar, the tactical officer, hailed from a planet the Oligarchy had destroyed. Not enough of his people had escaped to preserve their species.

The Oligarchy wanted to do that to humans too.

"It looks like they're stopping at twenty-four," Adar said. "Two wings."

"Is the flagship following?" Captain Wayward asked.

"Not yet, sir, no."

"Good. Tanice, hold fire for now."

Madison saw what the captain intended. If they pulled the fighters far enough from their flagship, they lost one degree of coordination. It made a difference.

The viewscreen filled with a blur between the *Star* and the asteroid field. An Oligarchy cruiser had slipped out of FTL and into their path.

Chance had more likely brought it to the right place at the right time than this battle. That failed to change the fact they now had to deal with a flagship and a cruiser.

"Let's not hit that thing, Hennrick," Captain Wayward said. "It would be messy."

"Yes, sir."

The cruiser slid upward on the screen as their ship's nose dipped to send them under it. Madison would have rolled the ship at the same time to use more thrusters at once.

"This changes things a bit," Captain Wayward said. "Tanice, open fire on the fighters. Get rid of them as fast as possible."

No matter what happened, the captain remained calm. Madison imagined he could stay serene even with the ship breaking apart around him and a hevit pointing a gun at his face.

She, on the other hand, gasped for breath. The situation had shifted at light speed from bad to horrible. And she couldn't do anything about it. No one would let her.

"The cruiser is launching an assault craft," Adar announced.

"We have no one signaling their intent to help, sir," Violine said. "We're on our own."

"Of course we are," Captain Wayward muttered.

Assault craft, which could press through ship shields, carried hevit troopers, the most feared soldiers in the galaxy. Except for someone with dragons at their disposal.

Kirehe and her dragons had proven more than capable of handling hevits. Even Skila knew how to help if they could find glitter or dust and a pouch for her to carry it.

But Captain Wayward had no idea about that. No one on his command crew did either. As he gave brilliant orders for evasion and escape, Madison thought of a different plan.

An insane plan.

She rushed around her uncle's chair to avoid Xavier and reached his left side. "Captain. Let them board. Keep shooting the fighters, move toward the cruiser, and let the assault craft dock."

"Madison, now is not the time to give up." His hands flew over his controls, changing configurations.

She touched his arm. "I'm not suggesting we give up. I have a plan."

"No one has a plan for resisting hevit troopers inside their own ship," Xavier snapped. "I'm calling Pirro."

"Uncle, please. Trust me." Knowing someone would come and try to throw her out, she gripped the impact handle on his chair. "You said you watched both of my executions. And you know I survived them. Trust that I can get us through this."

"Nine dead," Xavier snarled as he wrapped an arm around her waist and pulled. "Nine!"

Her grip tight on the chair, her arm screaming about how hard Xavier yanked, Madison begged her uncle to listen to her. They stood no chance of escape otherwise. "The ones who died in the arena panicked and didn't listen to me! Everyone who trusted me survived! Ask them later. They'll tell you. Captain, let me help!"

Captain Wayward met her gaze. "It's the most insane idea I've ever heard."

She tried not to grin too hard at him even as Xavier smashed his fist against her fingers. "Except for the last idea *you* had, right?"

The barest hint of an answering grin ghosted around the corners of his mouth and twinkled in his eyes.

"You're not actually considering this?" Xavier sputtered.

"Hennrick," Captain Wayward gave Madison a curt nod. "Put the cruiser between us and the flagship. Stay close to it. Sound the boarding alarm. And Xavier, put her down."

The moment Madison's feet hit the floor, she bolted for the cargo bay. And cradled her hand. Xavier had hit it hard.

CHAPTER 16

KIREHE

The mara dragons had a use on this big ship. Kirehe sprinted with the pack, following Madison. Blue-coats, including Gordy, clustered around a large iris on the side of the ship. They held rifles ready to fire at the iris. A red light glowed next to the iris.

Orange lights flashed. The hideous alarm noises had silenced. People stood ready in grim silence.

The ship shuddered. Metal groaned.

Oolaang arrived from a different direction, carried on the shoulders of the big fighting man from the brawl on Ghati Prime. "You called for me?" Oolaang asked.

"Yes," Madison said, her entire face alight with anticipation. "And thank you for bringing him, Pirro. I'm not sure we'll need you, but better safe than skewered."

Pirro shrugged. He carried a stick, a gun, and a knife the length of his arm. The big man gave the maras a wide berth and took up a position on the opposite side of the iris as Gordy.

Gordy grinned at Kirehe. He wore a blue coat like the rest of the crew. Standing with them, he fit in. "I should've guessed this was Madison's idea."

"If it's her idea, we're all pokked," a blue-coat said.

"Hey," Madison said as she panted to catch her breath. "My plans always turn out in the end."

"Not for everyone," another blue-coat grumbled.

Kirehe strode to the center of the iris. Her maras surrounded her. "No argue. We win. They die."

"Wise words," Pirro said.

"If Kirehe says it, I believe it," Gordy said. He offered her a six-inch piece of plastic.

When she squinted at him, he pushed a button on the end. Blue energy crackled into life to form a person-sized oval.

"It's a personal shield," Gordy said. "In case they fire before charging in. Drop it when you don't want to use it anymore. Don't touch the outside. It stings a bit. And Madison, get your ass away from the iris. You don't even have a gun, pilot."

Madison jumped like she'd forgotten the hevits would charge through the iris in a minute or less. She scurried to the side and hid behind the security team with the much more sensible Oolaang.

"This lady has a pokken pointy stick," another blue-coat said. "What's she going to do?"

Kirehe stamped the butt end of her spear against the floor as she experimented with the shield. "Kirehe kill hevits. No shoot Kirehe in back."

"No, ma'am," Pirro said. "Anybody willing to stand and face hevits is someone I don't want to cross."

"Is big, bad Pirro afraid of a lady with a pointy stick?" a blue-coat asked.

"Did any of you idiots see her fight in the arena?" Pirro asked. "Or notice she commands these things? If you're not afraid of her, you need to check with medical, because you might be brain-dead."

Madison giggled like a twit.

Kirehe appreciated this man's faith in her.

Gordy laughed. "Our job is to handle the injured ones. And try not to let your mouth fall open while you watch Kirehe. Hevit blood tastes like kut."

The blue-coats muttered behind her. Kirehe focused on the iris.

Hevits would avoid shooting at first, she suspected. They relied on stealth. Shooting revealed their positions. She expected no opening volley. If they shot first anyway, the shield would protect her.

In case they did the stupid thing, she sent the maras to the sides where they risked no harm from laser blasts.

While waiting, she rocked from one foot to the other.

A high-pitched whine began and grated on her nerves. She would have a harder time hearing the hevits with it. The flashing orange light turned to dark red.

The whine stopped and the iris opened.

"Just watch," Madison said. "She's amazing."

"Quiet," Gordy snapped.

Kirehe held up the shield. Through it, she saw a passage wide enough for three men to stand shoulder-to-shoulder, extending ten meters then connecting to the enemy ship.

Laser blasts pounded the shield, hitting it and nothing else. Kirehe braced it with her arm. She waited for the shooting to stop.

The moment it did, she heard the hevits. Their machine hum trundled down the passage.

She tossed the shield at one hevit and stabbed another. With the end of her spear, she slammed a third in the gut.

The maras rushed in. They swarmed over the hevits in a wave of claws and feathers. Blood splashed everywhere, turning the gray corridor red.

Behind her, blue-coats expressed their surprise with words Kirehe hadn't heard before.

Another hevit, another stab of her spear. She bashed one in the face. Its knife clattered on the floor. She rolled on her shoulder and picked up the knife.

Spear in one hand and knife in the other, she waded through the humming menace with her maras. Their blood and those of their brethren marred their feathers enough for even small wounds to render them visible.

Rifles spat their lasers behind Kirehe.

Gordy fell in beside her. He used the butt of his rifle to help.

Once, they'd fought each other. On this day, they fought side-by-side.

Kirehe tossed him the knife. He caught it by the handle. His movement became a slash across a hevit's neck.

Pirro stepped to her other side. His stick crackled with electricity and he swung it with precision to avoid Kirehe and cover as much space as possible. When he hit a hevit, the electricity crawled over its feathers and rendered the hevit immobilized for a moment. Pirro used his blade to stab it.

Though he could handle a hevit, he had no way to detect them. This man needed Kirehe or a mara nearby to find them. Then he could kill them.

The tunnel filled with hevit blood and bodies. Other blue-coats followed behind them, picking up dropped blades and stabbing the bodies to ensure they stayed down.

"I told you she's amazing," Madison said behind her.

Kirehe yanked her spear out of a hevit and cocked her head to the side. "They're all dead here. Check the rest of the ship?"

"Yes." Madison rushed to her side. She'd brought Oolaang. "Everyone, hold this line with shields up." She indicated the start of the tunnel on the Oligarchy ship side. "When we come back, abandon the assault craft at top speed. Until then, fire on anything that isn't us."

"Where do you want me?" Pirro asked.

Blood dripped from his blade and his arm. More spattered his face and coat. He was a true warrior.

"Here, please." Madison gestured to the security team. "Keep them in order. Watch our backs. Oh, and ask the bridge not to fire on the assault craft."

"You got it."

"Kirehe, Oolaang, this way." Madison pointed. "Gordy, come with us too. Just in case."

Ready to find and kill more hevits, Kirehe checked around the corner. She heard the machine hum yet saw two qusamadi.

Both male qusamadi had the dark, slitted eyes and pale blue skin of their race. Both had long hair, one orangey-red with subtle stripes of a lighter tone, and the other pure white. They held guns and had no other obvious weapons.

Kirehe slipped around the corner, whistling for her maras to follow. She thrust with her spear at one.

Both qusamadi squeaked and hopped to the sides.

The maras flowed around the corner.

"Attack!" one qusamadi called.

Kirehe heard the engines hum louder. She sprinted for the cockpit.

Fortunately, she knew where to find it. This ship matched the one they'd found on Veriscova Four. Both used the same layout.

In the cockpit, she found another qusamadi flipping switches. Kirehe punched the pilot across the face in the close quarters. She mashed the button to release the pilot's harness and dragged her out of the seat.

She smashed the pilot's head against the floor twice, then stabbed her with the spear. Leaving the corpse behind, she returned to the others. Four more hevit bodies and both qusamadi lay dead in a short hallway.

Gordy took their guns. "What took you so long?"

"Pilot. Dead."

"Your dragons picked up your slack, so I'll let this one slide." He stood and grinned at her.

Madison cleared her throat. "Whenever you're ready. It's not like we're in a hurry or anything."

Rila called out, "All dead."

"The ship is secure," Kirehe told Madison. "All enemies are dead." She gestured for Madison to go do whatever she wanted.

"Thank you. Competent, efficient helpers are so hard to find." Madison hurried past her with Oolaang. "Time to use what we learned,

Oolaang. Time to make their deaths worth it."

"What do you want me to do?" Oolaang asked. "Pirro didn't know anything."

Kirehe tuned them out. Oolaang's duties didn't concern her. She remembered liberating supplies from the other assault craft. Patting Gordy's shoulder, she nodded toward the other end of the ship.

"Take things?"

"Absolutely. You keep an eye on Madison, though. I'll get the security team to loot this boat in no time." Gordy flipped her a two-finger salute and jogged back to the other blue-coats.

"Maras return to big ship and wait for Kirehe," she whistled as she hustled to catch up to Madison.

Rila acknowledged her. Kirehe smiled at Rila's softer whistles and chirps to her pack. They had a functional alpha who did her job.

She found Madison and Oolaang at a door they hadn't opened on the other assault craft. Unlike other doors on this craft, they'd made this one red. Oolaang pressed a button to open it as Kirehe arrived.

Machine hum, too big to mistake for hevits, rolled through the door on a wave of warm air.

The room inside had a curved wall with a smooth, thick tube running parallel to the floor. Oolaang rushed inside brandishing tools. Madison followed him with her cybereye in her hand and a cable dangling from her eye socket.

"What is this room?" Kirehe asked. She took one step into the room to smell it and listen. Metal and grease dominated the space. Consoles with screens and switches covered the walls opposite the tube.

"The engine compartment." Madison stepped in front of a console and plugged the other end of her cable into a port. "In the big ships, these run vertical, but they have to make them horizontal for the smaller ones."

Kirehe turned her back on Madison and the strange room to keep watch. "What are you doing to the engine?"

"Me? Nothing. Oolaang is handling that part. I'm accessing the pilot controls."

"Why not do that from the cockpit? Isn't that what it's for?"

"Yes, that's what it's for." Madison tapped her eye socket. "Oligarchy ships don't always have plugs for this kind of input, and I need to do things I can't do with just my hands.

"So no one else can do what you're doing?"

"Sure they could. These plugs exist for a reason. They couldn't do it with their brain, though. Not without this kind of interface."

"I'm done," Oolaang said. "How much longer for your part?"

Madison hummed for a moment. "I'm almost done. Go ahead. Tell everyone to get off the ship. Ask Pirro to shut the iris as soon as Kirehe and I come through."

"Yes, ma'am." Oolaang hustled past Kirehe with his tool kit.

"Kirehe," Madison said, "when I'm finished here, we're going to run to get off this ship."

"Why?" Kirehe gripped her spear, ready to push Madison to keep her moving.

"Because I'm programming it to leave. And now I'm done."

Kirehe heard Madison pop her cable out of the interface. She turned and took Madison's wrist.

They ran.

When they reached the bridge, they discovered the last few blue-coats hurrying through the iris. Kirehe pulled Madison after them. She let go of Madison to reach her dragons.

The iris closed as soon as they cleared it.

Madison bent over to catch her breath.

Kirehe thought Madison needed to run more. They'd gone only a short distance.

All four maras pressed close to Kirehe and trilled their affection. She rubbed under their chins, one at a time.

"What just happened?" one blue-coat asked.

Madison grinned. "We just made some modifications." She checked something over Kirehe's shoulder. "No big deal."

Glancing in that direction, Kirehe saw a clock.

"In two minutes," Madison said as she walked backward toward the ladders, "that ship will go home to blow up." She turned and jogged, abandoning Kirehe and everyone else for no apparent reason.

"I can't believe that worked," Gordy muttered. "She's fonsegek."

Other blue-coats murmured among themselves.

"What are these creatures called?" a blue-coat man asked. He pointed to Heetay.

"Mara dragon," Kirehe said. No better time to introduce these people to her maras. "No eat you. Good dragons."

He flashed her an uncertain smile. "Can I pet one?"

Kirehe nodded and moved close to show him how not to annoy a mara. She whistled for Heetay to come. When he did, she modeled stroking the mara's neck.

The man touched Heetay hesitantly. Heetay waited patiently.

Kirehe took the mara's head and scratched the scales and feathers under his chin. Heetay purred.

The man touched Heetay's neck more and raised his brow. "The scales are softer than I expected."

"Care with touch," Kirehe warned, loudly so the whole group would hear it. "If no Kirehe, no touch. Animal. Not like loud noise. Child danger."

Gordy hadn't touched a mara yet either. He brushed a hand along Heetay's cheek and let Kirehe correct him.

Pirro held out his hand to Fobi. She let him touch her. "We all just saw what these dragons are capable of," he announced to the group. "Let's all remember these are dangerous predators even scarier than hevit troopers. Kirehe is their trainer, and when she's not around, they might get confused or scared. If you don't bother them, they won't bother you, is that correct?"

"Yes." Kirehe smiled at Pirro so they all knew she approved of everything he said.

Among her people, she knew Pirro would have risen among the warriors to become a leader of hunters. He had the good sense to survive and command respect. She patted his shoulder.

She also thought Gordy had these traits. The crew had known Pirro longer. If Gordy had joined the crew at the same time as Pirro, she wondered which of them might have risen to the top.

With a grin for Gordy, she gathered her maras.

They had saved the day. Despite that, they had to return to the cargo bay. This ship had no precedent for dangerous animals roaming its corridors.

In fifteen minutes, Kirehe expected the maras to revolt.

She led them to the yacht anyway.

CHAPTER 17

MADISON

It worked. Her insane plan worked. She reached the bridge and warned the captain in time to see the assault craft detonate on the hull of the cruiser. The surprise gave the *Star* enough cover to plot an FTL jump without interference from the flagship.

The ship jumped.

Captain Wayward's stunned bridge crew, all his most trusted people, stayed in their seats. Everyone stared at the viewscreen even though it showed only streaks of stars.

Xavier frowned at Madison yet he did and said nothing. She expected no apology. In his position, he'd done the right thing.

"Madison," Captain Wayward said, his voice soft and low, "what did you do?"

She shrugged like she hadn't run all over the place, risked brain infections, and unleashed horrors. "My job."

He snorted and stood. "Good work everyone. Time to collect damage and injury reports. What's our jump time?"

Under most circumstances, Naomi would've announced that information as soon as they jumped. "Forty-three minutes, sir." She sounded shaken.

"I'll be in my cabin for the next twenty minutes, then. Madison." He gestured for her to join him. The captain also nodded to his first mate.

Madison fell in beside him, half a step behind and to his left.

Xavier did the same to the right.

"I'd like an actual explanation of what you did," Captain Wayward said. "With real details."

"Yes, sir."

The three of them stepped inside his cabin. Madison sat in one of her usual chairs. Captain Wayward sat in his armchair. Xavier stood, forming the third point of a triangle, and tapped on his tablet.

"Kirehe and her dragons can hear the hevits. She says it's kind of an annoying hum. All five of them are capable combatants, so this means they can fight the hevits and it's not even that dangerous for them. Hevits are used to people not being able to see them."

She paused for effect.

"They demolished the hevits."

Much to her satisfaction, Xavier's mouth fell open. "No one can demolish hevits."

Madison shrugged, enjoying this. "Kirehe and her dragons can, especially first-wave ones. Seriously, you should watch some of her Rikor Six footage. She's amazing."

Xavier returned to tapping on his tablet with a light shake of his head.

"I took Oolaang onto the ship. I programmed the system to ignore remote and pilot commands, then input a flight path to return to its home vessel. Oolaang sabotaged the engines to initiate immediate self-destruct on impact. I set a timer for the instructions so I had time to warn you."

Captain Wayward sat with a tiny smile, one that spoke of surprise, pride, and a spark of joy.

"I can't believe that worked," Xavier muttered.

Madison raised her hands and made half of a picture frame with them. "Imagine flying to a flagship, letting Kirehe and her dragons fight their way through the ship with a security team, and setting up the flagship to explode as soon as we escape." She lowered her hands and shrugged. "Obviously, it's harder, and it would mean dealing with more than just first-wave troopers. We'd have to prep for that kind of thing, and we'd need support to keep the flagship busy long enough to get it done."

"Injury reports are in already." Xavier blinked at his tablet. "Light and minimal. Nothing serious. How is that possible?"

"I told you," Madison said. "Kirehe and her dragons are amazing."

"Damage reports are also minimal," Xavier said, "but we expected that. They didn't get through our shields. I'm dispatching crews to handle it."

"Thank you, Xavier." Captain Wayward gestured to the door for him. "Would you let Hennrick know he can go back to cargo piloting duty?"

"Yes, sir." Xavier nodded his respect and left the cabin.

Madison smirked. "You would've come up with something brilliant, Uncle Chris."

He shrugged. "The asteroid field would've given us cover."

"Not with Hennrick flying."

"You've been gone a long time, Madison. He's done similar maneuvers before."

"I'm sure." She could guess he'd pulled off those maneuvers by the skin of his teeth, and with damage to the ship. But she saw no reason to press. Her uncle wanted her back in the chair. She'd won her most important victory. "Where are we going?"

"Sanctuary. I want you at the helm when we get there."

Madison raised her brow. "I'm allowed to fly the ship again?"

"Yes." He chuckled. "I feel like you having to watch Hennrick handle that situation was enough of a punishment."

"It really was," she said with a grimace.

When she stood, he draped an arm around her shoulders. The weight reminded her of other times and other places.

He felt like a father at times like this. Her actual father had treated her this way, and Uncle Chris had tried his best to step into that role for her.

"Tell me why you think you can find the engine room on a

flagship?"

As they returned to the bridge, she explained the point of the mission she'd stolen his ship and crew to accomplish. Their failure had diminished their success, of course. They'd still succeeded at the original goal.

The cost had only turned out much higher than expected.

"They didn't die for nothing, Uncle Chris. I made a mistake, but we all learned from it. We can use it to fight back like you always wanted to. No more running and hiding. Not as much of it, anyway."

"I'm going to think carefully about your plan. I suspect it's not as simple as you want it to be."

The door to the bridge opened for them. Chatter filled the room like it always did right before and after a jump. People stood near or sat at their consoles, checking data or comparing tablet readouts. Xavier hovered over Naomi's shoulder. Violine flashed a mild glare at Madison.

The normalcy made Madison want to break down and cry again. For months in that gladiator pit, she'd craved this so hard it made her chest hurt.

"I never said it was simple," she said without sniffling. "I only said we can do it."

Captain Wayward gave her a gentle shove forward and headed for his chair.

Taking her time to savor each step, Madison descended to the pilot seat. Once upon a time, she'd flown from the door to her seat without regard for anything other than getting there.

She'd taken her position for granted. Uncle Chris had probably wanted her to see that and understand. Acting like she deserved the ship and the crew's loyalty earned her nothing but the kind of glare Violine threw at her.

Madison was not the ship's princess or the captain's heir. She was the pilot.

As she passed members of the command crew, she nodded to them. Everyone stopped talking around her, creating a floating bubble of quiet.

The pilot sat in the center of the room, at the lowest level. Blue cushions covered a bulky chair angled for a perfect view of the huge screen. She slipped into the seat and buckled the three-point harness over her body. She rested against her back and hips with enough cushioning to stay for hours without complaint.

Someone had plugged in a cable for her and left the cord coiled on the armrest. She disengaged her cyber eye and stuck it into a plug designed to keep it safe while she worked.

When she plugged into a small ship like the yacht, it fed her data and piped camera feeds to her brain. She managed it without issue because a small ship only had so much data to offer.

Wayward Star knocked her flat with all the information it shoved into her head.

Thank goodness she'd come before the jump ended, because she'd forgotten how it felt. The ship wanted her to know everything at once, and she could only process so much. All her presets had wiped. Hennrick had probably done that by accident when setting up his own profile.

She shut off the feed and closed her one eye.

Step one adjusted the chair to fit her better. The sides shifted. Pressure on her knees reduced. The foot pedals slid close enough so she could reach them properly.

Bit by bit, she took individual feeds of data and arranged them to suit her style. The process felt like unmaking rope. Instead of weaving a thousand strands together to make a whole, she unraveled the strands and slid them into channels.

By the time Naomi announced a two-minute warning for their exit from FTL, Madison had arranged all the streams.

The ship was her body.

She calibrated the hand and foot controls and tested them. Everything worked perfectly.

Tears rolled down her cheek again, this time from the joy of truly having returned home.

"Madison," Captain Wayward said, "It's been a while since we came here. Just a reminder that the entry is rough."

"Yes, sir," she whispered.

The ship slipped out of FTL and into the center of an asteroid field.

They could have jumped closer to the planet, or in any other direction. Taking this path had meant risking damage to the *Star*.

Her uncle liked to pull crap like this.

"Shields at twelve percent," Adar reported.

She didn't need his report. The ship told her. A few medium-sized rocks had clunked against their shields at the end of the jump.

With the ship as her body, "medium-sized rocks" meant chunks of stone, metal, and ice roughly half the size of the *Star*.

Scanners showed her the path to starboard. They also picked up an explosion from an Oligarchy frigate sliding out of FTL and into a rock the size of the *Star*. Captain Wayward had jumped to the location precisely to cause that kind of damage to anyone tagging and following them.

Madison hadn't noticed any frigates in the area before the jump, but she hadn't spent the entire battle on the bridge.

"Enemy ship destroyed on arrival," Adar reported.

Under her control, the ship dipped to starboard and twisted to fit through the gap between two giant rocks.

Another frigate exploded behind them.

"Second enemy ship destroyed on arrival."

A set of coordinates appeared, indicating where Madison needed to take the ship. The ship's system tried to find a safe path. It kept drawing and redrawing lines.

She shut off the path assist function. It distracted her too much.

"I hate this part," someone groaned, their voice pinched with tension.

"Relax," Captain Wayward said. "Madison can handle this better than the computer."

No pressure.

Madison studied the maps and scans as she maneuvered the ship. Within seconds, the best flight path stretched before her like a ribbon dancing through a ballet of death.

"Should we shift power from weapons to shields?" Xavier asked.

"Not necessary," Madison murmured.

Ultimately, Captain Wayward got to make that call, of course.

"No," Captain Wayward said, "let's hold onto the weapons in case anything else makes it through."

Three scout-sized ships arrived. One exploded as the frigates had. Another hit a large asteroid immediately upon arrival. The third bounced between several small rocks.

"Three more enemy ships detected," Adar said. "One was not destroyed on arrival. Monitoring."

"If you have a clear shot, take it. Don't risk it getting away."

Madison doubted Cradok would follow them blindly. He was a thousand years smarter than that. She would've liked to see the flagship explode from a giant asteroid in its belly, though.

She blocked out Adar's reports to dance through the spinning, swirling rocks. With the ship at her command, it floated and twisted to a melody only she could hear.

That rock spun just so. This rock slid at that speed. Those five rocks moved in concert. Fifteen more surrounded them.

They squeaked between a pair of giant asteroids with only centimeters of clearance on two sides.

The coordinates pointed to a massive planet.

Stardrifters tended to start settlements on small planets, as those stood more chance of being overlooked. A few big ones made their list. In this case, Sanctuary.

Sanctuary, otherwise known as Irid Prime, orbited a blue supergiant all by itself. The planet offered little. Nothing more than a ball of useless rock and sand, no one even knew why it had a breathable atmosphere.

If it had useful minerals, the Oligarchy would've mined it to a husk.

Instead, Sanctuary had giant monsters, devastating sandstorms, and rock too annoying and pointless to mine and refine.

It also had a Stardrifter settlement. Thanks to its size and crappy landscape, they could take the *Star* to the surface.

Madison hadn't visited Sanctuary in several years. Captain Wayward only came when they needed a deep, dark hole to disappear into.

For example, after fleeing a battle featuring an Oligarchy flagship.

They had no serious concerns about any Oligarchy navigators figuring out they'd come to Irid Prime. Tagging and following didn't broadcast location if the ship blew up in transit. Those two ships not destroyed in transit hadn't retained enough ship function to transmit anything back to the mother ship before destruction.

"Shields?" Captain Wayward asked as they cleared the asteroids.

"Twenty-one percent and still regenerating," Adar said. "At this rate, they should be back to full power within forty minutes."

"Excellent," Captain Wayward said. "Well done, Madison."

Glowing with satisfaction, Madison angled the ship to bring it into port on a desolate, empty world. This planet offered a temporary haven and salvation.

Kirehe would hate it.

CHAPTER 18

KIREHE

The cargo bay opened on a yellow and brown planet with air so dry it leeched Kirehe's flesh and parched her tongue in seconds. Their big ship hung in the air, held in place by giant scaffolds and tethers. Below, jagged fingers of brown rock reached from the ground.

Metal in brown, gray, and beige formed a curiously bumpy structure covering most of a vast, dry canyon.

All the dragons recoiled.

"Either we run here or we do not run," Kirehe told them in whistles and chirps.

Nihan leaned over the edge. "Fly. Need to use wings."

Rila trilled a sigh. "Run. Find good food?"

Kirehe hoped they could find prey. The rations bored her too. Without plants anywhere to see, she tried not to hold too much hope.

Skila hid in Kirehe's shirt with only the top of her head poking out. Her foreclaws gripped the edge. "Food?"

"We have to look. First, we reach the ground." She pointed where a small shuttle landed. No one had told her to do or not do anything. An announcement had indicated anyone could leave the ship here and all the cargo bay doors would open until dusk. "Too far to jump. Nihan, take the maras to the ground two at a time, then come for me."

Nihan scooped up Rila and Heetay with his foreclaws and flopped off the edge. He snapped open his wings and glided to the surface a few dozen meters below. Once he deposited both beside the shuttle, he returned for the other two.

On Nihan's third trip, Kirehe leaped off the edge. He caught her and brought her to the surface.

A cluster of blue-coats emerged from a nearby shuttle.

Madison wore a new blue coat like everyone else. She walked with the captain and his people. Kirehe spotted Rho waddling with Lylla, both also wearing blue coats.

"Kirehe!" Madison hurried to greet her with a brilliant smile and bounce in her step. "Everything is great!"

The cheer seemed out of place to Kirehe. "Is it?"

Madison hadn't come to tell her anything or make sure she knew where to go or what to do. As if Kirehe should somehow know or the dragons should somehow act like people instead of wild animals.

"Can the dragons roam here?"

Madison's expression fell. "Sort of? There are monsters here. Things bigger than Nihan. It also gets pretty rough at night. Bad enough that they close the settlement's access points at dusk. They'll close up the ship too. If you stay close, you'll be fine. Solid rock is safe. But I want you to see the inside. Sanctuary is a special place and they know it."

"Dragons inside many days." Kirehe thought Madison had forgotten everything important. "Need run. We go."

"Okay, but it's dangerous. Be back by dark. Move from water hole to water hole so you don't get dehydrated."

"We'll be fine." She nodded and turned to her dragons. "Nihan, fly. I run. Watch for predators."

The krata loped away from people and ships until he gained enough speed to leap into the air.

Kirehe whistled for her maras to run with her.

"Kirehe." Madison touched her arm and furrowed her brow. "This place is dangerous. People who go wandering don't come back."

"I'm not afraid of a sand place." Kirehe chirped at her mara pack to get them moving.

The maras formed around her and they left Madison behind, baked by the intense heat of the blue-white sun.

Madison shouted something. The sun, wind, and sand swallowed her words.

Nihan led them to a trail out of the canyon. Beyond the sheltered region, sand formed long mounds. Smooth rock offered certain footing in meandering lines among the mounds.

They flowed over the rock. Despite Madison's warning, Kirehe took the maras off the rock to test it. Their feet sank into the sand too much to run with speed. The effort made for good exercise, though.

At first, the heat baked into the ground soothed her toes, chasing away the chill of the ship's metal floors. The longer they ran, the less she liked the warmth. Her feet threatened to overheat.

Maybe she'd try boots after all. Someday.

They ran over a sandy mound to find more rock on the other side.

As they reached a long, rocky cliff, the ground trembled. Kirehe kept them moving at high speed.

"Big animal with many legs," Nihan roared as he streaked past overhead.

Kirehe chose not to look. If Nihan called something "big," he meant it. They ran along the cliff.

Nihan slipped below them, flying along the cliff face. In his wake, a large yellow-brown arm swiped the air the moment after his tail swished past.

The krata turned and chose to fly over Kirehe and the maras again.

Madison's warnings rang in Kirehe's head. Her suggestions had merit as good sense. Kirehe wanted to ignore them but also wanted to keep her dragons going.

"Find water," she called to Nihan.

He flew ahead and circled them. When he called with a shrill whistle to announce water, the maras turned of their own accord.

They reached a round pool in the rock too small for Nihan to climb inside. Tiny bubbles percolated from the depths to pop on the surface.

Nihan had already drank his fill, leaving the pool almost half a meter below the lip and more than ten centimeters below the line of wet rock. He perched beside it with his wings open and head turned up to let the sun bake the underside of his neck.

Kirehe jumped into the water and found it warm. Her feet failed to reach the bottom. Maras could swim. She doubted they could climb out on their own.

Skila climbed onto the top of Kirehe's head with her soaked feathers drooping.

"Nihan, greedy," Kirehe chided. "Let the maras drink first next time. They have shorter necks. Now you have to help them reach it and get out."

"Thirsty," Nihan whined. "Work hard."

"Rila work hard!" Rila stomped a hind claw on the stone. "Fobi work hard! Heetay and Wooni work hard! No reach! Bad krata."

Kirehe beckoned her maras to jump into the water. "Move legs in water. Always move. Nihan, give me a claw."

Rila leaned over the edge and reached toward the water. Her forelimb wasn't long enough. "Too far."

"I was stuck inside the big machines with you," Kirehe scolded them.

Nihan heaved a whistling sigh and flopped his forelimb over the edge. His claws plunged into the water and splashed everyone.

Fobi hissed at him. She straightened and blinked. "Danger," she chirped.

Kirehe launched herself at Nihan's claw. He flipped her out of the water and onto the rock.

In doing so, Nihan rolled onto his back. Beyond him, a huge creature with too many legs and a shiny brown shell clicked pincers as big as Kirehe. Spikes stuck at odd angles from the entire creature's body. Sand streamed from it as if it had risen from self-burial.

Skila squealed in fright and dove into Kirehe's shirt again.

"Kill big thing," she told her dragons.

Once again, she faced an enemy with no weapon. She wanted a new machete. Something that size could dangle from her belt without getting in her way.

Nihan flipped to his feet as the creature stomped a thin, spiky, four-jointed leg at his head. It caught his tail. He roared his anger and swiped his claws at the leg.

The creature had seven more legs with three joints each. Its enormous, round body hung in the center with too many giant eyes. When its mouth opened, the deafening screech grated on Kirehe's ears.

Kirehe sent her maras to charge a leg. How many did they need to disable to put it on the ground? Three? More? How much injury did they need to inflict before it considered them too costly to pursue for a meal?

Their enemy raised its leg out of the maras' reach. At the same time, the body lunged at Nihan.

With no weapon, Kirehe decided to try to distract the thing. She raced under its body.

Nihan snapped and slashed at the monster's pincer-studded maw. The maras darted from one leg to another as the monster lifted them to evade.

It tried to stomp Kirehe, missing her close enough to feel the wind from its passing.

The maras swarmed a leg. They scraped their foreclaws on its hard shell.

Kirehe thought the maras avoided using their jaws for fear of the spikes. She spun to avoid another stomp.

The monster raised the mara-swarmed leg. Fobi clung to it with all four claws and screamed her fright.

Rila, Heetay, and Wooni darted to another leg, also screaming their frustration and fear.

Nihan roared his anger. Kirehe heard a note of pain in his voice.

When she rolled to avoid another stomp, she saw streaks of blood on his scales and dripping from his mouth.

The krata snapped his jaws around the monster's leg and wrenched it to the side. Part of the monster's leg broke. Dark, sludgy ooze spewed from the ragged ends. Nihan tossed his piece of leg to the side.

Fobi clung while the monster flailed its leg and partial leg. She turned to gnawing her prisoner. Over the monster's screeches, Kirehe barely heard Fobi's teeth grinding against its shell.

Rila, Heetay, and Wooni each elected to attack different legs.

No matter how it danced, the monster had no chance to avoid all five dragons. Kirehe hurried out of the way. She had nothing to add to the situation anymore.

Nihan leaped into the air. Though he had no chance to gain enough altitude to fly without running first, he used his wings to jump. He swiped with a foreclaw at the creature's face. Three of his sharp claws slashed eyes. Clear liquid sprayed into the air.

The monster's screeches became the woeful cry of a fierce predator failing for the first time. Kirehe had heard such anguished calls from elder dragons no longer able to hunt for loss of acuity in their senses. They left their roosts with determination. One day or another, they never returned.

Under the combined assault of the dragons, the monster fell. Its pride or stupidity kept it from fleeing. Kirehe wondered if a creature with so much armor had any notion of retreat.

When it lost the ability to stand, Nihan snapped spikes off its back and slammed his foreclaw into the body.

Thick, blue-black blood spurted at him and flooded from the mass.

Her krata raised his head and shouted a war cry of dominance. The sound rattled Kirehe's bones.

The monster twitched. It subsided with a long, low moan of confused defeat.

All the noise faded. Kirehe waited a moment so her dragons could savor their victory.

"Taste first, then eat," she chirped.

Skila climbed out of her shirt. "Big. Ugly. Scary."

"Yes. Skila, keep watch for more." Kirehe noticed a line of stinging down her arm. The stupid thing had cut her with one of its stomps. She forced Skila out of her shirt and tore off what remained of her sleeve.

Once she'd washed the shallow cut down her bicep at the water hole, she wrapped it with the sleeve.

Her dragons had taken injuries too.

She should've listened to Madison. Why had she dismissed the warning?

Staying in a small space had affected her as much as her dragons. She needed to run like them. In the gladiator pit, she'd always had the option to run, lift things, spar, or practice on her own. On the yacht, she'd sat and stewed.

And, if she wanted to be honest with herself, she had to admit she felt abandoned. Madison had returned home and forgotten about her until she needed help.

Once the dragons and Kirehe had served their purpose of killing hevits, she'd disappeared again.

On her homeworld, Kirehe had served that same purpose. There, though, she had known it from an early age. No one had connected with her like Madison. Everyone had held her apart, including her.

Kirehe had promised to take care of the mara pack and Nihan. She'd taken them from their home and forced them to suffer in a box because she believed in Madison.

Because she thought Madison cared.

Madison had used her. And her dragons.

Those fleeting moments of contact, a kiss, an embrace, a smile, a laugh, had all served only the purpose of coaxing Kirehe into saving Madison's life.

While she had no doubt Madison cared whether Kirehe and her dragons lived or died, she hated the discovery that it extended no further. To Madison, Kirehe was a friend and nothing more. Someone to call upon in times of need. Otherwise, she served no other purpose.

Maybe they could find a way to live on this forsaken planet. This stupid monster hadn't beaten them.

No one would use them again.

Another monstrous thing howled in the distance.

CHAPTER 19

MADISON

Passing through the force field at the open gate of the salvaged metal walls of Sanctuary brought Madison into another world. Pleasant, slightly humid air flowing past as a light breeze forced her to notice the grit of the sand in her teeth and hair. Her nose ran.

Vibrant green vines clung to the three-meter walls. More plants, some with brightly colored flowers, grew from trenches along the edges of the corridor. Soft white lights hung in rows on the ceiling.

She hurried to catch up to Captain Wayward and his command crew in the passage. Kirehe had left when she would've loved this place. With some assurances, she thought the guards would've let her maras inside. Nihan couldn't have come inside, but he could've flown by himself and returned to the ship. This planet had few flying predators.

Sandstorms kept everything on or under the ground.

The passage opened into a town square where the walls ran all the way to the ceiling, fifteen meters up. Trees trained by growers over the years provided seats. White flowers and dark-leafed bushes heavy with bright red berries grew around them.

People sat on the tree-benches, stopping their conversations to take note of the newcomers. No one appeared to give Madison any special notice.

Captain Wayward hung back as his commanders peeled away. He put a hand on Madison's shoulder and guided her to an empty tree bench.

"Let's talk some more about Kirehe. I can't have her and those animals staying inside that little ship. It needs to be dismantled so I can put together another scout ship."

She sighed. At least he refrained from referring to it as the ship she stole. "You could retrofit it, you know. Oolaang certainly thought that would make sense. It's the right size. With some weapons and a few other upgrades, it would work fine."

He shrugged. "That would also work. But it doesn't solve the giant flying lizard problem. In fact, it neatly ignores the giant flying lizard problem. Which is the problem I'm most concerned about at the moment."

Madison had no plan for what to do with Nihan. She should have thought of that by this point yet she hadn't. The matter had taken no space in her mind.

"He's a krata dragon."

"I don't care what we call the problem. I care about solving it."

"He's useful, just not in space."

Captain Wayward arched an eyebrow at her.

She huffed and raised her hands. "I have no idea, okay? He won't fit in most of the corridors or rooms. A cargo bay is the only real option, and we don't have a spare one handy."

"We can forego having a scout ship for a while, but not forever. I need the use of that bay, Madison. We had a scout ship for a reason. It's a good reason, not a frivolous one."

Too late, she realized he did want to complain about the *Scout* after all. Accepting her presence on his ship again and letting her do her job hadn't happened because his anger had blunted. He'd done that because…

Who knew?

"I'm not sorry I stole your ship. It was worth it."

"So you claim." He sighed and rubbed his temple. "Who is Kirehe, exactly?"

Right. He'd said he wanted to talk about her. Madison had skipped to the dragon problem. "She's from Rikor Six. Human. There are people living in the jungle on that world outside of the resort. They're not under Oligarchy control and don't have spacefaring tech. Primitive, except for how she knows about plastic and genetics."

"And she saved your life."

"Yes. Two or three times, depending upon what you count. Also Jaco, Shmar, and Oolaang's lives. She did honestly try to save everyone else. Except Dani. Subjugator Cradok killed Dani personally."

At some point, she hoped to stop seeing Dani's dead, glassy eyes in her nightmares.

The part where the maras ravaged the rest of the crew could also stop surfacing anytime.

Captain Wayward nodded like he humored her. "And you, I imagine, also saved her life."

Madison squinted at him, knowing he wanted something yet unable to figure it out. "By coming up with the plan and getting her off the planet, sure. You could look at it that way."

"Where is she?"

"She took her dragons for a run across the surface." Madison sighed and slumped her shoulders. "I tried to tell her it's dangerous here. I'm not sure she believed me. She's so amazing, and so great at everything, she probably thinks this place is no problem like any other place. Her dragons are meat grinders. They can hear the hevits and know how to fight based on only that, which is incredible. Kirehe can do it too. I've never seen anyone fight like her before."

Captain Wayward set a hand on her shoulder without pressing down or trying to make her stop. "And?"

"And she's smart! She's weird, but also not. I don't think anyone has ever shown her affection before. Not shy, exactly, more like inept with people. But in such adorable ways. She's like…like a person-shaped dragon." Madison grinned despite worrying about Kirehe. "That's what she is. A person-shaped dragon."

"I see." He squeezed her shoulder and stood. "I imagine a person-shaped dragon needs to run around much like a dragon-shaped dragon does. At any rate, we should contact at least some of the other captains and find out how much damage you inflicted and what the fallout is. You're free to go get a drink if you'd rather. I know how much piloting through something like that can wind you up."

Madison shrugged. "I'm fine." As they headed deeper into the settlement, she glanced back at the corridor leading to the gate. "She'll be okay out there. I told her to come back before dark."

"I saw her fight. I'm sure she can take care of herself on a short jaunt." He draped an arm around her shoulders and pulled her toward the communications center.

Sanctuary could send messages to any captain at any time. As far as they knew, the Oligarchy hadn't noticed any of the infrequent signals. Based upon their usual tactics, the Oligarchy would have come to destroy Sanctuary if they ever did.

"Yes, of course she can. It's not like she ran out there alone. With her dragons, she's unstoppable."

Captain Wayward nodded. "You sound like you're trying to convince yourself."

"I'm not. I'm fine. Everything is fine. She'll be back before dark."

Still fretting about Kirehe, Madison watched the floor as they walked. As soon as she stepped inside the communications center, though, she focused on her goal. The other captains had information, and they needed it.

Screens covered an entire wall of a room salvaged from a ship's bridge. Spaceship technology hadn't evolved much since the battle of Irid Prime. Stardrifters had little time to sit still and perform research. What they'd upgraded, they'd done on the fly, under difficult circumstances and out of necessity.

Most advances failed when attempted a second time.

As a result, most of the materials discovered on the planet still served them well.

Captain Wayward greeted Sanctuary's communications officer.

Violine already worked at a console.

"Captain Wayward, the room is yours," the local woman said.

"Violine, let's talk to Bontemps. She usually has all the news."

"Yes, sir."

While they waited for Captain Bontemps to answer, Madison considered how to present her case for attacking an Oligarchy flagship to anyone other than her uncle. Even with him, he still sounded skeptical.

She'd proven the concept already. What more did he want?

Some kind of proof Kirehe and her dragons could handle more than first-wave hevits. That they could storm a flagship and get to the engine room without Subjugator Cradok killing or imprisoning them all.

Taking an assault craft had shown they knew what to do. Accomplishing the whole plan was another story.

The other captains would agree with him. Good job, Madison, way to find a weakness. Now figure out how to exploit it without getting nine people killed. Here's a pat on the head. Make it happen!

Madison rubbed her face. For now, she had to keep her mouth shut. Until Captain Wayward believed it would work, she stood zero chance of convincing anyone else.

Captain Bontemps of the *Good Times* appeared on the screen. Before taking over her own ship a few years earlier, she'd served on the *Wayward Star*. The parting…

Uncle Chris hadn't connected with anyone for a long time after he'd lost his wife. Mila Bontemps had, once upon a time, stepped into that void.

And then she'd stepped out of it.

Neither captain talked about it.

Captain Bontemps had short brown hair, only a little lighter than Kirehe's. She smiled like she knew things no one else would ever guess.

"Captain Wayward," she said with a polite nod. Her voice rolled with rich purring, something Madison had always liked about her. "I heard you've had a busy day."

At the moment, the sound, much like Mila's hair, made her think of Kirehe and her dragons.

They'd make it back in time.

Captain Wayward echoed her nod, acknowledging her as an equal. "Captain Bontemps. We left in something of a hurry. I was wondering if you could fill in some of the gaps?"

Captain Bontemps laughed. "Something of a hurry is one way to put it. The waves are saying you disabled a cruiser enough to force Cradok to stay. Bravo on that. Left us a grand opening to raid a transport that otherwise would never go anywhere without a flagship. Trade must go on, eh?"

With a glance at Madison, Captain Wayward asked, "Do you know how disabled?"

Bontemps's eyebrows jumped with amusement. "Hard to say, but a reliable source suggested they were emptying it instead of sending assistance. Highly suggestive, yes?"

"Quite." A small smile touched the corners of Captain Wayward's mouth. "Would you like to know how we did it?"

"By acting like lunatics, I assume." She smirked. "Well done, Chris, but as usual, I seriously doubt anyone else can duplicate your successes." The sparkle left her eyes and the mirth left her mouth. "I can also tell you that I've confirmed personally the reports about the Veriscova sector. Seven settlements. Gone. Each one had one or two Oligarchy assault craft, and a cruiser in the middle of it all."

Madison nodded with this grim confirmation of her suspicions. They'd taken the yacht's heading, gotten ahead with the faster FTL drive of a cruiser, and killed everyone who might have helped Madison, then set a trap on each planet for them.

No need to tag and follow if you could use the situation as an excuse to destroy everything nearby.

"I hate them so much," she murmured.

"There's a lot of chatter about the bounty on Madison," Bontemps added. "I'd be careful about where you go and where you take her. If you want support, you'll need to talk to captains individually, not in groups."

"Thank you, Mila," Captain Wayward said. "Can we count on your support?"

Bontemps sighed. "Honestly, Chris, much as I hate to say so, it depends on what you need. I have to protect my crew just like you have to protect yours."

"I understand. Thank you for your honesty. Do you know where we might find some scout-class weapons? They don't have any here."

Captain Wayward had moved on to actual business, a subject Madison had little interest in. Either they'd find weapons for the yacht or they wouldn't. She had nothing to add to the discussion.

She wandered out of the communications center and noticed Jaco passing by with some old friends from the crew. They knew nothing of his betrayal of Kirehe, which meant he could spend some time with people who didn't blame him for anything.

Anything other than listening to Madison, anyway.

No one would hold that against him, of all people.

He saw her and grinned. With a wave, he invited her to join them.

She glanced toward the corridor leading to the gate. Kirehe would return on time. Sitting and fretting about it wouldn't help anything or speed Kirehe.

Madison hurried to join Jaco and do something fun for a change.

Kirehe would return in time.

Probably.

CHAPTER 20

KIREHE

The dragons ate small bites of the monster. Kirehe tried a few squishy pieces. It had an unpleasantly sour tang. She could live with that. Cooking might make it taste better.

"Hurt?" she asked the dragons.

"Mouth," Nihan said. "Inside. Bite spike." He held up one foreclaw drenched in dark ooze. "Scrape."

Fobi had bloody cuts across her chest and neck. Wooni cradled his right foreclaw.

Kirehe set aside the frustrating and hurtful matter of Madison in favor of cleaning her dragons' injuries. The maras drank water first, then she had Nihan submerge his claw. She could do nothing about a cut inside his mouth. The shallow gashes on his foreclaw thankfully looked superficial enough to heal on their own.

Only Wooni had suffered a serious injury. A monster spike had pierced the flesh between his claws. Kirehe had to pull out the spike and use her other sleeve to bind his foreclaw.

"We should go back to the people." She examined the spike and found it fit in her hand like a knife. The spike had a point without a blade, making it better than nothing.

If she learned nothing else from this expedition, she now knew she would never again leave the cargo bay without her spear.

"Skila, what do you see?" she called to the kukiri.

Skila fluttered to her shoulder. "Yellow."

Yes, they'd plunged deep into this desolate land. Deeper than they should have. The cliff they'd followed forked within her sight, and she had no idea which direction they'd come from.

The blue-white sun hung near the horizon and cast long shadows behind them. Had it hung this low when they left? She hadn't noticed. Or maybe it had moved much faster than she expected.

Even if Skila couldn't see it, Nihan might find and reach the settlement in time. The maras stood no such chance.

They would stay together. The maras and Kirehe needed Nihan for protection, and Nihan needed them for morale.

Still, she asked Nihan to take to the air and look for the settlement, or at least a landmark he recognized. She stayed with the maras and spent more time inspecting the maras for injuries. Rila had scraped her tail.

Kirehe spent several minutes picking up broken feathers and trying to match them to maras. Fobi had two, Heetay five. Fobi's snapped feathers warranted no special concern. Both came from her body and did nothing for balance or speed.

Heetay had three broken major balance feathers on his tail. This serious problem led to her sitting and trying to find some way to imp the feathers back into their flesh. She had no supplies, no plants to cut up for strings, and only spikes to cut things.

Until they returned to the big ship, she had no way to help him. When he ran, he would veer to the left, most likely, and then bump into his packmates. The whole pack would trip over each other and fall.

Unless Nihan reported the settlement close at hand, they needed a place to shelter for the night. Most prey animals on her homeworld found holes to pass the darkness in sleep.

On this planet, with things like that eight-legged monstrosity roaming the sands, she and the dragons counted as prey animals.

Nihan returned. He landed beside the maras and stuck his head into the water hole to drink more. When he raised his head, he pointed with his healthy foreclaw.

"Big ship. Not see. See remember place."

He hadn't spotted the settlement, but he'd spotted a rock formation he recalled flying over. They'd ventured farther than she expected.

"Dirt flying." He pointed in a different direction. "Like birds. Dirt."

Her dragons had no word for sand, of course. Their homeworld had no such thing. She thought he'd seen a cloud of sand picked up by the wind. If the wind blew hard enough, the sand would sting flesh and maybe even scales.

"Never mind the people. We need to find a place to rest. Not here. Scavengers will come. No safety." She paced to the edge of the cliff and checked over the side. A wall of rock might have caves.

At the base, at least thirty meters down, she saw a plate of gray metal sticking out of the sand.

"Nihan, come here." She pointed for him. "See if that has a hole to reach inside. Try prying the metal open."

The krata huffed a whine. "Claw hurts."

"Don't use that claw."

"Mouth hurts."

"Don't use that either."

He whined again.

She patted his cheek. "We need a place to stay safe overnight so you can heal. You're the only one who can do this. Nihan will keep us safe."

Her krata sighed and flopped off the wall. He used his wings to glide to the base of the cliff. On the ground, he investigated the metal, sniffing, poking, and prodding it. Blowing on it made sand puff in his face.

He growled at the metal and swiped it with his good claw.

"Don't kill it, Nihan," Kirehe called to him. "Open it."

"Stupid," he chirped.

She laughed. "You beat the big monster twice your size, but the metal beats you?"

Nihan jabbed his claws into the metal and tore it upward. Before he ripped off the flap, he stopped. "Open. Happy?"

"Can you get inside?"

He growled too low for her to hear. Then he attacked the metal, tearing it in strips until he had a gap wide enough for his body to fit through with his wings furled.

After checking the size, he withdrew and launched himself at the cliff. His claws plunged into the rock, sending chips flying in every direction. "Big space. Cool."

"Nihan, you're the best dragon."

Skila squeaked with affront. "Skila best dragon!"

"Skila is the best kukiri." Kirehe patted her tiny head. "Let's get into that metal hole. Nihan, carry the maras. I'll climb."

Nihan huffed a long-suffering whistle.

Skila chirped her acceptance.

Kirehe swung over the edge and scaled the rock wall. Even with her injured arm, the rock had enough creases and jagged ledges to make her descent only a minor challenge. She'd climbed trees with fewer handholds.

By the time she reached the metal hole with sand stuck to the sweat on her brow, Nihan had carried all four maras inside. The sun sank deeper, throwing much longer shadows over the mounds.

Big things screeched and bellowed. The ground rumbled. Wind growled.

Kirehe reached the edge of Nihan's hole and leaned inside. The dragons hunkered together several meters below her.

At her whistle, Nihan stood on his hind legs. She jumped into his foreclaws. He caught her.

The air felt much cooler and tasted less like grit. This space smelled and sounded steady. Serene. Almost stale. Aside from the quiet, it reminded her of the sleeping room in the gladiator pit. She'd hated that place but had always felt relatively safe in that one room.

"Smells empty," Nihan said.

"Can you close the hole?" She pointed at the wide, irregular oval of light overhead.

Instead of complaining, Nihan jumped, caught his claws on the wall, and climbed to the hole. Metal shrieked and groaned as he wrenched the flaps into place. Her poor krata worked so hard.

His effort blocked them in. It also blocked anything else out.

Strips of light through the tears in the metal offered enough to see, at least until the sun set.

Kirehe tested the ground with her foot. A thin layer of sand covered metal similar to the wall in the big ship. What little she could see in the gloom also reminded her of the cargo bay with the yacht.

Something snuffled, wet and distant.

Her maras scrambled to their feet. Nihan landed and hissed at the room.

Kirehe wanted to start a fire for more light yet had nothing on hand to burn, let alone to make a spark. In this dim light, all her dragons could still see shapes, at least, even Skila. Their ears and noses worked fine.

They fought hevits with only hearing, of course. In that case, the subtle shimmers of their feathers still betrayed them. The hevits could only keep their weapons camouflaged so much. When they struck, she often caught a glint of metal in time to react.

Despite how much it annoyed her, Kirehe needed to see to fight well.

"What is it?" Nihan asked as the strange sound continued.

"Animal," Kirehe said. "Under us. Check for passages. Maybe it's nearby but can't reach us."

She moved in a tight group with the dragons to investigate the noises and room. They found four metal walls at an odd angle, suggesting a squared room tilted to one side. If Kirehe oriented correctly, she thought the room stuck into the rock.

If true, that meant the rock had formed after the room. They had discovered something quite old.

On her homeworld, metal rusted long before anything like rock could grow over it. This place, of course, had little water. Perhaps metal never rusted on this planet.

They shifted across the floor, finding places in the middle where sand covered the metal at least several inches deep.

Nihan stopped and used his wing to prevent the rest of them from continuing. "Here. Below."

Kirehe squatted and listened. She agreed with him. The noise seemed close. "Dig."

She stepped out of the way while four maras and a krata burrowed into the sand. They dug much longer than she expected.

The snuffling stopped. The dragons became a single, furious, writhing shadow.

"Hurt claw," Nihan snarled.

Something near the size of a mara squeaked in distress. One of the shadows flipped and separated from the mass. The noise waved across the room. Sand flew in every direction.

Kirehe shielded her face from the sand as the dragons abandoned their hole to converge on the source of the noise.

Nihan growled. Kirehe heard crunching and squealing, snapping and thumping.

The noises ended. Something squishy landed on the ground. A smell like rotting fruit burst into the air. Bones crunched.

Nihan swallowed something.

"Dead," Nihan said. "Deep hole. Dirt drain. More hurt."

The maras chirped distress. They wanted a safe place for the night. Instead, they got a scary, dark hole full of unfamiliar and unknown dangers.

"How deep is the hole?"

"Not know. Prey bite claw, Nihan bite prey. Head taste good."

"Good food?" Rila asked.

"Go ahead," Kirehe said. She pulled the unusually quiet kukiri out of her shirt and set Skila to see about eating too.

Her maras ate with chirps of satisfaction.

Kirehe shuffled forward to the edge of the hole. She lowered to her hands and knees and patted the ground. An unexpected empty space of darkness confused her.

Nihan had opened a gap to another chamber. Below them.

The snuffling creature may have excreted a substance keeping the sand in place. She had no other good explanation for the phenomenon.

Kirehe wanted to explore more to determine the extent of their cave. If other creatures lurked within it, she wanted to know about it.

But the hole was much too small for Nihan.

They still had some light. She gripped the edge of the hole and lowered herself through it. Her toes touched the ground. When she tapped a few times, she heard soft sand.

Though Nihan couldn't fit through the hole himself, he could reach a foreclaw down for her.

She let go, determined to discover whatever she could before the light failed.

CHAPTER 21

MADISON

Sanctuary had a good bar. They kept it clean and smelling like herbs. Anytime someone threw up or spilled a drink, a bot came through and cleaned it. Lemon and lime trees lined the walls, and anyone could take a fruit anytime they wanted. Several colorful birds lived among the indoor trees, all chirping and squawking in the background.

Madison gnawed on a lemon. She liked the peel best and had missed them on Rikor Six. Once in a while, she could get her hands on candied peels.

Jaco sat beside her, laughing with their friends. Captain Wayward had several crewmembers around their age, and they all stuck together.

Usually.

Madison had nothing to say to them. Aside from her lemon, she kept thinking about Kirehe. No one came back from the desert. She believed Kirehe could, of course.

She also believed Kirehe would stay close to Sanctuary to make sure she could return by dark. Had she warned Kirehe enough? Maybe she should've made it sound worse.

"Where's that woman with the monsters?" Taniya asked.

"Her name is Kirehe," Jaco said. "And they're dragons, not monsters. She's probably out running with them. They need more activity than you can get cooped up on a ship."

"Nora said she killed a bunch of hevits and that's how we escaped."

"I was at my duty station in weapons control," Jaco said with a shrug. "I didn't see anything." He nudged Madison with an elbow. "But she was there. She saw it all. It was even your idea, wasn't it, Madison?"

"Yeah." Madison lowered her lemon and stared at it. "Kirehe and her dragons can hear the hevits. They make some kind of noise most humans can't pick up." She wondered if Kirehe or the dragons would like lemons or limes.

She reached to the nearest tree and picked another lemon to tuck into her pocket.

No one said anything for a minute or so.

"Maybe Madison needs some rest. She did a lot today." Jaco took her wrist and tugged it to get her to stand with him.

"What?" Madison huffed. She stood, though. "I'm fine."

"Sure you are." Jaco pulled her toward the door.

She paused to pluck a lime and stuff it in her pocket. "What? I am."

He pushed open the door and dragged her out. "Uh-huh. What's on your mind? Because you've barely touched that lemon, so I know something's eating your brain."

Madison checked her lemon. She hadn't done more than scrape some zest off the surface. Stupid fruit. Something that dumb shouldn't give her away.

"Kirehe's outside."

"Okay. And?" He released her wrist.

They walked through a curtain of vines studded with tiny yellow flowers to reach a garden. Narrow metal paths lined wide sections of dirt exploding with ferns and flowers. Tomato plants heavy with ruby red fruit and pea plants bursting with wide pods grew from the ceiling. They combined to create a peculiar woody yet floral scent.

"What do you mean 'and'? She's outside. Running around with her dragons." Madison huffed and pointed despite not knowing which direction to indicate. "There are things bigger and badder than Nihan out there."

Jaco stuffed his hands in his pockets. "Did you warn her?"

"Of course I warned her! And she still ran off. Without even a peck on the cheek or anything! Kirehe just turned around and walked away like I'd told her nothing more than she might get cold without a scarf."

Instead of saying anything, Jaco snapped a pea pod off the plant and ate it. His crunching echoed too loud.

Madison wanted to slap him for his calm.

"We could steal the yacht," Jaco said as he snapped off another pea pod. "Fly it over the surface to look for her. Maybe she won't see that as us thinking she can't handle herself. It's not like you think she's a little kid who can't be trusted on her own."

She glared at him. "I don't think that. I just don't think she took me seriously when I explained the dangers. I'm not sure she's ever encountered anything she can't kill or injure enough to drive off. She rides a pokken dragon!"

"You know, I get that you're worried, and I know this place is dangerous." He handed her a pea pod and took another one. "But you should hear yourself." He leaned close and whispered, "Maddie, you're in love with her."

"I know that, you idiot!" She threw the pea pod at him.

He flinched and grinned at her. "Then stop acting like a twit. You're moping around like your princess escaped your ship."

She smacked his arm. "I am not."

"Yes, you are." He poked her shoulder. "Either do something to distract yourself and trust her to handle herself or come up with a plan to help her. This whole 'woe is me' thing is gross. It's wrong for you." He shrugged. "If you need my help for whatever plan you've got, I'll do it. She matters to me too."

Madison huffed and gnawed on her lemon. Taking out the yacht now would annoy her uncle. Assuming it could still fly. Bijou had already dismantled parts of it. Those parts may have included necessary flight components, especially if one of the other small ships needed replacements.

They could take one of the other ships. Except that would also annoy her uncle. Probably even more. At least the yacht kind of technically belonged to Madison. She'd seized it. In her conversations with her uncle so far, she hadn't formally relinquished it to his possession.

She had, of course, flown it into his ship. Which made it his.

Even if they did steal a ship and take it over the surface, they also had to return by dusk. The Star shut its cargo bays at night because of the sandstorms.

Besides, she had no idea which direction Kirehe had gone, whether she'd decided to explore caves, or how fast dragons ran at top speed. They could be anywhere.

Madison would never find them. Even with the *Star*'s high-powered scanners, she might overlook them.

"Whatever," she snapped. Defeat sucked. Sitting useless while other people did things also sucked. "I'm just going to watch for her. At least that's kind of like doing something."

"Do you want me to come wait with you?"

Jaco wanted to sit and wait with her for someone who still hated him. He was her best friend in the whole universe for a reason.

"Nah. Go have fun or something." She flashed him a fake smile. "Go regale people with the amazing tale of our escape so I don't have to do it."

He hugged her. "I'm sure she's fine. Have a little faith."

"Yeah. Fine." Madison let him go and headed for the gate. She sat near the guards with her back against the wall. Once she told them she wanted to watch for someone, they ignored her.

People used ropes and the scaffolding to climb the outside of the *Star*, performing repairs and maintenance. Everyone came to Sanctuary for that. Stardrifters had no option for building space docks. Anytime someone tried, the Oligarchy swooped in and destroyed it, then the settlement, then anything else nearby.

Few planets could support a ship of its size in the atmosphere. That unusual facet explained what made Sanctuary special, in a way.

A long time ago, the humans had gathered a fleet to challenge the Oligarchy in a last-gasp effort to end the war and win their freedom. They'd set up an ambush and planned it for months. The lakhan in command had fallen for their trap.

And yet, the human fleet had failed.

Legend claimed Irid Prime had once supported life. Not the giant monsters living on it these days. Birds. Mammal-like animals good for eating. Trees. Plants with berries and edible roots. A full ecosystem bursting with water and living things.

They'd used the Irid system for the ambush on purpose. The nearby asteroid field had, reportedly, covered a lot more space at the time. Irid Prime had supported a sizable colony. Ground-based weapons had held so much promise against the Oligarchy ships.

And yet, the human fleet had failed.

The massive battle had destroyed Irid Prime. And the backbone of the human resistance. The remains of that fleet's ships lay scattered across the planet's surface, mostly hidden by the shifting sands.

Sanctuary was built from and atop the bones of that failed fleet.

Uncle Chris liked to tell the story with the addition that the humans had taken a lakhan flagship down with them. They'd killed a lakhan.

Madison believed it. The rest of Captain Wayward's crew did too. They followed him because of that conviction.

Even if no one had ever seen it, she refused to accept the lakhans as immortals. Maybe Subjugator Cradok participated in that long-past battle, as the lakhan who finished the job. But that didn't make him a god. It made him an exceptionally long-lived person.

Her plan would work. She knew they could sabotage a flagship. Getting to the engine room of one and performing that sabotage would take serious effort and work. Kirehe and her maras needed help.

One of the guards crouched beside her. "We're closing the gate in five minutes," he said.

Lost in her thoughts, Madison hadn't noticed the sun slipping out of sight behind the ship. The last blue rays of light painted long shadows on the rocky ground between the settlement and the ship. Harsh yellow lights glowed to mark the location of the gate and its force field.

Madison blinked. Time had slipped through her fingers.

She leaned forward to see more of the *Star*. The cargo bay door slid shut. They didn't know.

Nihan could fit through the gate, though. Even if he had to stay in the town square for the night, Kirehe and her dragons would be fine.

"You have to wait. She'll come back."

The look on his face made her want to slap him. She didn't want his pity. "If we can't see anyone," the guard said, "we shut the gate. That's the policy."

No one remained on the ship's hull. The last shuttle returned to its dock, stranding everyone where they were for the night. Lights along the hull winked off to keep any creatures from deciding it might make a good snack overnight.

"Just five extra minutes," she said.

The guard patted her on the back like he'd done it for many people before her and would have to for many more. "I'm sorry. She shouldn't have wandered into the desert. No one comes back. You know that."

Madison did know that. But Kirehe would come back. Any moment, Nihan would glide out of the sky to land with Kirehe on his back. The maras, run ragged trying to keep up, would follow.

In the growing darkness, she heard the rumble of a sandstorm. Something enormous screamed into the night. Maybe Nihan could make that noise. She hadn't heard him do it, but that meant nothing.

"She'll come back," Madison said, as firm in this conviction as her belief lakhans could be killed.

"She has two minutes."

"At least look. What if she's just down that way?" Madison knew she sounded desperate. Like that day when she'd awakened without her sight.

She'd begged the nurse to check one more time, over and over. Her parents had to have survived. Had they checked the debris? What if her mother still lay gasping for breath, waiting for rescue?

Except she'd awakened three days afterward. And it had happened in space.

That scraping, scrabbling desperation had eaten her for weeks. Clinging to pointless hope. Begging for a different answer. Devising plans with flawed premises and no chance of success.

This felt the same.

The guards humored her. Both men moved outside and stood watch there.

Something else huge roared in the distance. Even Madison couldn't pretend it might be Nihan. Not this time.

When the yellow lights flashed, they stepped inside.

One pressed a button on the wall. "Gate is clear. No one incoming," he said.

"But she's still out there," Madison whimpered.

"I'm sorry," the guard said. "Pour one out for her tonight."

The gate slid down from the ceiling. When it reached the floor, it clanged with finality.

Not even the amazing, magnificent Kirehe and her amazing, magnificent dragons could survive a night on the surface of Sanctuary. Especially not without gear to protect them from the cold.

Madison sobbed into her knees.

CHAPTER 22

KIREHE

The space beneath the initial room reminded Kirehe of a corridor on the big ship, except sideways. She ventured a short distance from the hole before giving up. They had too little light.

If she could find something shiny, she could direct light where she wanted it. Until then, she had dragons with injuries to tend. Also, she noticed the temperature continued to fall as she delved deeper.

Exploring on her own in the dark with only a small spike for a weapon sounded stupid even without the growing chill in the air. She turned back and whistled for Nihan to lift her out of the hole.

"Sleep here," she said once she got her feet on the floor with the dragons. They could live with the smell. Besides, the maras had devoured enough to reduce the strength of it. She doubted anything else would come through the small hole in the floor. Whatever might fit, they could handle.

The corpse would probably attract scavengers, though, and she wanted all of them to actually sleep.

"Rila, Heetay, push the dead thing into the hole."

She heard them following her orders in the failing light. When they finished, she gathered them in the corner of the space. They nestled together as they had in the yacht. Nihan draped his wing over them like a blanket.

Skila chirped a quiet song to wish them all good night.

In the shared warmth of her dragons, Kirehe fell asleep.

She woke when Nihan rumbled annoyance. A harsh, bright band of light lay across his eye.

Together, they rose and stretched.

Kirehe's arm ached like any minor injury. She unwrapped Wooni's claw and checked it. The flesh looked fine with no infection showing. He spent a minute licking it to clean the wound. When he finished, she retied the makeshift bandage.

All the dragons had parts to lick clean of their own blood. Kirehe checked her arm and found a nice scab.

Skila flitted around the room. Watching her in somewhat better light this morning, Kirehe decided they'd fallen into a cargo bay. That being the case, she expected to find materials the captain might want.

If she brought him useful things, he might dislike her less. Eventually, she might persuade him to take her and the dragons back to Rikor Six despite the danger.

Yes, she needed to befriend the captain on her own. She couldn't rely on Madison for that.

That thought hurt. She pushed it aside. Madison was a person. Dragons made more sense than people ever would.

"Nihan, open the hole. We're not leaving right away, though. Tend injuries, explore this place, then go back to the big ship."

In the dim light, she saw blood crusted on his foreclaw. He ignored it to climb up and pry open the flaps. With more light, she inspected the injury and found several shallow punctures in an arc. The scabs had cracked while he worked.

"Nihan fine," he chirped. "Hurt not bad. Stay. Kirehe and maras explore." He settled on the floor and licked his claw to stop the ooze of fresh blood.

She patted his cheek. "Nihan is the best dragon."

"Skila best dragon," the kukiri grumbled as she landed on Kirehe's shoulder.

"Skila is the prettiest dragon." Kirehe rubbed under the kukiri's chin, ruffling her feathers.

Skila hugged Kirehe's finger. "Kiki best dragon."

"Yes, Kirehe is the best dragon of all. Come. Wooni stay. Heal with Nihan. Heetay also stay." His broken feathers made him a liability if they met an enemy. "And Skila. Come find me if there's danger."

As Kirehe deposited the kukiri on Nihan's snout, Skila chirped, "Watch! Good watch."

Nihan snorted.

Skila fluttered into the air with an annoyed whistle and landed next to the two males.

Kirehe grinned at her family. "Rila, Fobi, we explore."

With Nihan's help, they dropped into the hole to find whatever secrets lay inside this strange metal haven.

The two maras ranged up and down the corridor. Fobi returned with a piece of shiny metal.

"Pretty," she said.

Kirehe took it and judged it good enough to angle the light. "Yes, pretty. Good find." She piled sand to make a stand for it and pointed it down the corridor.

With her two maras close at hand, Kirehe plunged down the corridor. They walked over doors with more doors overhead. A thin layer of sand covered the floor, grinding against the calloused flesh of Kirehe's feet.

She wondered how to get any of the doors open without Nihan. They needed a piece of metal to wedge into the seams. Aside from the one shiny surface Fobi had found, the ship seemed intact.

Unlike Captain Wayward's big ship, this one had no ladders she could find. They wandered until Kirehe discovered a gaping open hole with a square shaft running sideways. In one direction, the shaft grew dark. In the other, thin beams of light lanced the tunnel.

They climbed into the shaft and headed toward the light. Not far up it, they encountered another open doorway. Kirehe pressed ahead in the shaft. They passed one more open doorway before reaching a wall blocking any further progress.

Kirehe led her maras through the last open doorway.

Beams of light from the outside slashed across the floor at random places. Near each, thin puddles of sand covered the floor.

Rila paused. "Hear?"

Kirehe stopped and listened.

Bone or claws scraped across metal in the distance, much like Nihan's when he walked. Krata dragons had no significant abilities to maintain stealth on the ground. In the air, they could glide in complete silence. On the ground, they made noise no matter how hard they tried to avoid it.

"Big?" Fobi chirped.

"Maybe." Kirehe rose to the balls of her feet and slipped forward.

Her maras followed her example and flanked her. They made only a whisper of sound as they stalked closer to the source of the noise.

They turned down a corridor to the left. With every step, the noise grew louder. Kirehe heard something breathing with exertion.

Through an open doorway, they found a six-legged beetle three times the size of a mara. Two thin strips of light shone on its dull, sand-colored shell. It rocked back and forth on its legs as if it tried to roll something too heavy or square.

Kirehe had never seen a beetle so large.

At least they could surprise it from behind. Trying to crush fist-sized beetles with rocks had taught her how strong the shells could be. They would need stealth to kill it.

She had a small monster spike and two maras. The beetle had unknown weapons at its disposal. For all she knew, this one could stab with its short antennae or bite with large pincers. She scanned the floor for sand and debris.

There and there, she would avoid the small sand drifts.

Together with Fobi and Rila, Kirehe stepped into the space. They had to climb a short distance to reach the floor. Or, Kirehe, supposed, to reach the wall which had become the floor at some point many years earlier.

Now she knew without a doubt she'd made the right choice in leaving behind the two male maras. Either would have fouled this hunt one way or another in their current conditions.

They crept forward. At the point when Kirehe wanted to charge, she reached to both sides and patted her maras on the back.

The trio sprinted forward and slammed into the beetle, hitting with their sharp things.

Kirehe's spike scored a tiny hole in the carapace without stabbing through it. Rila leaped onto its back and jammed all her claws into the shell. Fobi chomped her jaws around a back leg.

Only Fobi caused real harm. She snapped the leg, forcing it to bend at an unnatural angle without severing it.

In retrospect, Kirehe should have also attacked a leg. The creatures on this planet seemed to have many of them, and all served as a weak point.

The beetle shrieked and tried to turn.

Rila scratched at its face.

Kirehe danced to the side and grabbed for the other back leg. It stepped out of her reach.

Fobi bounced forward to attack a middle leg closer to the body.

The beetle bucked. Rila flew forward. She landed with a clatter of metal and plastic.

Chomping the middle leg, Fobi shrieked her rage. The beetle screeched and turned toward Fobi. Kirehe snatched the injured back leg. She shoved her monster spike at the place where the leg joined the body.

Her spike sank into flesh and released a spray of hot, sticky, blue-green blood onto her face and chest.

The middle leg crunched under Fobi's assault.

Rila charged into the fray again, leaping at the beetle's face with her foreclaws and her fangs bared. She hit a meter-long pincer. Instead of letting that stop her, she snapped her jaws shut and scraped at it. Hard shell cracked. She fell to the floor with the shell still clamped in her jaws.

More blood spurted from the limp flesh dangling at the beetle's mouth. Its second pincer twitched.

Fobi shook her head, trying to tear out the middle leg.

Kirehe ripped out her spike. As soon as she held it free, she thought better of the choice. She punched the spike back into the hole, shoving it into the beetle all the way to her shoulder. Turning her wrist back and forth, she swept the spike through the beetle's body as much as possible.

The beetle's screeches grew less intense. Its body sank to the floor.

Rila rushed its head again and tore it apart. Fobi yanked out the leg and tossed it aside.

They'd defeated the giant beetle.

When Kirehe removed her arm, she let it hang at her side, dripping blue-green blood and oozing gobs of cream-colored meat. That tactic had worked but it left her with a stinking sheath of disgusting slime over her arm.

She shook her hand. When that accomplished little, she smeared the whole limb against the wall.

"Good," she told her maras.

Peering over the beetle while Rila and Fobi tasted the meat, she saw chairs. Rila had landed among them. Their tables remained bolted to the wall.

The room otherwise offered nothing of interest. Kirehe wanted useful things. Captain Wayward could get chairs anywhere.

She chirped to get Rila and Fobi's attention. The two maras, both also covered in blue-green and beige gore, raised their heads. A string of meat dangled from Fobi's fangs. She slurped it into her mouth.

"We keep moving. Stay quiet. Listen."

"More eat?" Rila asked. She bared her teeth in a grin.

Kirehe snorted. "You've eaten more in the past day than in the past two weeks. We move."

The trio used the open doorway on the other side of the room to leave. They skulked through empty rooms and corridors until they reached a strange room full of chairs molded to the wall, all facing in one direction. Strange shapes dangled from several of those chairs. Broken glass littered the floor. On the far end, shards of glass hung from parts of an otherwise blank wall.

She saw no moving creatures, so she slipped deeper into the room. The equipment in this room defied her understanding. Once she reached the center, though, she saw one thing she knew Captain Wayward would want.

This thing, he would find exceptionally interesting, she thought.

Kirehe knew she appreciated it.

CHAPTER 23

MADISON

The night limped past. Madison tossed and turned for an eternity. According to the clock, she gave up trying to sleep after two hours. For another eternity, she paced with frantic energy, unable to think straight.

Until she saw a body, she had no ability to believe Kirehe had died in the desert.

The monsters ensured no one ever saw a body.

This contradiction kept her awake.

She left her rented room and headed to the gate, knowing it had no viewscreen. Part of her expected to hear someone pounding on the wall.

In her head, an entire fantasy played out.

Nihan pounded on the wall. Madison ran to fetch a guard. They opened the gate. The dragons piled in, carrying Kirehe, who'd passed out from an injury and the cold. Madison took her to the rented room and wrapped her in blankets. Kirehe woke. They kissed. Poof, and happily ever after.

By the time she reached the gate corridor, she sprinted through hallways.

Two different guards stood watch at the gate. They stared at her. She stared at them.

"It's the middle of the night," one guard said as if she must have lost track of time. "The gate is locked until dawn."

She nodded. "If someone came during the night, would you open it?"

"No."

"Why not?" Madison prepared for some soulless answer about following orders.

"Because some of the things out there at night can mess with your mind." He sounded so patient, like he fielded this question all the time and knew people needed softness to handle the answer. "We can't trust what we see or hear. You should go back to your bunk and get some rest."

Madison hated him. He gave her a real answer instead of one to argue and rant about. She turned her back on the guards and wiped her face.

"She's fine," Madison whispered.

Except she knew Kirehe had no chance out there. Why did the universe do this? Finally, she'd found the one person she wanted. Then the stubborn woman had run off to her death.

She wandered without paying attention to direction and wound up sitting on a tree bench.

"Madison? I can't sleep either." Lylla shuffled to her side from behind her. "The bed is weird, and I can't stop seeing numbers."

Lylla needed her. Madison straightened and plastered a fake smile onto her face. "Weird how?"

"I don't know." Lylla shrugged as she sat beside Madison. "It's just not right."

Madison could summon whatever she had left to do this. She forced herself to breathe. "Numbers?"

"They keep swirling inside my head." Lylla rubbed both her temples. "Ever since I started plotting those courses for you, I keep dreaming about numbers. They dance and spin with stars. I could give you a point-by-point course to Veriscova Four right now. It's like I opened a door and stuff streamed in, and now it won't shut again."

The girl's new ability needed exercise. Like Kirehe and her

dragons needed exercise.

"Did they give you a learning tablet? You could enter them into that."

"No."

At least she could worry about someone else's problems instead of her own.

Madison hopped to her feet and took Lylla's hand. "Let's find you something to do that. I'm sure someone here has something you can borrow for now. In the morning, we can go back to the *Star* and get you something there."

Lylla nodded. "Thanks. I would've gone to Kirehe, but I don't know where she went."

A small, stupid, helpless noise spat out of Madison's mouth. She tripped over nothing and stumbled forward.

"I think she stayed on the *Star* for the night," Madison said in a rush. "Because of the dragons."

She lied. Why did she lie? To spare Lylla's feelings?

"Okay. I'll find her tomorrow. Watch out, the floor is a little uneven."

The galaxy had become a little uneven.

Finding something for Lylla to use to input her numbers kept Madison busy for a while. When she left the girl, Lylla had a tablet in her hands and a broad smile on her face.

Madison returned to wandering. She could have found a way to explain more firmly to Kirehe. She *should* have done that. Kirehe and five dragons lay dead on the surface, probably half-eaten and frozen, and it was Madison's fault.

Her thoughts spiraled deeper and darker. Twice, she returned to the gate, wanting them to open it so she could leave. If Kirehe stayed on Irid Prime, Madison wanted to stay on Irid Prime too.

Eventually, she curled into a corner and rocked herself. She nodded off.

Light and noise woke her much later. People passed nearby, not noticing her between two flowering shrubs. She rubbed her eyes as she stood, thinking about one thing only.

She needed to take the yacht and skim the surface. If anything remained of Kirehe or her dragons, Madison would find it.

Her entire body ached from how she'd slept. As she hurried to the gate, she tried to stretch out the kinks.

"Madison!" Jaco called. He caught up to her. "Where are we going?"

We.

"To find Kirehe."

"Okay. Let's go."

At least she still had a friend.

No one stopped them from leaving Sanctuary. They passed through the forcefield and into the dry, baking heat of another glaring day on Irid Prime.

With Jaco in the lead, they ran for the two small shuttles parked nearby. Anyone wanting to get from the ship to Sanctuary or the reverse could use them anytime. Pilots sat inside, waiting to fly the small craft.

As they reached the closer shuttle, Jaco hit the button to open the door. He turned back to offer his hand to Madison.

His gaze drifted past her. He raised his brow and grinned.

"We maybe don't need to go looking," he said.

Madison stopped and turned to see where he pointed.

Nihan flew to the gate with Kirehe on his back. On the ground, Madison thought she saw shimmers of the maras running toward them.

"I guess they're tougher than Irid Prime," Jaco said.

Tears sprang to Madison's eye. She thought her heart stopped, or maybe it gushed. Her fingers and toes tingled.

The giant dragon backwinged and landed in front of the gate. Kirehe climbed off his back with a long, wrapped bundle slung over one shoulder. She patted Nihan's shoulder.

Madison noticed Nihan favoring one front claw. Kirehe had lost her sleeves, though she'd wrapped one around her free arm. Dried blood and blue-green stuff crusted with sand stained her clothes and spattered her flesh.

Without realizing she'd started running, Madison jogged to Kirehe.

Her warrior princess whistled with her dragon.

"Kirehe! You're alive!"

"Yes. All of us are fine." She sounded distant. Normal? Sure. Her gaze ignored Madison in favor of the incoming maras. With a few more chirps and whistles, she patted Nihan again.

Nihan trotted to go meet the maras.

The dragons mattered to Kirehe. Madison knew that. Kirehe would see them safe and comfortable before attending to anything else.

Skila popped her head out of Kirehe's shirt and chirped.

Kirehe chirped something in response. "Where is Captain Wayward?"

"Inside Sanctuary, as far as I know." Despite Kirehe's no-nonsense, officious manner, Madison craved her touch. "Can I hug you?" she gushed.

"Hands full," Kirehe said. She turned and marched inside the gate.

Of course. Kirehe carried something about the size of a large body. Madison knew better than to try to unseat cargo for something as dumb as a hug. Kirehe didn't even like hugging that much.

"I'll show you where he most likely is." Madison hurried to lead Kirehe inside Sanctuary. She'd wanted to do this the day before. "The place is amazing."

"Are you okay?" Jaco asked.

Madison had forgotten about him. She glanced back to see him pointing at Kirehe's arm. Her dumb self should've asked.

Kirehe scowled at him. "Small hurt. Good scab. No bad."

Her warrior princess still hated him for his betrayal. He kept apologizing to her but needed to do more. Madison would have to think about that because Jaco would never figure out how to appease Kirehe.

At some point. When she had nothing better to do.

Jaco gulped but soldiered on anyway. "And the dragons? I saw Nihan can fly, but he was limping?"

Kirehe nodded and growled in the back of her throat. "Also small hurt. Much whine. Good scab. Wooni bigger hurt. Heetay break feathers. Need medicine but no bad. Send to big ship." She checked the walls. "Nice inside. They like much, I think. If guards say yes, come here later."

"I'll ask for you," Jaco said. "Least I can do."

She grimaced at him. "Thank you." The words sounded like she found them bitter.

Jaco tossed a significant look at Madison like he'd done her a favor before he turned and jogged away.

Madison couldn't stop checking to make sure she had Kirehe and not a figment of her imagination. She wanted to show Kirehe the whole settlement at once.

"That way, there's a—"

"Captain Wayward, please," Kirehe said. "Heavy thing."

Yes, of course. Madison had again forgotten about the bulky bundle slung over Kirehe's shoulder. Obviously, it weighed a fair amount and forced her to walk with much heavier steps than she preferred.

Kirehe only seemed distant because she'd spent the night surviving in the most inhospitable place imaginable. She and her dragons needed rest and food, and they had injuries.

As soon as they handled this delivery, Madison would pamper Kirehe with a hot bath and fluffy towels. They'd snuggle for a little bit. Kirehe would nap. Then they'd go tend to the dragons.

On second thought, Kirehe would probably fret over the dragons until she saw them tended. Only then would she allow Madison to do anything for her.

Madison plotted what she could accomplish to get to the snuggling part as quickly as possible. From Sanctuary, she could contact the ship and ask someone to bring food for the dragons. Kirehe wouldn't object to a short pause for her to do that.

By now, most of the crew knew the dragons had helped defend

their ship, so Madison had no doubt she could get someone to help.

Maybe she could even convince Kirehe to leave the dragons with food until after Kirehe took care of herself.

Probably not, but she could try.

They reached the captain's favorite place to relax on Sanctuary. The garden featured his late wife's favorite purple and blue flowers nestled among ferns. A sweet, citrusy scent drifted on a gentle breeze through the grotto. Water flowed down a smooth silver wall to splash into a narrow channel at the base.

Captain Wayward lounged in a reclined chair. Rho squatted on the floor beside him. Both looked up from a chat when Madison entered the secluded space.

Kirehe stopped inside the space, the full force of her attention on Captain Wayward. "I have gift."

Madison moved to the side, not sure what Kirehe thought her uncle would want from the surface of the planet. Her curiosity kept her quiet and still.

Captain Wayward and Rho both leaned forward to see.

With care, Kirehe lowered her bundle to the floor. She fussed with the wrapping until it opened. Once it did, Madison realized she'd wrapped her bundle in an orange and white cloak.

The object inside defied her ability to process. Madison stared at a shriveled gray thing, trying to comprehend the shape.

"Is that what I think it is?" Captain Wayward asked in a whisper. He crept forward to crouch beside it, blocking Madison's view.

"It's so well preserved." Rho moved to its other side and prodded it with a finger. "Dry heat dessicated it without destroying it. And nothing ate it. Look, you can see an old scar here."

His attention on the gray thing, Captain Wayward asked, "Kirehe, where did you find it?"

"Inside broken ship."

"You found a crashed ship, got inside it, and brought this back?"

Kirehe nodded. "Not heavy. Only big."

"Madison." Captain Wayward shook his head. "You said she was amazing, and I believed you, but this is beyond anything I ever expected."

"What is it?" Madison asked.

Her uncle shifted to let her see. The shape suggested a person, but the sunken flesh and odd angles still confused her. She frowned at it. "But what actually is it?"

"A lakhan corpse," Kirehe said.

Madison blinked at her, feeling stupid and elated at the same time.

CHAPTER 24

KIREHE

Since watching Viriok get up after Nihan bit him almost in half, Kirehe had wondered about the lakhans. Others insisted they couldn't die or be killed.

Then she'd found a corpse.

Even now, after dragging the corpse back to Nihan, getting all of them outside that ship, and flying the stupid thing back to the others, Kirehe still savored the sight.

A dead lakhan. The tyrants could die. They healed and they had advanced medicine, but they could be killed.

She would kill as many of them as possible.

Somehow.

"I wonder if there are more," Captain Wayward said. "Kirehe, was it a big piece of a ship? There might be parts or even information stored in the ship logs."

"Big piece of ship. Many levels. Walk on walls." She flipped her hand to try to explain the ship lay on its side. "Parts under rock. Much dark. Creatures."

Captain Wayward stood and smiled at Kirehe. "Can you find it again?"

Kirehe nodded. Though they'd had difficulty before nightfall, Nihan had found their way home this morning. He could find it again. "Nihan good find path."

"Nihan is…?"

"Big dragon."

"Ah." Captain Wayward got the same gleam in his eye as Madison when pieces of a plan came together in her head. "Can Nihan carry people?"

This gift had accomplished exactly what she'd hoped. "Kirehe and two more, yes."

"Which means you could take one person and some gear. Excellent. Madison, get this corpse moved to the communications center. Rho, go tend to Kirehe's dragons and make sure Nihan is fit for flight. Kirehe, come with me."

Captain Wayward strode out of the grotto with a swish of his cloak.

Kirehe followed him. If he wanted her to rush back out to the broken ship, she would rush back out to the broken ship. Nihan would whine, but she could tempt him with the chance to eat more of that thing he'd killed. They might find another.

"If I can only send one person with you, then it should be an engineer. You know Oolaang already."

"Yes. Nihan like small man."

"Skila like small man too!" the kukiri in her shirt chirped.

"Skila stay with maras," Kirehe whistled. "Keep them out of trouble. Help Heetay with his feathers. Skila is best dragon at feathers."

"Yes!" Skila climbed out of her shirt and onto her shoulder. "Kiki is best dragon. Skila is best dragon more!"

"You'll need lights, weapons, and some containers, I expect," Captain Wayward said. Though he addressed Kirehe, he seemed to speak to himself more than her. "For your dragon to carry, bags might work best. A tablet capable of capturing video. If we have one that can transmit back to the ship, that would be ideal."

They left Sanctuary and took a tiny ship to return to the big ship.

Walking alongside Captain Wayward on his own ship, Kirehe noticed members of his crew stopping their travel or tasks to stand aside and let them pass. Every single one acknowledged their captain. His people showed respect for him in the same ways her people showed respect for their elders.

"Kirehe?" Captain Wayward stopped near the ladders. He looked her over like he hadn't truly seen her until this moment. "Do you want to be part of the crew?"

She had complicated things to say in response to that question. "Kirehe want safe. Want dragons safe. Kirehe also want fight bad masters. Home good when bad masters gone. Ship good for fight."

He nodded like he'd never heard anything so profound. "I think I understand. Get yourself cleaned up. I'll send someone to the cargo bay with a crew uniform for you. As soon as you and Nihan are ready to go, meet Oolaang on the surface near the shuttles. It would be best to avoid staying out all night this time, so use your judgment to make sure you get Oolaang and Nihan back to the ship before dark."

"Yes, good. Kirehe like not blood on face or sleep in cold ship." She brushed sand from her skin.

"I feel the same," he said with a nod and a smile.

Others had said something specific when he gave orders. "Yes, sir."

When he nodded, she turned and used the ladders to return to the cargo bay. An hour later, she carried her spear on Nihan's back as he flew to meet Oolaang near the tiny ships. She wore a new blue coat with soft cloth underneath.

They gave her boots.

She had spent at least ten minutes trying to decide if she wanted them.

In the end, she'd decided to try them later. When she had nothing important to do.

Bare feet let her feel vibrations through the ground and use her toes when she climbed.

The clothing felt good, though. She liked it. No wonder everyone wore their coats all the time. Hers settled around her body like a fine glove. Every piece hugged her body without impeding movement.

Oolaang waved as Nihan landed near him. Proving how much the dragon liked the small man, he landed with his back to Oolaang to avoid blowing debris and sand at him.

Kirehe climbed down to inspect the objects around Oolaang. No matter what Captain Wayward wanted them to bring, she had the final say over what Nihan carried. Even if he disagreed on that point.

When he learned to speak to Nihan, he could ask Nihan to do things.

"I'm so glad to see you!" Oolaang wore a pack on his back and offered another to her. Along with the dark-lensed goggles he always wore over his eyes, a close-fitting blue hat covered the rest of his head. He also wore a belt with a pistol and several pouches. "This has food and water for you."

"I like see Oolaang." Kirehe took the pack and shrugged the straps over her shoulders. "Nihan too. What else bring?" She tested swinging the spear with the pack on her back and found it acceptable.

He pointed to a box beside him. "Can we carry a box? Because if not, we can pull out the important things and hold them separately."

"Nihan has hurt claw. No carry."

"Okay." Oolaang pulled a bag out of the box and stuffed a few things inside it. "Lights, a tablet, hand tools, rope, and…that should do it. Do you want a gun?" He held up a pistol clipped to a belt.

The belt appealed to her. Pouches offered extra space to carry things. Her new pants had pockets, but this would give her even more pockets. Still, she had no real use for a gun. "Kirehe trust spear." She held up her weapon. "But take belt."

Oolaang grinned. "I love my belt. I've missed my belt." He helped her put on the belt so it hung on her waist, above her hips. "You look like you belong now. Maybe we can get Nihan something blue so everyone knows he's part of our crew."

Having some kind of identification for Nihan sounded like an idea to consider. Later, though. Kirehe helped Oolaang climb onto Nihan's back with her.

"Captain Wayward asked us to survey the area and see if there are any other ships we can get into near the one you found. If so, we can go back tomorrow and investigate as many as possible. The more lakhan corpses we can find, the better, and we always want more data."

"Nihan look while we search broken ship."

"Good idea."

Nihan loped until he gained enough speed to leap into the air. They flew. Without having to wait for the maras, they covered the distance much faster. He reached the open flaps of their overnight haven in half an hour.

"Nihan drink, fly. Look for more like this. Come back, drink, wait inside."

"Kirehe and small man safe," Nihan said. He left them to climb the rock and drink from the water hole.

Kirehe tied the rope and helped Oolaang climb down. She escorted him past the minor remains of the dead thing. Her dragons had finished most of it before leaving.

As they moved through the ship, she led, listening for any new creatures inside it.

They had a wandering line of dried blue-green blood drops to follow back to the beetle corpse. Once there, she brought Oolaang to the site of the lakhan corpse.

"Most of the stories about this battle claim the humans lost horribly and the lakhans involved left the planet as a graveyard. The fighting destroyed the ecosystem, rendering it useless." He shuffled across the room, peering up at the odd chairs. "A few even specifically say the lakhans all left because they couldn't even find anything worth mining."

"Victory means tell story," Kirehe said with a shrug.

"A fact many lose sight of when studying history. There are three accounts from humans who survived the battle, which is how we knew at least one lakhan was killed here. Compared to the official lakhan historical statements on the subject, though, the human accounts sound farfetched. Of course, there have always been humans like Captain

Wayward. People willing to take big risks, I mean. To try unbelievable things.

"I suppose that's why he was so willing to trust those accounts. They were about people like him. Other Stardrifters, ones on other captains' ships, call him 'The Madman.' He tries things and escapes things other people never would. His worst crime, of course, has always been trusting those human accounts of the battle."

Kirehe so far had seen in Captain Wayward a cautious man who avoided risk. She wondered what had happened to the one Oolaang remembered.

"Madison's mother once told me they named her for Captain Wayward as something of a joke."

She squinted at him. "No understand?"

"*Mad*-man. *Mad*-ison. Can you lift me? I think I see a place to plug in my cable."

Still confused by the joke, Kirehe picked up Oolaang and held him while he connected a cable to a box. When he said she could, she set him on the floor to fuss with his tablet.

"Her mother was a lovely person," Oolaang murmured while he tapped on the tablet. "She was an engineer, like me. Helped fix the ship. She had the poor taste to fall in love with our captain's older brother, the previous Captain Wayward." He raised his head with a mild blush darkening his tan cheeks.

"I'm sorry. I didn't mean that how it sounds. There's nothing wrong with falling in love with a Wayward. You having done it is perfectly fine. Diana had a sense of hu—"

"No love Madison," Kirehe snapped.

Oolaang stared at her. "Oh. I thought..." He trailed off without finishing his statement.

"Wrong."

The silence between them grew tense and uncomfortable.

Kirehe pointed to the tablet. "Do. Back to big ship by dark."

With a small, hesitant nod, Oolaang returned to his work.

She lifted him a few more times for his cable. He wriggled in other places and removed small parts to return with them.

Wind whistled as it blew across cracks in the outer wall. Thin streams of sand spilled into the ship at random moments, never lasting long.

Kirehe did not love Madison. She didn't even know how much she liked Madison at this point. She and Kirehe, and all the others, had worked together to save each other's lives.

They all owed each other a debt of gratitude.

Nothing more.

Madison's actions had made clear she felt nothing else. The most important person to Madison was Madison.

Oolaang's voice interrupted her brooding. "I'd like to see if we can find any other important parts of the ship," he said as he deposited another mysterious part into his bag. "Especially the engine room. This is the bridge, and the ship is angled like this." He faced away from the glass shard wall and cocked his head to one side.

"According to Madison's schematics, I think the engine room should be near where we entered. Which means it's most likely separated from this piece of the ship. Or possibly, it blew up."

"Try new broken ship?"

He slung his bag over his shoulder. "Yes, I think so."

Kirehe nodded and led him back the way they'd come. "Monsters in new broken ship."

Oolaang gulped. "Probably, yes. You can handle them, right?"

"Yes." She longed for the distraction of a fight.

CHAPTER 25

MADISON

Leaning against the back wall of the communications center, Madison tried to pay attention to the conversation between Captain Wayward and three other captains. He'd already contacted Captain Bontemps. She wanted a serious plan before committing anything.

From these three, her uncle had expected similar reactions.

"I'm not saying I don't believe you, Chris," Captain Roberts said with a sigh. "That's clearly the corpse of a lakhan. I'm just saying it doesn't help us much. If you put it back, we can let all of this nonsense die down again."

Captain Vane snorted. "Unlike that ingrate, I'm one hundred percent behind you. Madison's escape was the banner moment we needed to galvanize our efforts. This corpse is like a second major victory. What can I do to help?"

Roberts rolled her eyes.

"You're an idiot, Vane," Captain Halsey grumbled. She jabbed a finger at Uncle Chris. "Madison's escape has turned the Oligarchy's armada into a search and destroy mission. They've wiped out entire settlements on the outside chance she might show up there. And we're supposed to be all happy and ready to sacrifice everything and everyone because now we know lakhans can be killed? We've tried, Chris. We've tried. So now we're sure they can be killed. Great. It's still damned hard to do."

Uncle Chris stood with his hands clasped behind his back as if he faced a trial with a foregone conclusion of execution.

Madison wanted to slap them all. Even Vane. He said a lot but hadn't offered anything concrete and didn't argue with the other two on Uncle Chris's behalf. He just kept saying how much he wanted to fight the Oligarchy with Uncle Chris.

The door opened. Sanctuary guards hauled three more lakhan bodies inside the room.

Kirehe followed them with a fourth. She wore a crew uniform. The clothes made her look even more gorgeous than usual. They showed off how her muscles bulged. Even with streaks of sand-crusted blood and other muck, Madison wanted to devour her.

"And now you've got the monster girl," Halsey said. "Did you know there's a bounty for her too?"

Roberts nodded. "Chris, I respect you and consider you a friend. But even I have to admit…the bounties for all three of you combined? That's damned tempting. If you give up on this crap, the Oligarchy will let it go at some point."

Madison stormed out rather than continue to listen to those idiots. She stomped on the floor a few times outside the center, exorcising her aggression while waiting for Kirehe.

Her warrior princess burst out of the center with a stony, annoyed set to her face. Madison felt the same way.

Kirehe breezed past her with nothing more than a nod.

For a moment, Madison blinked and watched Kirehe's backside move away. The view usually made her smile. This time, she had to jump and jog to follow Kirehe.

Something had gone wrong. Maybe Nihan needed medical attention or one of the maras had done something stupid in her absence. Madison should have checked on them, probably. Except she had no idea what to do if they wanted to fight each other or whatever mara dragons did when bored.

"Kirehe, wait. What's wrong?"

"Nothing is wrong." She shrugged.

Madison had to keep running the match Kirehe's ground-devouring pace. "Then what's actually wrong?"

"Still nothing."

"Wait." Madison put a hand on Kirehe's shoulder. "Would you slow down for five seconds, please?"

"For what?" Kirehe sounded…complicated. Not precisely angry, not precisely preoccupied, not precisely frustrated, and more than all three at once.

"So I can talk to you? I've barely seen you in days."

"Yes. Isn't that what you wanted?"

Madison thought someone had slapped her from how little she'd expected that retort. "What? No."

Much too fast for Madison to react or even track, Kirehe whirled. She jabbed a finger in Madison's face and forced her to the wall. Her body pressed vines against the metal and her boot sank into soft dirt.

"I came with you because I trusted you," Kirehe growled. "I liked you. But you used me. As soon as you found your home again, you abandoned me even though you knew I have nothing and no one else out here. Kirehe, fight the hevits. Kirehe, make your monsters dance. Kirehe, stay in a box. Kirehe, I forgot you even exist.

"I didn't leave my homeworld for this. But now I'm here and I'm making the best of it for myself and my dragons. These fancy toys work for Captain Wayward now. At least with him, I know where I stand."

"You think I used you?" Madison sputtered. "What?"

Kirehe narrowed her eyes and bared her teeth. "I know you did." She spun and stormed toward the gate.

Madison's mind whirled and spun, trying to find a way to attack a problem she didn't understand. She pushed off the wall and ran to catch up.

"I didn't use you." She had to huff and puff to breathe because Kirehe insisted upon using a ridiculous walking pace.

"That's a lie," Kirehe snarled.

"Okay. At first, I used you. Because you're beautiful and capable. Then I got to know you."

Kirehe plunged through the gate. Nihan waited outside. He swished his tail like a giant puppy happy to see his mistress.

The heat of the fading day stole what little breath Madison had. She swiped at Kirehe's shoulder and missed. The effort took what energy she had left, forcing her to stop and brace her hands on her knees to catch her breath. "Please stop, Kirehe. I can't keep up."

Thank goodness Kirehe stopped. She turned with her fists on her hips. "Maybe I'll talk if you decide it's not too much of a hardship to come visit me in the cargo bay."

She left Madison and climbed onto Nihan's back. The big dragon flapped his wings hard enough to knock Madison off her feet and sting her face with blowing sand.

Madison curled her body against the onslaught and waited for it to pass. When she deemed it safe, she scrambled to her feet.

Nihan circled overhead.

"Using a dragon is cheating!" she shouted at them.

They banked and turned toward the *Star*.

Madison sprinted for the single shuttle on the ground. Kirehe and Nihan would reach the cargo bay first. She would reach it second. Or third, she supposed.

Whatever. The point was, she had every intention of going directly to that cargo bay before Kirehe could decide Madison actively hated her.

She rushed into the back of the ten-person shuttle and ran to the front. The Sanctuary pilot sat in the cockpit, surrounded by thick glass unsuited for space. She ate something crunchy from a packet designed to keep food free of sand.

"Hey," Madison said, sticking her head as close to the pilot as she could, "can you take me to that open cargo bay instead of the airlock? Right now?"

"Nope. We follow protocols around here to avoid crashes and stay safe. Buckle up."

"Please?"

The pilot snorted. "Do you have something to bribe me with that's worth more than my job? Because that's about all I'd take to do something stupid like that."

Madison sighed. "I'd do it."

"But you're insane. Everyone knows that. Buckle up or this bucket's going nowhere."

"Fine." Madison sat and strapped herself into a seat.

The shuttle stayed on the ground.

"Are we going to lift off anytime soon?"

"Hold your throttle, princess. You know how this works."

Yes, she did. The shuttle had to check in and wait for permission to leave. The ship had only one airlock suitable for small shuttle docking. If the other one used it, this one had to wait. When they had multiple ships docked, they brought out extra shuttles so no one had to stand around outside for long.

Sitting in a stupid little shuttle, waiting for it to take off, she buried her face in her hands and tried to understand what Kirehe meant. Because she needed a plan to fix that.

Why would Kirehe think Madison considered it a hardship to visit the cargo bay? On the yacht, Kirehe had told everyone to stay out. The dragons hated the confined space and she'd worried they might lash out. While Kirehe could handle them in the throes of a temper tantrum, no one else could.

She'd asked Kirehe to come sit with her. Without intending anything more risqué than cuddling, she'd asked Kirehe to share a bed with her.

In both cases, Kirehe had declined in favor of tending her dragons. Madison had respected that. She'd considered going in there anyway and decided she liked all her limbs intact.

The moment she'd thought of something valuable Kirehe could do for Captain Wayward, she'd gone and asked Kirehe to do it.

Kirehe felt used and ignored. Why?

Madison tried to remember everything since the escape from Rikor Six. How long had they spent in FTL jumps? How many days had passed? How much time had she spent with Kirehe?

Apparently, the answer to the last question was "not enough."

Everything had seemed fine when Madison had fetched Kirehe to repel the assault craft. She hadn't said anything or acted weird. In fact, Kirehe had jumped at the chance. So had the maras.

Maybe Madison just hadn't noticed anything. She thought over how Kirehe had acted this morning and realized she hadn't seen the anger and frustration. The day before, she hadn't seen anything either.

When Kirehe had complained about being cooped up in the ship, Madison had seen it as nothing more than cabin fever. Everyone got that. No one else chose to solve it by going for a run on a planet like Sanctuary, but Kirehe had a lot of unique about her.

Madison appreciated that about Kirehe.

Did she tell Kirehe things like that enough? Maybe not.

The shuttle lifted off.

She needed a plan. Something bold. Daring. Worthy of a dragon warrior princess.

"Hey, Madison," the pilot said as they covered the distance to the *Star.*

"Yeah?" Madison lifted her head.

"Thought you might want to know. There's another ship coming in. *The Schooner.*"

Captain Janssen had found them. Madison groaned and shelved all plans of finding a way to woo Kirehe again. "Thanks for telling me."

"Do us all a favor and try not to get Sanctuary blown up for a second time, yeah?"

"That's the plan."

The shuttle docked with the *Star.* Madison unbuckled and rushed out. She paused for a moment, debating which way to go.

Kirehe needed her.

Janssen and his crew wanted to snatch her for the bounty. If they could get away with it, they'd grab Uncle Chris and Kirehe at the same time.

Especially after that thorough trouncing on Ghati Prime.

Captain Wayward, already standing in the communications center, would know about Janssen's arrival. Nothing she had to say would change anything. He'd helped them on Ghati Prime, so he already knew the situation. If he wanted her to prepare to get the ship elsewhere, he'd have someone announce it.

Her running to the bridge made no sense. What would she do there? Plug in and panic?

She needed to explain this to Kirehe anyway. The concept of a bounty might not make sense to her. Madison certainly hadn't bothered to explain that part of their situation.

Come to think of it, she'd failed to explain a lot. Maybe fixing that would lead to fixing the other stuff.

Determined to get this solved one way or another, Madison sprinted to the cargo bay.

Maybe she'd try apologizing. That usually helped when she'd screwed up.

CHAPTER 26

KIREHE

Once Nihan reached the cargo bay, Kirehe decided to stay on the *Star* until morning. She wanted to take the maras into Sanctuary so they could see it, but tomorrow. Today, she had broken feathers to fix. They all needed rest anyway.

Skila chirped a stream of chatter to tell her everything she'd already tried to fix Heetay's feathers. Unsuccessfully.

Rho sat with Wooni, which surprised Kirehe. Her mara slept with his head on their lap. The rest of the maras arrayed around them, resting, as if to protect their packmate. Heetay curled around his tail, completely miserable.

"He allowed me to take care of his foreclaw," Rho said. "It's washed and treated. I added some ointment to ease the pain and he conked out."

Kirehe shushed Skila with a finger on the mara's beak. She crouched beside Wooni and laid a hand on his neck to check his breathing and heartbeat. Both felt slow yet strong. The mara would be fine. "Suffer much. No sleep good."

"I'm not surprised. Would you like me to go?"

Kirehe shrugged. "Which you want is good. Know how fix feathers?"

"Is that what's wrong with this one?" Rho nodded to Heetay. "No, but I have steady hands and plenty of supplies." They pointed to a plastic box beside them.

"You do for pack like Tau?" Kirehe shifted to Heetay and patted his flank. With her direction, he wriggled closer to Rho.

"You mean was I a medic for my family?" Rho nodded and smiled with sadness. "Yes. I obtained medical training. My role in my family was to raise the children for my remica. Knowing how to treat injuries is helpful for that. Especially when they reach exploring age."

"Young maras dumb," Kirehe agreed.

Rho chuckled. "Young macricas too."

"Yes. Hold here?" Though she had no spare feathers to replace Heetay's, she could set him up to grow new ones.

The pack had managed to keep him from falling over for the run out of the desert, so she knew he'd be fine.

"You want new family?" Kirehe asked.

Rho smiled and used their hands as Kirehe directed. "I believe I have one already, thank you. It's not the one I expected, and I'm not always sure how to fulfill my purpose among them, but it's family nonetheless."

"Kirehe same."

"Kirehe!" Madison shouted.

The sound, so unexpected in the situation, startled Kirehe enough to jab Heetay.

Heetay groaned. Wooni moaned. Nihan grumbled. Rila and Fobi both growled.

"Madad too loud," Skila scolded, further annoying the rest of the dragons.

"Hush," Kirehe whistled. "Quiet," she said to Madison.

At least Madison had come to visit.

"Sorry," Madison said as she shuffled closer. "Hello, Rho."

"Madison." Rho fetched a thin tube from her box. "This will ease the pain for him. You rub it on the site." She squeezed a small lump of white goo onto Kirehe's finger.

Kirehe smeared the goo around the three broken feather shafts. The goo made her finger tingle like extra blood flowed to the spot and swirled with excitement. She thought his scales felt unusually bumpy and rough with that finger.

Heetay murmured in pain. Then he sighed with relief.

The other dragons settled.

For whatever reason, the goo soothed his pain and also made her finger more sensitive. Strange. Kirehe opened her mouth to try to explain this to Rho and ask why.

"I came to the cargo bay," Madison said, using Kirehe's language.

Rho may have picked up a few words, but they wouldn't understand much.

"Yes," Kirehe said, "and you annoyed the dragons."

"I'm sorry." She scuffed her boot on the floor. "Not for that."

Kirehe raised her brow and turned to regard Madison.

Madison rubbed her forehead and sighed. "No, wait, actually, yes for that. I didn't intend to annoy the dragons. There's no emergency, so yelling was rude and unnecessary. Except there kind of is an emergency, but not that kind." She paused and crossed her arms. "I'm going to start again."

Kirehe watched with some bemusement as Madison sucked in a deep breath, turned around, walked back to the door, and paused there for several seconds.

"What's she doing?" Rho whispered.

Because she only marginally understood, Kirehe shrugged. "Madison."

Rho chuckled.

Uncertain how long Madison would take, Kirehe returned her attention to the broken feathers. This time, though, Madison wouldn't startle her. She listened.

When Madison's boots pattered across the floor, Kirehe expected the interruption.

Madison stopped beside her and crouched. "Hi, Kirehe." She spoke with a low voice unlikely to disturb anyone this time. "I'm really sorry that I made you feel abandoned. I didn't do it on purpose. I want to fix that, but right now, I have something else I need to explain because it's important that you understand what's going on. Is that okay with you?"

Maybe Kirehe had expected too much or misinterpreted Madison.

Understanding people gave her a headache.

The ache in her heart, the one she'd neatly ignored without Madison present, eased.

"I accept your apology." Kirehe finished doing all she could for Heetay's feathers. She rubbed his leg. "We can talk about it later if this other thing is more important."

"It's kind of time-critical." Madison switched to the foreign language. "Captain Janssen's ship just arrived. His crew are the people we fought on Ghati Prime where Captain Wayward stepped in. They were trying to take me to collect the bounty on my head."

"Oh dear," Rho said.

In Kirehe's language, Madison asked, "Do you understand what that means? That I have a 'bounty' on my head, I mean. We mentioned it several times, but I don't know if you grasped the concept."

Though Kirehe didn't know the word, she'd picked up at least some of the idea. "The Oligarchy wants you very dead?"

Madison grinned. "Well, yes, but that's not a bounty. That's situation normal. They want all humans dead or enslaved. This bounty thing means the Oligarchy is offering a significant reward to anyone who brings me to them alive so they can execute me, or gives them information about where I am. That reward includes citizenship in the Oligarchy, which is something they've never offered to any human that I know of."

"That would mean giving up." Kirehe grimaced. "Becoming the enemy." She could imagine no worse crime than turning her back on her people to save and enrich herself.

"Yes. And that's something I would never want. But there are a lot of Stardrifters who hate the way we live. They hate how much they have to work and suffer and fear. An offer like that can be…tempting."

Kirehe spat on the floor. "Only to terrible people."

"In fairness, plenty of Stardrifters are terrible people." Madison shrugged. "But that's beside the point. What matters right now is some of that kind of Stardrifter have arrived on this planet. Also, there's a bounty for you too. I guess you pissed off Viriok enough that he wants to make an example of you too. Added to the bounty my uncle has had forever, which they increased, our ship is kind of a hot target right now."

All this information made Kirehe curl her lip. Greed made people act like idiots. "You're warning me that we probably will have to fight and flee. Dragons may be useful in this situation. Are we still supposed to avoid killing fellow humans?"

"Any day before today, I would've said yes. If they're coming to drag us to the Oligarchy, we'll do whatever it takes to stop them. On the bright side, they'll probably try to do it as an ambush."

"This is the bright side?"

Madison grinned again. "I'm pretty sure we can take them when we're expecting it."

This seemed to defy the meaning of "ambush" but Kirehe chose not to argue. "What would you like me to do?"

"Since the captain hasn't sounded an alarm yet, I'm assuming he plans to meet Janssen and his people. Come with me back to Sanctuary, armed and ready for violence. Bring whichever dragons feel up to it and have them act scary. We might be able to intimidate them into doing the right thing."

Kirehe had wanted to bring her maras into the green place. Jaco had promised to ask for permission.

She doubted Jaco had remembered to handle it.

Regardless, she would bring at least one.

"Rila, Fobi, Nihan," she whistled. "I need your help again. This time, we scare people and fight back if they attack."

"Tired," Rila whined.

Nihan groaned.

Fobi whimpered.

"I'm tired too. We work more now to work less later. We see bright green things inside there." She pointed to the dull metal shell of Sanctuary.

Rila sighed and clambered to her hind claws. She nudged Fobi with her head.

Nihan flopped his wing over the side. "Nihan fly all."

By the height of the sun, they might wind up spending the night inside Sanctuary. Kirehe stood and touched the krata's wing. "Nihan bring us to the ground, walk inside, act scary. No more fly."

He flopped his head over the side, letting it dangle.

"He looks like a toddler," Rho said. "A tired, cranky baby."

Kirehe chuckled. "They say to leave you," she chirped, "because you can't do it. I say Nihan is best dragon and can do anything."

"Skila best dragon!" Skila landed on Kirehe's shoulder and swished her feathery tail across Kirehe's back.

"Skila is best shoulder dragon," Kirehe said.

With a long-suffering sigh of a whistle, Nihan rolled off the yacht's roof and landed beside Kirehe. He hunched his shoulders, making sure she knew how grumpy he was.

"Carry Rila and Fobi. Madison and I ride to the ground."

His head lifted. "Madison ride?"

"Bad dragon." Kirehe smacked his shoulder with a laugh and beckoned for Madison to come. She picked up her spear. "Glide only. No time for flying. Too tired, remember?"

"Kirehe no fun."

"Do you ever feel like you've stepped into a big, noisy family with lots of jokes you'll never understand?" Madison asked Rho.

Rho laughed. "Every single day."

"He's not going to do loops this time, right?" Madison asked as she held her hand for Kirehe to take. Every muscle in her body clenched tight and tense.

Kirehe took Madison's hand. She liked the feel of Madison's soft skin with oddly placed callouses. "I told him to glide, and he claims he's tired. If he's obnoxious, I'll keep you safe."

"Great. That's just great. He's going to fly upside-down or something. I know it."

With a chuckle, Kirehe helped Madison climb onto his back.

"Maybe." She sat in front of Madison with her spear across her lap. "Hold on. I only fall on purpose."

Madison slipped her arms around Kirehe's waist and pressed her body close. "I'm sorry I hurt you," she murmured. "I want to make it right."

The warmth and apology Madison offered mollified Kirehe. Something dumb had kept her out of the cargo bay, probably. The captain's orders, weariness, trying to fix things, or anything else could have distracted Madison.

Kirehe put her dragons first. Madison put her ship first.

She turned and kissed Madison's cheek. "We'll fix it in the morning."

One mara in each foreclaw, Nihan leaped off the big ship. He opened his wings and used them to glide to the ground near Sanctuary's gate.

Madison pointed to a shuttle headed toward them. "That's probably Janssen and his people. Let's get ready for a fight here. It's outside Sanctuary, so the guards won't interfere."

Kirehe helped Madison climb off Nihan's back. He set down the maras.

Madison stood facing the shuttle. Kirehe stood beside her with the end of her spear on the ground. Rila and Fobi flanked them. Nihan spread his wings and stood over all of them like a giant, angry shelter.

As the shuttle landed, several blue-coats jogged out of Sanctuary's gate. Captain Wayward led a six-person Star security team to Madison, Gordy among them. He'd also brought Pirro.

"I'd thought we might meet over drinks, but this is more dramatic," Captain Wayward said. "I approve."

A dozen people filed out of the shuttle. They wore the red and brown of Janssen's crew. At the front, a man with a short cape fluttering in the breeze of his passage led the rest.

Kirehe noted the guns they carried in hand, ready to use. She wished she had a shield.

CHAPTER 27

MADISON

Janssen led his crew across the wide path to Sanctuary. He'd overfilled the shuttle. Eleven of his people followed him in a tight group, including Famke. In an unexpected choice, he hadn't brought his bosun. Maybe she'd come in a second shuttle?

"Christopher!" Janssen called as he and his crew neared them. He waved in cheerful greeting. Of them all, only he carried his gun holstered on his belt. "What a charming welcome you've assembled for us."

Captain Wayward took a step forward.

Madison snatched a handful of his coat before he could get farther from her. "Are you sure it's a good idea to go meet him?"

"It's a terrible idea," Captain Wayward said with a smile. "Let go, please."

She sighed and let go of her lunatic uncle.

On his own, Captain Wayward paced forward to meet Captain Janssen. "Only the best for you, Adrian," he said.

They met a few meters away from the group and shook hands.

"You keep giant lizards now?" Captain Janssen asked.

"They have their uses." Captain Wayward shrugged. "Efficient killers of hevit troopers, I have to say."

Captain Janssen looked up at Nihan's bared fangs. "Interesting. And impressive. Do you have any proof of that?"

"I have some dead hevits we haven't disposed of yet. Would you like to see them?"

"I would love to. We came, of course, because of a rumor you have a dead lakhan, so I'd like to see that even more."

"They're inside. I've actually got five of them now. If we look, we can probably find more. My engineering team is working on accessing data from their ships."

Two men held a polite conversation. Nothing untoward existed between them. One had definitely not tried to kidnap the other's niece. The other had obviously not beaten his crew handily.

Madison had seen similar meetings before. Beating up the crew who'd transgressed typically resolved any bad blood between captains.

In this case, Madison wanted something more than two gentlemen having a chat and never acknowledging what had happened. With her neck on the line, she preferred a more concrete statement.

"Excuse me, sir?" She took a small step forward.

Captain Wayward glanced at her. He gestured for Janssen. "I believe my pilot would appreciate some sort of direct statement from you."

"Of course." Janssen placed his hand over his heart and bowed his head. "My most humble apologies for the behavior of my crew. If you have proof that lakhans can be killed and hevits can be fought, then we are here to help take the fight to the Oligarchy in whatever way possible."

"We're happy to have your support, Adrian." Captain Wayward shook his hand again.

Famke stuck out her tongue at Madison. She had bruises on her face. Then she grinned.

No hard feelings.

Madison turned to Kirehe. Her stomach tensed.

Meeting a crew who might want to abduct her and hand her over to the Oligarchy hadn't made her nervous. Her uncle's backing had given her confidence. Nihan looming over her had helped.

Facing Kirehe twisted her into knots.

"They're not here to fight. I want to come with you, but it's better if I go with them. Would you stay with me in Sanctuary tonight? I have a rented room. It's not the most comfortable place ever, but it's private. I think it's big enough for two maras to stay with us."

Each fraction of a second before Kirehe answered stretched into an eternity of agony.

Obviously, she'd refuse. Madison needed to prove herself more. She'd taken too long to reach the cargo bay. Her entrance had annoyed Kirehe too much to endure a lousy bed for the night.

"Yes," Kirehe said.

Madison grinned. She had to contain herself to avoid jumping or shouting.

"I'll send Nihan back with the maras," Kirehe continued, oblivious to Madison. "Rila needs more practice taking care of her pack."

The most amazing person ever turned and whistled to her dragons.

Captain Wayward escorted Captain Janssen inside. Except for Madison and Kirehe, their crews followed them inside. Everyone greeted each other.

Gordy patted Madison on the arm as he passed her.

Famke paused on her way to Madison. She used a subtle point of her finger to indicate Kirehe and a raise of her brow to make it a question.

Once upon a time, Madison and Famke had indulged in a fling.

Nothing about Famke had ever inspired as many feelings as Kirehe did.

Madison nodded to the mimed question of whether she had a thing with Kirehe.

Maybe Famke hadn't joked about a date as much as Madison had thought on Ghati Prime. She'd probably wanted to bed Madison before handing her over. In Famke's mind, it had likely seemed a good chance for one last time to create a memory to hold onto.

To her surprise, Famke grinned and flashed Madison a thumbs-up. "She's hot," Famke mouthed as she passed.

With an answering grin, Madison nodded.

Nihan scooped up the maras and jumped into the air. Skila licked Kirehe's cheek, then followed the big dragon.

Kirehe turned and took Madison's hand. "Show me more of this Sanctuary place. And apologize more. I like that."

Madison laughed as she squeezed Kirehe's hand. "I worship at your feet."

They used the gate and caught up to the two crews.

"Captain Wayward," his chief engineer said out of Madison's sight. "Oolaang's rigged up a device to access the lakhan recordings. They're not in great shape, so we're working on that. We expect to have at least one ready for you by morning."

"Excellent work," Captain Wayward said. "Make sure Oolaang sleeps. You know how he can be with a project."

"Yes, sir. I remember."

"Lakhan recordings?" Captain Janssen asked. "You've been busy, Chris."

"One of my people stumbled across them on this very planet," Captain Wayward said.

If they'd believed the stories he told and the journals he had, Madison thought they should've found a way to survey the planet sooner. She wished it had ever occurred to her to go looking for evidence. Kirehe had done it with dragons. A small armed crew could've done it years ago.

Everything would've changed.

She never would have met Kirehe.

Maybe those secrets had waited for a reason. She leaned close and whispered, "You're amazing."

"You say this a lot. It sounds like you're confused. I'm Kirehe."

The joke took a moment to hit Madison's brain. She covered her mouth and kept her laughter quiet to avoid interrupting the captains.

"You know what? I don't care what they have to say. As long as no one is going to try to drag me to the Oligarchy, we can go."

The group filed into the communication center. Madison hung back and kept Kirehe outside it. Famke stopped at the door.

"I would've drugged you enough not to feel anything," Famke said. "I'm not a monster."

Madison shrugged. "We kicked your asses."

Famke pointed to her face. "Uh, yes. I know." She grinned. "As soon as he heard about the lakhan corpse, everything changed. You're safe so long as we have anything to say about it. His big plan was to sacrifice you, gain citizenship, and then work to undermine the Oligarchy from within. Blowing it up from without is just as good. More satisfying, for sure."

"Glad to hear it." Madison shook hands with Famke. "You should get in there and see them for yourself."

"Enjoy," Famke said with a sassy little smirk. She disappeared inside the communications center.

"Enjoy what?" Kirehe asked.

Madison giggled and pulled her away from the area. "The tour, silly. I want to show you around."

They walked through Sanctuary. Madison showed Kirehe the many different gardens, all with different combinations of colors and plant types. Kirehe had never seen any of the plants before and pointed out a few that reminded her of home.

The pair shared a meal and retired to Madison's room.

Having Kirehe beside her, even when their touch remained chaste, made Madison forget about everything else. She reveled in the warmth, acceptance, and affection of someone she thought she could spend five lifetimes learning about.

In the morning, they shared another meal in the commons, a huge cafeteria with a gentle breeze and plenty of plants. The captains and a significant number of crew from both ships also ate there, all mingling as friends. Several locals also sat among them. Gordy and Jaco ate with Madison and Kirehe.

Captain Roberts had arrived in the night. She and her crew joined them all for breakfast. Many glanced at Madison over and over. They calculated. Their eyes gave them away.

Oolaang burst into the room. In two hands, he held two boxes connected by cables. The other two kept the double doors from hitting him in the face.

"Captain Wayward!" he shouted into the room, breathless and excited. "I've got the first recording! You need to hear this."

Everyone shut up.

"Play it for us," Captain Wayward said.

Kirehe slipped off her seat to help Oolaang climb onto the Captain's table. Oolaang held one box aloft and pushed a button on the other.

The first few seconds hissed and came out garbled.

"…most dangerous enemy we've faced since our civil war! I need more of you to commit now." The voice filling the room reminded Madison of Subjugator Cradok and Arena Master Viriok. This speaker had the same harsh, cruel feel to his tone.

"These humans," a woman said with a growl. She too had that peculiar lakhan quality. "They're weak, they only live a handful of decades, their offspring are time-consuming and worthless, and they have inferior weapons. How did this happen?"

"Arrogance."

Madison shivered because she recognized Subjugator Cradok's voice. The other two sounded similar to him. Having met him face to face, having seen him murder Dani, having heard him laugh at her, she would never forget his specific voice. He still haunted her nightmares from time to time.

"We underestimated them." Cradok laughed, bitter and mirthless. "Our enemies have been pathetic for so long, we forgot how to fight. How Corvik must cringe as He watches us scrabble like fools to hold this sector."

Madison, like many others in the room, straightened at the mention of "corvik." The gladiator pit had used that word as a team name. Kirehe had fought for them.

"I'm too busy with them in this sector." Speaking of Arena Master

Viriok, he sounded frustrated and annoyed. "They're like cockroaches. Find one, and fifty more wait out of sight, multiplying. I'm not leaving to help you. That would be a retreat. I'll never reach the Hacariot to stand in Ackrion's glory."

Another of the gladiator teams used the name "ackrion." Had Viriok named the teams for four of their gods?

"I'll come," a different lakhan woman said. "But I want assurances my ships and soldiers won't be deployed foolishly. And have you captured all those blasted navigators yet? They're an incredible pain—"

Her voice garbled and the recording ended.

"There's sand damage," Oolaang said. "That's all I've got for now. But there are more recordings. We have more to come."

The room erupted into chatter. Kirehe helped Oolaang to the floor. Oolaang rushed out of the room, probably headed back to the ship.

Madison met Jaco's gaze, then Gordy's. Humans had fought back the Oligarchy at one point.

She knew how to do it again. Sort of. Destroying that assault craft had taken a peculiar and particular set of talents and circumstances. Madison's ship interface, Kirehe's dragoncalling, and Oolaang's knowledge had made it possible.

To expand their victories to a wider scale, they needed more.

Not more people with a cybernetic eye or the ability to hear things regular humans couldn't, though those would help.

More people with special skills and abilities. Weird tactics. Surprise assaults. Curious weapons.

Lakhan ship schematics. Surgical strikes.

Sacrifices.

Madison stood and stepped onto the table. She stomped her foot to get attention. People quieted.

"They were afraid of humans," she said into the near-silence. "Whatever else you remember from that recording, never forget that part. Humans worked together. They formed an armada. We know that much from how many broken ships litter this planet. That armada killed at least five lakhans. They destroyed flagships.

"We don't know exactly why they failed, but we do know they were able to succeed more than the histories claim. What's more, we know that when the Oligarchy won, they didn't stamp out humans. They didn't even destroy all our ships. If they had, we wouldn't be here today.

"Those humans who fought here centuries ago took on at least six lakhans. Imagine if we target just one and strike fast enough to keep him from calling for reinforcements. Subjugator Cradok is offering an impressive bounty for my head. I know that, and I don't blame anyone who's tempted by it. But he's offering that because he knows *we're coming for his.*"

The room erupted into applause and cheering. Stardrifters jumped to their feet and shouted their enthusiasm.

Captains Wayward, Roberts, and Janssen all smiled at her.

They had three ships full of people ready to fight.

To win this battle, they needed more. A lot more.

CHAPTER 28

KIREHE

Though she had only understood some of the recording and Madison's speech, Kirehe liked the outcome. More people wanted to fight. Fewer people wanted to give up.

Despite wanting to spend more time with Madison, she returned to her dragons. Madison had things to do. The dragons needed Kirehe.

Lylla came to sit with her for a while. Skila entertained the girl and helped buoy her spirits. Not until the next day did she see Madison again.

Madison entered the cargo bay with soft steps while Kirehe checked Wooni's foreclaw. The flesh healed well, thanks to Rho's ministrations. In another week, she expected him to regain the use of his claws. The wound needed several more weeks to heal fully.

"Sorry I haven't been able to stop by sooner." She sat beside Kirehe. "Uncle Chris is trying to convince as many captains as he can to participate in a conclave. That's when as many ships as possible meet up in space. All the captains collect on one ship and yell at each other. He's got a lot of them saying yes already, but I kind of doubt they'll all show up. It's a big risk.

"Anyway, Oolaang got some more recordings cleaned up. I thought maybe you didn't quite catch a lot of the first one and haven't heard about the later ones."

Kirehe nodded. "They used words I don't know." And, she had to admit to herself, the sound of Viriok's voice made her too angry to think straight. If she ever had another chance to kill him, she would take it.

"The lakhan on that ship recorded several meetings between a number of their kind. At some point, one of them used the name of another lakhan I've heard of, Yuechki. She and Cradok manage this part of the Oligarchy's empire. So that's three lakhans still alive who were around then. They talked a little more about this civil war we've never heard of before. But never mind that. It was a long time ago.

"Reading between the lines, we're pretty sure there aren't that many lakhans still around. Not sure how many, because they don't use numbers, but they were concerned about attrition. As in they aren't breeding anymore. Which means every lakhan we kill brings us closer to eradicating the entire race."

"We have to kill one first," Kirehe said. "Until we manage that, no one will truly believe we can win."

Madison sighed. "That's the damned truth. No one with even a gram of sense is going to volunteer to face Cradok, even with the whole mara pack supporting them."

Kirehe said nothing. She would volunteer for that. With four maras and her spear, she thought she could handle Cradok. Doing so might get all of them killed, but she would take him down with her.

"The only other thing you might care about concerns Lylla. It sounds like the human fleet had a bunch of people like her. The lakhans took some captive and tried experimenting on them. Lylla is likely descended from those people, one way or another. With how Viriok is, I'm betting he knew her ancestry and kept much better track of her than it looked like. Which may explain why she never knew her father."

This information seemed unlikely to help Lylla handle her situation. The girl missed her deceased mother and knew as little about Stardrifter life as Kirehe. Together, they complained about the homes they missed.

Some mysterious father with a special gift offered nothing positive. Daydreams of another prisoner to rescue someday and bond with sounded dangerous.

Kirehe shrugged. "What do you need me to do?"

"Right now? Keep the dragons content, stay ready to fight, learn more Lakhan Basic, and occasionally let me kiss you." She flashed a grin before continuing. "We're leaving Sanctuary today. Captain Bontemps hasn't shown up or responded to any calls, so we're leaving three of the corpses behind and only taking two to the conclave. In case she or anyone else arrives after we leave."

"This Bontemps disappearing is not a concern?"

"Not really." Madison shrugged. "We're all notoriously unreliable. Any number of things could've happened to her, including damage to the ship from a lousy jump someplace."

Several questions buzzed in Kirehe's head, most centering around the idea of Stardrifters as "notoriously unreliable." How they expected to fight the lakhans with such uncertain allies, she had no idea.

She thought they should spend some thought worrying that Bontemps might betray them.

"We'll expect the cargo bay door to close soon," Kirehe said.

Madison nodded and stood. "I'll be busy on the bridge for the next while. I'll make sure someone brings you all a meal."

The ship needed its pilot. After talking with Madison, she now understood this. Her duty to her uncle and the *Star* demanded a great deal of her time.

"I'll stay here so I'm easy to find." She raised her brow at Madison.

Madison grinned and leaned down. "I promise I'll come see you."

Kirehe closed the distance and kissed Madison. "You'd better. I'll send Rila to cause trouble if you don't."

Laughing, Madison left her.

For a while, no one bothered her and the dragons. She threw a small stone for Skila to fetch. Nihan draped himself over the yacht and slept. The maras remained inactive.

Then the cargo bay door shut. Kirehe moved so she could hold onto the yacht. The ship engines fired, humming a low rumble.

Everything shook.

Skila dove into Kirehe's coat.

Force pressed her to the floor.

Nihan whined.

All the rattling and shaking and pressing ended after about a minute.

Another few minutes later, the ship jumped. Her stomach rolled. The dragons all grumbled.

"Jump time," a woman's voice said everywhere, "is ten hours and twenty-six minutes."

They had nothing else to do except wait.

Kirehe sat with the raptors and used a tablet Lylla had left with her. The device had a routine intended to teach children Lakhan Basic, the language everyone else spoke. She used it for a while.

The dragons slept. So did Kirehe.

"Exiting jump in two minutes," the everywhere voice said after ten hours and twenty-four minutes.

In two more minutes, Kirehe's stomach turned. Then more nothing.

"Want hunt," Rila whined.

All the dragons whined about their boredom. Kirehe tried to ignore them.

An eternity later, the everywhere voice spoke again. "Kirehe and Mara, report to Airlock Delta for security detail."

She smirked and stood. Picking up her spear, she whistled for the maras to join her.

"Skila help!" The kukiri landed on her shoulder. "Skila best dragon."

"Nihan stay."

"Nihan stay bored," he grumbled.

"Nihan rest."

"Wooni go?" He held up his foreclaw, still covered with a bandage.

Kirehe frowned at it. If he clawed anything with it, he'd probably reopen the injury. "Wooni stay. Keep Nihan company. Heetay decide if stay or go."

Heetay swished his tail back and forth. He ran in a small circle, then reversed direction. Despite the missing feathers, he didn't wobble or weave. The mara had adjusted. "Heetay go."

With three maras, Kirehe left the cargo bay. They arrived at the designated airlock to find Captain Wayward and Madison. Gordy and his squad of six men waited with rifles and extra guns holstered on their belts. Pirro carried a lakhan corpse over his shoulder. Oolaang also waited with them. He held his two boxes connected by a cable.

"Excellent," Captain Wayward said. "We're all here."

Pirro cleared his throat. "Captain, I feel like I'm the only one who's going to ask this. Are you sure this is a good idea?"

"Not at all. This is a terrible idea. We should absolutely continue to meet with screens between us." Captain Wayward shrugged. "Unfortunately, that would leave us debating for a long time about minutia. It would also mean everyone can sit in their ship, feeling secure on their own. Meeting like this is forcing us all to take a risk."

Madison nodded. "Running and hiding is all we've done forever. It's time to take a few risks."

Captain Wayward touched a panel to open the airlock. "That's why the rest of the command crew is staying behind."

Kirehe nodded to Gordy in greeting.

"Do you want a gun?" Gordy asked as they crossed a bridge to another ship. He kept his voice down as if he preferred for the captain not to overhear.

"No. Spear is better." Kirehe rubbed under Skila's chin. "Go to Madison," she chirped. "Stay with her. Come find me if trouble. Relying on Skila."

"Watch Madad for Kiki," Skila said. She leaped off Kirehe's shoulder and fluttered around people to land on Madison's shoulder.

Madison swiped the kukiri and stuffed her into a pocket. Skila chirped and hid.

"I'm not saying spears are a bad choice," Gordy said. "But they have a much shorter range."

Kirehe shrugged. "Run. Kirehe and maras fast."

He chuckled. "That's true. At least take a shield. I brought a spare for you."

She took the handle he offered. "Kirehe like shield. Good tool."

"I'm fond of them too. We were told to patrol outside the meeting. Do you want to join us for that?"

As she'd heard no other directions, Kirehe nodded. "Show. Kirehe do. Maras follow."

"I can work with that."

They trooped onto a ship a lot like the *Star*. Kirehe had no way to judge the size or shape.

People with guns in red and purple coats escorted them deeper into the ship.

"Who is big ship?" she whispered to Gordy.

"We're inside the *Vane Sequence*. Captain Vane runs it. He's got the biggest ship, as far as I understand. It sounded like he also showed up first and he's on board with the whole fighting idea."

"Good. Need fighters."

"Agreed."

The escorts stopped at a double-size door. A woman in the lead opened it for them. Captain Wayward, Madison, Pirro, and Oolaang stepped into a large gray room with plenty of space. Chairs and tables littered the space in clumps. Viewscreens on the far wall showed the outside, including the *Wayward Star*. Another ship arrived from the other direction.

Gordy held out an arm to prevent Kirehe from following the others inside. "We're the guard detail. It's rude for us to go in."

"Tomas," Captain Wayward said as he moved forward to greet a man in a red and purple coat.

"It's good to see you, Chris."

The door shut.

Kirehe wanted to stand in the way so the door had to remain open.

Gordy directed two of his people to stand by the door. He sent another two walking between the meeting room and the airlock. His final two, he had walk the same path, but half a minute later.

"The Star is going to disengage from the airlock," Gordy said once his people had their assigned jobs. "To make room for another ship. It'll stay close. You and I are going to walk the path to where our shuttle has docked. In case of emergency, we'll need to get our people off this ship, into that shuttle, and back to the *Star*."

Some of those words made Kirehe think she didn't understand him correctly. "Why we walk to big ship?"

"Pirro said that's a gesture of trust on our part." He pointed the way for Kirehe.

She led her maras.

The ship smelled funny. Not as clean as the *Star*. Kirehe supposed a bigger ship took more effort to clean. Or maybe Vane's people liked to roll in filth.

They followed a path with only a few turns and one ladder down to the next floor.

Her maras liked the ladders. They could climb with all four limbs and their teeth, which made them swift both up and down. Kirehe took longer.

At the small bay where their boxy shuttle waited, Gordy introduced her to the pilot, Hennrick. The long, low bay had other small shuttles already, in a few different shapes. All but two had the red and purple markings of the host ship. The two on the other end had maroon and black markings.

Another captain had arrived already, Kirehe assumed. She wondered why they had two shuttles when Captain Wayward had only one. The other captain might have brought more soldiers, or maybe decided to use the opportunity to trade goods with the captains.

The annoying hum of the force field protecting the bay from

space kept her from exchanging more than a few simple words with Hennrick and Gordy. Worse, the bay smelled of grease and fuel, which covered everything like a thick blanket.

She tasked Fobi with following and guarding Gordy. The pair returned to walk the shuttle path as his squad did with the other path.

Kirehe waited about a minute and retraced their path with her two maras. The task promised a great deal of boredom, but at least they got to keep moving.

CHAPTER 29

MADISON

Despite her protestations otherwise, Madison sighed with relief when she saw the *Good Times* arrive on the viewscreen. She liked Mila. Even after becoming Captain Bontemps, Mila still remembered Madison's birthday.

Pirro laid out the lakhan corpse on a table so everyone could see it and poke it as much as they wanted.

Then they waited.

Madison stood and chatted with a few other junior command crew members as if she had no more importance to the situation than any other ship's pilot.

Captain Wayward spoke to Captain Vane, and then to Captain Bontemps when she arrived. Roberts and Janssen arrived soon after her, then Halsey and Orsino. Captain Zanmi showed up, and so did Captain Potsai. Each brought three to five people in their command entourage and six to ten guards.

No one else showed.

Fifteen captains had said they'd come.

Maybe the other seven needed more time. Everyone else had managed to arrive within an hour of each other, though.

"This is excellent," Captain Wayward muttered to her in passing. "I expected fewer."

Captain Vane clapped his hands twice.

The chatter in the room died.

"Thank you all for coming on short notice. A few others might still show up, but we may as well begin. Captain Wayward?" He gestured to her uncle.

Captain Wayward smiled and beckoned the rest of his peers closer.

The meeting began.

The lights around the eight captains faded, leaving them standing in a pool of bright white. The rest of the room faded to a dim gloom.

All the rest of the crewmembers except Madison faded toward the walls. Some sat in couches or chairs. Others stayed standing. They would listen and take notes as needed. Unless one had something important to say, they would remain silent.

Madison, on the other hand, needed to stick with her captain.

Oolaang also remained close to Captain Wayward.

"I heartily appreciate the presence of each and every person in this room. We all took a risk in coming here." He gestured for Madison to step forward.

She stood to his left.

"You all know my pilot. There's a significant bounty on her head. I think we're all aware of the reason, but I'd like to clarify it so we're all working with the same facts. Madison, my niece, infiltrated an Oligarchy ship, was captured, foiled two execution attempts, and then escaped. She and her friends are the first people to ever escape Rikor Six that we know of."

Madison beamed like the prize pony he wanted her to be.

"We've all gotten used to the idea that the lakhans are infallible, immortal beings. I present this corpse and Madison as undeniable proof that neither assertion is true. They are not gods. They are merely much more experienced than any of us. Please allow my engineer to play some recordings we recovered from their ships on Irid Prime."

He gestured to Oolaang.

"Chris." Captain Zanmi raised her hands. She had dark skin, a quick smile, and colored feathers dripping from her tri-corner hat. "I know you're excited about this, but we need to think this through. Yes, there's a dead lakhan on the table. That doesn't suddenly give us the ability to fight them better than we did a few days ago."

"She's right," Captain Halsey said. "A corpse doesn't give us new tactics or better weapons. We're outgunned. That's the entire problem."

Potsai and Orsino nodded. Roberts rubbed her temple.

"Why did you come?" Vane said with a roll of his eyes. "To try to talk him out of this? Has that ever worked? If all you're here for is arguing with him, you wasted everyone's time by coming."

Janssen laughed. "I happen to think Chris has the right of it. We're outgunned because we never work together."

Captain Wayward raised his hand. "If you'd all indulge me a bit more. These recordings are quite illuminating. We can argue all you want afterward."

"Oh fine," Potsai said with a flip of her hand. "Play your recordings."

Oolaang had collected all the recordings onto one file. He activated his makeshift player for the room.

Lakhan voices filled the air, making Madison cringe. Cradok's laugh slithered down her spine, cold and cruel. She saw Dani lying on the floor, her eyes suddenly glassy and blank.

Madison crossed her arms to avoid betraying herself.

Voices murmured in the background as the crewmembers whispered about it.

In the space after one section ended, Zanmi yelled for everyone to shut up and listen.

They all shut up and listened.

Oolaang played a section Madison hadn't heard before.

"...must be our last stand against these wretched humans. If we don't stop them here, we'll never stop them." This female had, according to other sections, come to the aid of the lakhan in charge. "Are you coming or not, Cradok?"

"I'm on my way," Cradok said. "I've had a distraction that caused a delay. Viriok is also on his way. We'll both arrive late, unfortunately, unless you delay and wait for us."

"Waiting at this point would be a mistake." This lakhan had called for help in the first place. From other sections, he'd assumed command of the Oligarchy forces in the sector. His plans had selected the time and place for the battle.

"The humans have a significant number of their largest ships gathered for repairs over Irid Prime. We'll never have a better chance to end this grand conflict than we do now."

Cradok harrumphed. "Have you considered the possibility they gathered the ships to lure us in? It could be a trap."

"They've proven a worthy adversary," the woman said, "but they've never shown any willingness to sacrifice a planet in their defense. The humans have an idiotic need to take care of each other no matter the cost. Irid Prime is the site of a sizable settlement. Scans have confirmed over a million of these cockroaches on the surface."

"I agree with Brivede," the command lakhan said. "If this is a trap, it's a suicidal trap. The humans would never do that. They don't sacrifice others, they only sacrifice themselves like morons."

The recording section ended. Madison waved for Oolaang to pause it. They'd already heard the most important parts anyway.

"Did you hear them call us morons and cockroaches?" she asked the room.

Captain Wayward put a hand on her shoulder. "More importantly, they assumed we would kneel and lick their boots. When we didn't, they assumed we would fall. Our people didn't do that either. It took at least six lakhans working in concert to defeat those humans. There are, as far as we know, only three in this sector."

"The humans had a lot more ships then," Halsey said. "We've all seen how much trash is on Irid Prime."

"We all assumed it belonged only to human ships," Captain Wayward said. "Now we know there are parts of at least five lakhan flagships buried there. And dozens more smaller Oligarchy ships. No one has ever investigated it all before."

"The humans still lost, Chris," Orsino said. "They faced the Oligarchy and they lost. What's the actual message of hope here? That we should go jump to Cradok's flagship and sacrifice ourselves to kill him?"

"Of course not." Captain Wayward displayed much more patience than Madison felt. "That would be stupid. I'm asking you to imagine the galaxy without the Oligarchy. With freedom for settlements to flourish, establish their own rules, and trade whatever they want, whenever they want with whomever they want."

"That's a fool's dream," Zanmi murmured.

Captain Wayward sighed. "It's a dream at least three survivors of that battle shared when they wrote their journals. All of you, every single one, called me a madman for repeating their stories, for daring to believe them. I'm showing you concrete evidence those stories were true. You can say you're a coward, but you can't deny the proof you can see with your own eyes. We challenged them once, and we can challenge them again."

Potsai snorted. "And then we're back to the part where we still have nothing to defeat them with."

"What are you people afraid of?" Madison snapped. "Death? That's always hanging over our heads. One mistake and a ship is blown up. Everyone dies. That's the situation already. Right now, every death means nothing. Nothing!" She jabbed a finger at the floor, imagining she poked everyone of these cowards in the chest. "We're all going to die. Even the lakhans. What if every death meant something instead? What if every death brought us one step closer to freedom?"

"What if we worked together to build up our weapons?" Captain Wayward asked. "What if we pooled our resources? What if we brought together all the best strategic minds among our crews and listened to their ideas? What if we carried out raids designed to get us specific materials for specific purposes to advance our technology? Use your imagination for five minutes and consider the possibilities."

Oolaang held up his box. "May I say something, please?"

No one objected. Captain Wayward gestured for him to speak.

"I'm an engineer. I'm sure all of your engineers can tell you what I'm about to say. Maybe they already have. We could have better weapons, more efficient engines, and faster jump drives. Those things are all possible. To get them, we need to be able to perform research and experiments. A ship always running and hiding and never able to get specific materials can't support research or experiments." He raised his box. "The Oligarchy does those things. They talk directly about experimenting on humans with unusual skills and abilities, like the navigators."

Madison wanted to hug him. Two of his hands shook, suggesting he might need it.

Oolaang stopped and frowned at the floor. "That's all I wanted to say. Thank you. Did anyone want to hear the rest of the recordings?"

"I do," Zanmi said. "I'd like to have some of my crew study them. Do you have copies of the files?"

"Just the one for now," Oolaang said. "I finished cleaning it up and putting it all together only a few minutes before we arrived."

Captain Wayward gestured toward the door. "You should go make copies for everyone."

"Please do," Vane said. He gestured toward the door. "I know I'd like to listen to it."

Oolaang offered the captains a polite bow and shuffled to the door.

Madison wanted to leave with him. These people needed a few blows to the head. Seeing and hearing the lakhans at their most unguarded gave Madison enough fire to want to go find a lakhan and punch them in the face.

Instead, she had to restrain herself from punching these other captains in the face.

She watched Oolaang while the captains fell to squabbling again about impossible, improbable, and uncomfortable.

Tension drained from his small body. He reached the door and adjusted his grip on his boxes.

The door opened.

He paused. His foot shifted back.

Madison had no view through the door. She leaned forward to see what had given him pause. Her pulse quickened and she gulped.

None of these people would have betrayed them. They couldn't have.

They'd all showed up.

How could anyone see a lakhan corpse and still choose the reward over freedom?

Oolaang scrambled to run back to the captains.

Skila chirped her distress, the sound lost among the arguing captains.

Suddenly, Madison knew what she'd see. She checked the captains instead.

"Right on time," Captain Vane said. "Captain Wayward, you have my deepest apologies."

"For what it's worth," Halsey said with a shrug, "mine too."

At least they hadn't bothered to pretend surprise or innocence.

"What the hell have you done?" Bontemps snarled.

Captain Wayward sighed like he'd expected this. "If I have anything to say about it, history will remember this."

Two pharedimi, one man and one woman, in maroon and gold-edged black uniforms stood in the doorway.

"You won't," the woman said with a smirk on her perfectly symmetrical face. "Subjugator Cradok sends his regards for your cooperation."

Along the walls, members of the crews suffered blows from invisible enemies and fell to the floor. Pirro hit the floor as fast as anyone else.

At least they appeared to want everyone alive. In Madison's view, that gave them a chance. Something to work with.

Several of Vane's and Halsey's crew carried at least two dozen subdued or dead members of other crews inside the room. Six wore Wayward blue.

That left Gordy, Kirehe, and three maras on the loose. Plus their escape shuttle and its pilot. Hopefully.

Madison tugged Skila out of her pocket. "Find a way out."

All her hope launched from her hands on brightly-colored feathers.

CHAPTER 30

KIREHE

The patrolling bored Kirehe and both her maras. At first, she reminded them they performed an important function. As time wore on, she doubted the value of their task. Back and forth and back and forth seemed like a waste of time and energy.

They crossed paths with Gordy and Fobi several times. Kirehe reminded the mara each time to follow and protect Gordy.

As they met in a corridor yet again and exchanged more bored greetings, an unexpected whirr and clunk sounded both in front of and behind them.

Two thick gray walls slid across the hallway at high speed, blocking them inside a twenty-meter section of corridor. Each new wall section had a red light glowing at the top.

Gordy launched himself at the wall too late to affect it. He hit with his side and grunted in pain. Rubbing his shoulder, he said, "They're emergency cut-off walls. Used to contain hull breaches or fires." He pointed at one of the red lights. "That means they're secured."

The maras moved to the other wall and scraped their claws against the metal. High-pitched shrieks from the assault hurt Kirehe's ears. None of her maras liked the sound either. They stopped.

"No smoke," Kirehe said into the fresh quiet. "No wall break."

"I know." Gordy knocked the butt of his rifle against the corridor wall, listening to it. "Two distinct possibilities here that I can think of." He crouched and hit the floor with his rifle. "Either Captain Vane betrayed us or someone else betrayed us and took over enough of his ship to use it against us."

Kirehe leaned against the wall and listened. The space sounded empty. She checked the other wall, and it sounded different. Thick. Solid.

"For Madison?" she asked.

"For Madison and Captain Wayward, yes. The Oligarchy wants them both. And also you, from what I've heard."

She hefted her spear and slammed it against the empty-sounding wall. The sharp point scratched the metal with a shriek almost as bad as that made by the mara's claws.

The maras hissed at the horrible noise.

Kirehe inspected the spot and discovered no sign of actual damage. They would not escape this way.

Gordy stood and shook his head. "The walls in a spaceship are tougher than a spear." He scanned the walls on both sides. "I want to complain about the bad luck that put us in a stretch of hallway without a door, but that probably happened on purpose."

While he rapped a knuckle at intervals along the wall for inscrutable reasons, Kirehe paced the length of their prison.

"There are ways around this," he said. "Pichet Three's settlement was built in and around sections of a damaged ship. I'm not sure what I have the tools for at the moment, though."

Only a few steps into her survey, mechanical hissing echoed off the walls. Vague yellow smoke drifted from several spots in the ceiling.

"Gas," Gordy said. He yanked a knife from its sheath on his belt and jogged to the closer of the two doors. "Probably supposed to knock us out. Try to breathe through a sleeve."

Kirehe raised her arm to do as he suggested. "What you do?"

"The quickest, dirtiest option." With one hand holding his shirt up over his mouth and nose, Gordy ran his fingers over the junction between the security door and the wall. "It closed this way, didn't it? I think it did."

From his gesture, she understood his meaning. The door had spawned from the other side and slid into the side he inspected.

"Yes."

Perhaps he lacked the words to explain his task simply.

"Others dead?" Kirehe scowled at the thought of Madison having survived so many things only to die from betrayal.

Betrayal had almost cost Kirehe's life. She wanted to believe Jaco had learned from it.

"Doubtful." Gordy slid his knife along a seam, the tip disappearing between the two metal plates. Every few seconds, he cleared his throat with a growl.

He meant to pry off the outer layer.

Kirehe coughed at the stinging stench of the sickly gas. Her eyes watered as it filled the space.

Her maras covered their noses and lowered their heads with tiny whines of distress.

She could do nothing about this vile, wretched problem. Nothing at all.

"The Oligarchy," Gordy said as he shoved his knife deeper into the tiny gap, "prefers humans as captives, not corpses. They want slaves, like on Rikor Six. Whoever they can take alive, they do it. Death is for the ones who fight. Take them by surprise and they never get a chance. Kill one person as an example and the rest fall into line."

"You fall into line?" She had a hard time picturing Gordy giving up for any reason.

"No. I was injured. They shot me unconscious."

"Also Kirehe."

He nodded. "Most of the gladiators were caught that way." With a heaving grunt, he wrenched off a piece of metal. The interior of the wall held machine things and wires.

Kirehe rubbed her eyes. The gas smelled like rotting eggs. It burned her throat and made her thirsty.

After flicking his fingers across several wires, he cut them all.

The red light flashed.

He sheathed his knife and systematically rubbed together the exposed ends of cut wires.

On his fourth try, the door whooshed open.

Such a simple act had saved them. Magic, as far as Kirehe could tell.

"We have to assume everyone else is down or captured," Gordy said as they all rushed through the open doorway. "If we're fast enough, we'll get to that meeting room before anyone is removed from the ship."

As soon as Gordy let go of the wires, the door slid shut again.

"Need new way to shuttle," Kirehe said with a frown.

Gordy nodded. "On the bright side, we've trapped the gas in there. But our priority is evacuating our people. Here's hoping we don't have to carry all of them, because that's a lot of people."

Carrying people to the shuttle would take a long time, especially if they had to make several trips. Kirehe wanted to ask if he knew how to wake up people once they'd taken stun blasts. She needed words she didn't know.

The maras stopped and listened at the first intersection.

"Smell ugly feather machines," Rila whistled.

Kirehe held up a finger to silence everyone. She heard no hevits.

Though she shared the hearing capabilities of a dragon, they had a much more advanced sense of smell. She trusted their noses.

"Rila smell hevits," Kirehe told Gordy. "No hear hevits."

"I'm guessing that means they passed through," Gordy said. "The lakhans know your dragons can detect the hevits. They must've locked us in so they could bypass us without a fight."

He pointed ahead, up their original path. "Have the maras pay attention, but let's focus on getting back to the meeting room."

Kirehe chirped for her maras to explain the idea. "Not walk into face?" she asked Gordy.

"Face?" Gordy squinted at her, then his expression cleared. "Oh, you mean— Yeah. We'll try, but I don't know any other way into that meeting room than the front door. Vane's crew will try to stop us. There may be other captains against us too. Realistically, we have to assume it's us against everyone."

"Humans fight humans and not enemy." Kirehe grimaced. "Dumb."

"Yes. I agree with you."

They hurried up the hallway keeping as quiet as possible.

"It occurs to me," Gordy said, "that for them to successfully stop us both in the same place, they had to have cameras watching us. If anyone was still monitoring those cameras, they know we're loose. They'll send someone to deal with us."

Kirehe paused long enough to peer down a side corridor. "Kill humans?"

Gordy sighed as he checked the opposite hallway. "I want to say no, but I don't think we have that luxury. If you see the red and purple coats, those are Vane's people. They made their choice. Anyone else, knock them out unless we're sure they're enemies. Blue coats, go ahead and trust."

She accepted this advice, finding it sound.

"People," Fobi chirped. She pointed at the next side passage.

"Maybe enemies," Kirehe muttered to Gordy. She activated her shield.

Shield up and spear ready, Kirehe leaped around the corner.

Laser blasts flew at her face. At least four weapons fired, most hitting the shield. Some hit the wall or floor around her.

Kirehe held her body sideways so the shield covered it.

Four attackers guarded a door fifteen meters away. Two knelt outside the door. The other two stood inside it, firing through the gap. Beyond them, a wall showed the back of a room or another corridor.

She moved forward with smooth, sideways steps. The blasts impacted the shield hard enough to make it wobble in her grip.

Gordy and the maras stayed out of sight. Heetay peeked one eye around the corner.

When Kirehe had only another meter to reach the doorway, the two shooters inside the room stopped firing. Their guns disappeared. She heard their boots clomping on the floor, the sound receding.

The tactic confused her. If they moved back to continue firing when she entered the next room, they would shoot their allies. Otherwise, they had abandoned their allies to her.

With a swift, fluid movement, she flung her shield at one attacker, leaped past both, and speared the other from behind. She held up the one wriggling on her spear as a shield.

Gordy hopped into sight and fired at the second attacker, knocking her down.

The other two attackers had retreated down a corridor. They fired a few pulses at Kirehe from a fair distance, hitting their speared comrade, then turned and ran.

Kirehe planted her dying enemy on the floor and yanked out her spear. She leaped over him, stomped on the edge of her shield, and caught the handle as it bounced in the air.

"Let them go," Gordy said. He patted the two downed enemies' bodies and took things from their pockets. With the dead man, he pulled something small from the corpse's ear, wiped it off, and stuck it into his own ear. "They know we're loose and uncontained."

"Yes, I agree."

"Kill this one?" Rila asked. She prodded the unconscious woman.

Kirehe waved off the maras. They had no need to kill someone downed by multiple stun bolts. If the ship survived, this foe would wake far too late to affect them.

"I'm listening to their security team talking." Gordy tapped his ear. "They're panicking because they know you're loose. Apparently, you're terrifying. There's an argument about whether they made the right choice."

"They choose wrong," Kirehe said.

"Agreed. We need to get to that meeting room, and we need to take a different path to do it. Enough of them are arguing for staying the course they chose that I don't want to go where they expect. Also, we're off their cameras right now. A map of the ship would be incredibly useful right now."

On the off chance it might work, Kirehe patted the wall like that one man had shown her.

To her great surprise, the wall flickered with a screen showing boxes and words.

Gordy chuckled. "I'm so glad we're on the same side." He checked the map. Several times, he tapped it. The view changed in response to his touch. After a minute or two of this, he wiped his hand over the surface, shutting it off. "This way."

With his direction and the shield in hand, Kirehe took the lead. They would reach Madison in time to rescue her. She also wanted to rescue Captain Wayward and the rest of his people on the ship.

"They attack big ship?" she asked as she peered around a corner.

"You mean ours?" When she nodded, Gordy made a thinking grumble. "Before the double-cross, it would've given them away. After, it depends on when the Oligarchy forces got here. If a cruiser showed up and dropped off bad guys, then left, they won't return until they receive confirmation of Captain Wayward and Madison in hand. Or a request for backup."

They ran up a corridor with the maras and stopped at another corner. As soon as Kirehe poked her shield into the space around the corner, laser rifles fired.

Kirehe resigned herself to an annoying, difficult slog.

CHAPTER 31

MADISON

Madison did her best to act like a scared person who had less than air between her ears. She pulled Oolaang with her and took several small steps toward the walls. Captain Wayward seemed to sense she had a plan, or at least a thought, because he punched Vane in the face.

The captains all shouted. Roberts slugged Halsey. Bontemps raised her gun and pointed it at Vane.

The tiny whirl of chaos attracted attention, allowing Madison to take Oolaang to relative safety. They dropped to a crawl and headed for the wall. At a couch as close to the wall as possible, they hid on the other side.

"Don't let them take the records," she whispered.

The fuss in the middle of the room faded.

"I'm done," Captain Wayward said. "I believe even you can understand the impulse."

The pharedim woman laughed. "Yes, I certainly can."

"Why would you do this?" Janssen asked. "Betray your own kind for them?"

Vane snorted. "That's rich for you to ask. I heard you tried to ambush them on Ghati Prime."

"How do we get out," Oolaang whispered.

Madison suspected someone would notice her absence soon. The best parts of the bounties came from handing over her head, after all.

Oolaang, on the other hand, could easily slip away unnoticed.

Bright feathers waved from a nearby clump of unconscious bodies. Skila dipped in and out of sight.

The little dragon had understood.

Madison pointed to the dragon for Oolaang. "You go."

"What about you?" Oolaang asked.

She shook her head.

He gulped. "I believe in you." Oolaang crawled over the closest unconscious people and searched the floor around them.

"It's nice to meet you, Captain Wayward," the pharedim woman said. "I sincerely wish it had happened a long time ago."

"The feeling is most assuredly not mutual," Captain Wayward said.

"Where is Madison Wayward?" the pharedim man asked. "I saw her a minute or two ago."

"Was she here?" Captain Wayward asked. "I can't remember."

"Oh please," Captain Halsey said. Pain pinched her voice. Good. "She's in the room. Maybe she fled for the wall and one of your goons zapped her."

"Not that it matters," Captain Wayward said. "I'm the one you want anyway. The bounty on her is mostly about me."

Madison heard that and knew her uncle would try to sacrifice himself so she could escape. In return, he hoped she had a chance to rescue him.

Oolaang waved to get Madison's attention.

Skila swished her tail from the slats of a vent set low on the wall. Oolaang gripped the vent with three hands and eased it free.

For whatever reason, the vent had no screws or rivets holding it in place. Maybe Skila had removed them from the inside.

"You know, Chris," Halsey said, "I see now why you don't wear a hat. Your head is too damned big."

"Search the room," the pharedim man barked. "Find Madison.

Check every single body if you have to."

Oolaang dove into the vent with his boxes. Madison might fit. Probably not.

As much as she wanted to evade capture again, she lurched to the vent and replaced the cover. "Find Kirehe," she whispered.

Kirehe would save them. Somehow.

Madison clicked over her options. Kirehe needed time.

Did the *Star* know something had happened? No. Pirro had their communicator, held by the bosun out of courtesy and as a show of good faith. Everyone else had done the same. A tradition Vane had known about and used against them.

Pirro had gone down too fast to signal anyone. Even if he faked it, he would've risked notice to fiddle with it and shut off the speaker.

None of the communicators in the room had shouted warnings, so no Oligarchy ships had arrived yet. These pharedimi and hevits had already been on the ship when the *Wayward Star* showed up.

Until Oligarchy ships arrived, they had time before anyone fired on the *Star*. As soon as they found Madison and felt they had her under control, they'd call in the Oligarchy ships.

Kirehe needed time. Madison needed that communicator.

She crawled to the next couch. Pirro lay over there. If they were both lucky, he faked his unconsciousness to wait for the right time to act. Others may have done the same.

Hope seemed futile at the moment, but she had nothing else to cling to.

Someone groaned nearby as an invisible hevit moved their body. Madison ducked under a table and waited. She heard cloth rustling and soft things thump on the floor. The sounds moved away from her.

As soon as she judged the distance to the sounds as far enough, Madison slipped to the next chair, then another table. She ducked behind a couch and saw Pirro less than a meter from her.

She wanted to call his name and have him spring to his feet. He'd fight his way to the door and get reinforcements.

No, the hevits wouldn't allow that.

As silently as she could, she slipped to his side and reached for his pocket.

He opened his eyes and winked at her. She nodded and took the communicator.

Whenever Kirehe reached them, they'd have Pirro's help.

Back behind the relative safety of the couch, Madison switched off the communicator's speaker and turned on the receiver. Violine would hear everything from this point onward.

Madison tucked the communicator into her coat pocket. The fabric wouldn't muffle it too much.

At this point, she had no other objectives than stalling for time. She crawled under a table and waited.

"How is that even possible?" the pharedim man roared. "She's in the room. Find her!"

"Looks like your little princess is a coward, Chris," Halsey said.

"Shut up," Roberts snapped.

"Was Madison here?" Captain Wayward asked. "You keep saying that, but I honestly don't remember her joining me."

"Don't listen to him," Vane said. Did he sound a little panicked? "She's here. He let her speak. She was standing right there."

"Are you sure that was Madison? I do have more than one pilot, you know."

Madison wanted to laugh. Uncle Chris would try to convince them water wasn't wet if they gave him the chance.

"I have to say that I'm not completely sure it was Madison either," Captain Janssen said. "He has another young redheaded lady on his crew that I, for one, find quite fetching. What's her name?"

"You mean Gita?" Bontemps asked. "She's a pretty little thing."

"Goodness, are there more than two?" Janssen asked, sounding delighted.

"My crew has several redheads, as it turns out," Captain Wayward said.

"Silence," the pharedim woman growled. "Madison Wayward! You have until the count of three to show yourself or one of these captains dies."

"Won't you feel stupid for killing prisoners when you find out she's not even in the room," Bontemps said. "I'll bet your lakhan daddy will love to hear about that."

Someone growled in frustration.

Madison heard the smack of a slap.

"Tear. The room. Apart," the pharedim man snapped. "And bring up the damned lights!"

Madison breathed. She waited. If she thought she could fit through the vent, she would've tried before this. Soon, the hevits would lift the table and find her. Even if she tried to play a game of hide and seek with them, she knew she'd lose.

She had no idea how many hevits the pharedimi had brought and couldn't see or hear them.

They won.

It was only a matter of time.

She heard the scrape of plastic on metal. It sounded distant. Plastic cracked like a bone.

"Is it necessary to destroy my property to find her?" Vane whined. "Do you think we have extra tables lying around?"

"Shut up, Captain Vane," the pharedim woman snapped. "Be grateful it's your furniture and not your neck. You said this would be easy. You said you'd prepared everything. And now here we are, searching for one of your promises. We're all extremely lucky I didn't call in Subjugator Cradok yet."

If that didn't tell Violine everything she needed to know, Madison had no idea what would. Violine might not recognize all the voices, but she would know Vane was a traitor and Captain Wayward needed rescue.

The sounds of destruction moved closer. Lights grew brighter around her table. Any window of escape closed.

No one would kill her immediately. She took solace from that fact.

Subjugator Cradok and Arena Master Viriok needed her to die messily and convincingly in front of cameras. They would apply much more control to her execution this time, but it would happen in the future. Not today.

Her uncle faced the same situation. No matter what, he would die after Cradok took care and made preparations.

Of course, she'd given a little speech about not fearing death. When they found her, she would hold her head high and make sure Halsey and Vane knew she had meant every word.

Oolaang had escaped. Even if Kirehe had to abandon Madison, she could save Oolaang. He had a copy of the lakhan ship schematics she'd pieced together. He'd also seen the internals of those old ships, and he had the recordings.

If she died because no one could save her, she knew the fight would continue.

The table flew upward. Madison caught the vague shimmer of a hevit.

She waved with a bright smile. "Hi."

Unseen hands hauled her to her feet.

Everyone looked at her. Chunks of broken plastic littered the room. Six of eight captains knelt on the floor with their hands held behind their heads. Halsey and Vane stood to the side, both triumphant and grumpy at once.

The two pharedimi glared at her.

"Hey, were you all looking for me? Sorry, I must've fallen asleep under there. The floor is surprisingly comfortable."

Behind her, the hevit dropped the table. She jumped but held in a squeak of surprise.

Something prodded between her shoulder blades. Eager to avoid sprawling at anyone's feet, Madison shuffled forward.

"Those hevits are pretty strong, aren't they?" she asked, still smiling as brightly as she could muster.

"Don't bother trying to get her to shut up," Halsey said. "It won't work."

Madison let her smile grow because she had an opportunity to give Violine more information. "Hey, Captain Halsey, you sure had me fooled. Here I thought you were just being obnoxious because you're a bitch. Turns out you're a traitor to your own people too. How about that. Anyone else? I mean, this is the time to reveal all your clever machinations, isn't it?"

"She's right," Captain Wayward said. "Wouldn't you rather we go to our deaths knowing about it? There's not much glory in a silent betrayal."

"If you won't shut up," the pharedim woman said, "at least blather quietly." She raised a communicator to her face. "Subjugator Cradok, we have them both in our custody, along with five more captains and a significant number of skilled slaves. Their ships are, as commanded, unaware of the situation. We await your arrival."

Cradok laughed over the communicator, as cold and cruel as Madison remembered. He sounded exactly the same as in the recordings.

Hevits shoved her to her knees beside her uncle. She raised her hands on her own.

"I'm looking forward to seeing Madison Wayward again."

"They have a fetish for full names," Madison said. "Has anyone ever noticed that?"

"Yes, it's definitely her," Cradok said. She could almost hear his smirk. "Your audience will end differently this time. I only wish I could kill you more than once."

"The feeling is mutual," Madison said in an annoying singsong voice. "But I'll settle for once. Hey, do you take last requests? Also, can I still punch Captains Halsey and Vane in the face? Because I didn't get a chance, and I would love to do that."

Halsey pulled her gun and pointed it at Madison. "I can kill her right now. It would save us all a lot of time and grief."

"I have plans for Madison Wayward," Cradok said. "If anyone harms her or Captain Wayward before they're delivered to me, kill them."

"Yes, Your Benevolence," the pharedimi intoned together.

"Prepare for my arrival in ten minutes."

Halsey holstered her gun with an annoyed sigh. "You're such a brat," she muttered.

"At least we have something in common," Madison said.

Kirehe had ten more minutes before Cradok arrived. Violine had ten more minutes to prepare everyone.

Ten more minutes.

Tick, tick, tick.

CHAPTER 32

KIREHE

Their path seemed too easy. Kirehe kept pausing at corners to check for enemies. They moved up hallways with caution. The tmaras sniffed everything.

No one else opposed them.

"They've lost us on the cameras," Gordy said. "There's a fair amount of panic that we're going to sneak up behind them."

"Gordy, Kirehe, I'm so glad we found you both together," said a voice above them.

"Kiki! Madad danger!" Skila whistled, also above them.

Kirehe looked up. She saw a vent in the ceiling.

"Oolaang?" Gordy asked.

"Yes. Captain Vane double-crossed us, which you've probably figured out. Captain Halsey also betrayed us. There are two pharedimi in the meeting room and some hevits. I don't know how many. They've got all the captains, Madison, Pirro, and everyone else who was inside there. I'm not sure about the security teams outside, but I'd guess they're all down. I have my recordings and I need to get them back to the *Star* so the lakhans don't take them."

Gordy swore.

"Move," Kirehe said. "Spear vent."

Oolaang squeaked. "No, don't do that. I can get it open. Just another moment."

The vent fell. Kirehe caught it and set it aside. Skila fluttered to her shoulder.

"Madad danger!" the kukiri repeated.

"Yes, I heard you," Kirehe chirped.

She and Gordy helped Oolaang reach the floor with his boxes.

"We don't have any good options here," Gordy said. "Taking Oolaang back to the meeting room is asking for them to take the recordings. If I take him to the shuttle, that leaves you to find the room on your own, and we're exposed to hevits. Then if the shuttle leaves, that means you and everyone else are stranded here."

Kirehe frowned. She didn't like the choices either. "Gordy take Oolaang and Fobi to shuttle. Oolaang use shuttle. Fobi find Kirehe. Bring Gordy. Kirehe like Gordy in fight. Like more small man safe. Madison steal shuttle."

Gordy nodded. "You're right. Madison is a pilot." He offered her a hand.

They gripped forearms.

"I'm pretty sure the earbud will just distract you," Gordy said, "or I'd hand it over."

"Skila find Madison. Kirehe and maras kill bad people. Fobi find Kirehe. Bring Gordy. Kill more bad people."

"I am so glad you're on our side," Oolaang said in an awed whisper.

"Let's go, small man." Gordy offered to let Oolaang climb onto his back.

Oolaang held his boxes and also held onto Gordy. "If you have an extra gun, I can watch your back."

Gordy handed him a pistol.

Kirehe sent Fobi to protect them.

"Take me to Madison," Kirehe whistled to Skila as Gordy and Fobi left.

Skila cocked her head and checked the vent. "Kiki big."

"Yes, I'm too big for that." Kirehe rubbed under Skila's chin. "Find another way. Skila is the best dragon for finding Madison."

The kukiri trilled with happiness for a moment before settling to become serious. She sniffed the air, wiggled her haunches, and swished her tail. Then she pointed a tiny claw in the direction Kirehe and Gordy had headed before stopping.

"Madad."

Kirehe resumed her forward progress.

With Skila's guidance, they reached a corridor where Kirehe heard hevits ahead. Rila and Heetay confirmed they smelled and heard the feather machines, and also humans. Even if they hadn't needed to go that direction, Kirehe would've detoured to deal with them.

They slipped up the corridor. She peeked around the corner. Two of Vane's crew stood with their backs to her. The hevit noise sounded farther away. Around the next corner, possibly.

To her surprise, more hevit hum came from the other direction, moving fast. She jerked her body fully into the safe corridor and raised her spear. Rila leaped at the hevit.

Vane's men called a question.

Rila missed with her pounce. She landed in sight of Vane's men.

Kirehe deflected the hevit without stabbing it.

Heetay surged at the hevit. He snapped his jaws around part of it and shook his head.

Feathers shimmered. Blood sprayed, landing on the hevit and revealing it. Kirehe stabbed. Vane's men screamed and opened fire. Rila bounced to the safer hallway.

The hevit's feathers lost their camouflage. Kirehe flung the body at Vane's advancing men. Two more hevits charged.

One hevit slammed its body into Kirehe and shoved her against the wall. A feathery arm pressed against her neck.

Skila screeched and darted at it. Her tiny claws scraped tiny lines of blood across it. Clear liquid sprayed Kirehe's face. The pressure on her neck ended. It made pitiful honking noises of pain.

She kicked the hevit, forcing it to stumble a few steps. Heetay raked his claws across it. The other hevit lay on the ground, blood pooling beneath its visible corpse. Rila stood on the dead body of one of Vane's people. Beside them, the other human moaned in agony and rolled on the floor, trying and failing to hold his organs inside his gut.

Kirehe wiped goo and blood off her face with her coat sleeve. "Traitor die," she snarled at the dying man.

"I'm s-s-sorry," he stammered, his voice high and breathy.

"Sorry no fix." She stalked past him.

Rila and Heetay followed her.

"Bad men," Skila chirped. "Danger Madad. All die."

"We will not hunt them," Kirehe whistled. "Only kill the ones in our way."

Rila chirped her understanding. Heetay followed suit.

Skila bared her teeth and growled while swishing her tail and mantling her wings. "Bad men die."

Kirehe grinned at her bloodthirsty little kukiri. Later, they would talk all about not hurting people without a good reason. First, they had to secure that promise of a later. "Yes. Traitors bad. Which way?"

The kukiri settled again and pointed around the corner.

At the corner, Kirehe peeked to see what they faced.

They'd found a door. Beside it, a button glowed with a red light.

So far, every red light she'd encountered on a ship had meant a locked door. That suggested it wouldn't open unless she pushed the button.

After checking in the other direction and softly directing the maras to stand watch, she slipped to the door and pressed her ear against it.

Enough hevits were on the other side of the door that she could hear them. She heard voices also.

"Smell Madison?" she asked all three dragons.

They sniffed the air.

"Yes," Rila bobbed her head.

Heetay also bobbed his head. "Near."

"Skila best dragon." The kukiri raised her head, presenting her neck for more scratches.

If Kirehe understood the situation correctly, they'd found a back door to the meeting room. As soon as she pushed the button, it should turn green and open the door. Inside that room, she would find an unknown number of hevits, two pharedimi, six friendly captains, two enemy captains, Madison, and many crewpeople.

They needed to get all the blue-coats to the shuttle bay. She hoped to find all of them inside the room. If they had to range across this enormous ship to search for anyone, she doubted they would escape so easily.

"Wait for Gordy," she murmured as she rubbed under Skila's chin. With one extra person and one extra mara, they stood a much better chance. Especially since Gordy understood much more of the full situation than she did.

While they waited, she explained as much as she could. The maras had seen inside the meeting room, at least. They had some idea of what to expect.

Gordy and Fobi found them within a few minutes. A few new blood spatters decorated Gordy's coat. The flesh along his jaw darkened with a small bruise.

"Oolaang is safely away. Security is officially panicked," Gordy said as they arrived. "Cradok's ship is incoming and they know you're still loose but can't find you. Everyone is terrified you're going to get them all killed. Half of the security personnel are ready to renounce Vane and try to get onto other ships. Also, the *Star* has moved to prevent Vane's ship from jumping away and is preparing to fight until we can get the captain and Madison over there."

Kirehe pointed to the door. "Meet room."

He nodded. "That's what the map says too. Do you have an insertion plan already?"

She shrugged. "Run. Kill. No die."

Gordy chuckled. "Not the worst plan I've ever heard. Let me have the shield. I'll cover you. Bring people to me if you need to. We'll take this path back to the shuttle bay. Hopefully, there'll still be one available."

Since she had no objection, Kirehe handed him the shield. No one would expect the door to open this time. Her entry would include no barrage of laser blasts.

"And Kirehe." He touched her shoulder. "As soon as you get in there and start things, it's going to turn into a massive pile of chaos. Focus on the hevits first because no one else can detect them. The pharedimi are the next biggest threats."

"Thank you. Good words." She mirrored his gesture, touching his shoulder. "No die."

"No die," he repeated with a firm nod. "Whenever you're ready."

Kirehe whistled for the maras to follow her and stay together. They would roll over the hevits in a wave of death.

She took one deep breath, then another. This felt like entering the gladiator arena. The anticipation sang in her blood. There, they fought to entertain. Here, she fought to save lives.

With one more breath in and out, she smacked the button.

The door slid open. Hevits flanked it.

"Will you all just shut up?" a pharedim woman shouted with clear, pure exasperation.

Seven people, including Madison and Captain Wayward, knelt on the floor in the center of the room with their hands behind their heads, all with their backs to Kirehe. Bright lights focused on them. Dimmer light glowed around them.

Dozens of bodies lay on the floor along the walls. More of Vane's crew stood guard over the bodies.

Furniture offered random cover from gunfire, though some littered the ground in broken pieces.

The pharedim woman paced in front of the kneeling line. Another pharedim stood with his back to the line, speaking to two humans in two different coats. One wore the red and purple, making him likely the traitor Captain Vane.

Kirehe speared one hevit. Heetay jumped the same one. Rila and Fobi pounced on the other. Both hevits fell swiftly in their surprise.

Together, they rushed another pair.

"What was that?" the pharedim woman asked.

The next two hevits also expected nothing. Kirehe and Heetay slew one while the other two maras took down the other.

Gordy fired into the room.

As he'd said would happen, chaos erupted.

Kirehe focused on the hevits. A sudden surge of shouting, screaming, and laser blasts made them difficult to track. She followed the maras. Their noses would lead.

She expected the hevits to focus on the most dangerous thing in the room anyway. They would come to her.

At least a third of the bodies on the floor moved as if they'd pretended their incapacitation or already recovered and waited for the right moment to act.

Gunfire erupted across the room. Kirehe and her maras swarmed a single hevit, giving it no chance to react. Through the mess, Kirehe saw one of the loyal captains stagger from a blow delivered by empty air.

She sprinted to the obvious hevit enemy. Spear held first, she leaped at it and sliced across its flesh as she landed. Blood stained the feathers. Kirehe stabbed the hevit and put it on the floor.

Kirehe whirled to find herself face to face with the pharedim woman.

In her experience, pharedimi could fight.

Hevits could also fight, they merely relied upon their stealth too heavily to present Kirehe and her maras with a serious challenge. Fearsome against humans, the hevits only slowed down those who could detect them.

The pharedim woman threw her first punch. Kirehe stepped aside and kicked. Her enemy swept Kirehe's foot aside, deflecting the blow with her arm.

The true battle began.

CHAPTER 33

MADISON

Madison's favorite kind of chaos exploded across the room.

The pharedimi and hevits had surprised everyone at first, removing the combat part of their fight. With Kirehe's better late than dead arrival, the Stardrifters had a chance to remedy that oversight.

She dove to the side with her uncle, both scrabbling to put more distance between them and the pharedimi.

Kirehe had a knack for attracting hevits. Madison didn't need to worry about those things anymore. Not much anyway.

Captain Roberts tried to launch himself at the pharedim woman. He staggered from nothing, indicating he'd taken a hevit blow.

And then Kirehe was there. She appeared out of nowhere, flying through the air like a goddess of destruction and salvation. Her mouth formed a growl too distant to hear despite its intensity. She killed the hevit with two swift, sure blows and whirled to face the pharedim woman.

They traded blows, each capable of dodging or deflecting the other. The single battle took place in a bubble of furious emptiness, each woman focused on nothing other than her opponent. Compared to Kirehe's gladiatorial fights on Rikor Six, this one held the distinct air of gritty reality.

The two women fought to kill.

All the facial expressions, big gestures, and body movements Kirehe had learned to use for the crowd, she'd left behind. This battle was not meant to entertain.

Nonetheless, its brutal glory transfixed Madison.

"Let's go," Captain Wayward hissed. He tugged her coat.

Madison blinked and remembered the rest of the universe. Kirehe fought to give Madison and her uncle a chance to flee. Gordy held the back door for them.

"We have to get the crew," Madison said.

"Pirro has that in hand." Captain Wayward nodded at the big man.

Pirro ran across the room with a blue-coat body slung over his shoulder, firing a rifle he hadn't brought with him. Another two huffed behind him, hauling two of their fellow crewmates. One more brought up the rear with another rifle.

Vane's and Halsey's crewpeople seemed uncertain who to target, which gave everyone else an advantage.

As far as Madison could tell, Kirehe and the maras had eliminated the hevit problem. She noticed the main door sliding open. Captain Vane bolted from the room, probably headed for his bridge.

Halsey stuck with the male pharedim. They retreated toward Halsey's people waiting by the door.

"What about Vane and Halsey?" Madison asked her uncle as they wove through hevit bodies and flitted from broken table to couch to chair for cover.

"Let them go," Bontemps shouted from nearby cover. "Worry about getting your own crew back to your ship."

While ordinarily she would agree, they needed to start acting like a proper team. "No," Madison said. "Everyone gets to their ship or this is all for nothing."

"She's right," Captain Wayward said. "Either we work together now or we never will. Pirro! We need a clear path to the shuttle bay! No one gets left behind."

"Aye, Captain! We've got a path back here."

The majestic stalemate in the center of the room ended with Kirehe catching the pharedim's foot enough to knock her a hair off-balance. The pharedim stood no chance once she'd made that singular mistake.

Her dragon warrior princess kicked the pharedim in the gut. As the enemy recoiled, Kirehe plunged her spear into the pharedim's side.

Kirehe yanked out her spear. She cracked the shaft against the pharedim's neck. When the pharedim crumpled, Kirehe slammed the spear into the pharedim's chest.

The other pharedim blinked and betrayed his sheer terror. He turned and fled past Halsey.

Halsey gulped and ran. Most of her crew followed her. A few people, of both Halsey's and Vane's crews, dropped their weapons and put up their hands in surrender.

Sudden silence in the room threatened to deafen Madison.

"I renounce Captain Vane!" one woman shouted. "Can I join one of your crews?"

No one answered for several seconds. Crews picked up their own people and carried them to the back door.

The seven captains all glanced at each other.

They could use the help of people who wanted to atone and knew more about Vane or Halsey.

Madison jumped to her feet. "Yes! For now. Help us carry people, pick a ship, and individual captains will decide how you need to prove your loyalty."

"Agreed," Captain Wayward said.

The rest of the captains nodded and murmured their assent.

"Let's go, people!" Gordy shouted from the back door. "Cradok is still on his way!"

Everyone snapped into action.

Madison helped an injured member of Janssen's crew stumble down the twisting, turning path to the shuttle bay.

"Captain," Gordy said. When seven different people looked, he added, "Wayward. Captain Wayward. I sent Oolaang and his boxes ahead on our shuttle. We'll have to take one of Vane's."

"Good," Captain Wayward said. He hauled a member of Bontemps's crew over his shoulder. "Madison, you're going to need to fly it for us."

"Oh no, Captain," Madison said. "I'm not sure I can handle that."

Several people around her chuckled.

"Do you want me to send it home to blow up afterward?"

Captain Wayward shifted his burden as they jogged through the corridors. "As tempting as that sounds, no. Shut it down until we have a chance to sweep it for bugs and trackers, then get to the bridge and keep the ship intact until Naomi can plot a jump."

Madison had a different navigator in mind. She needed to get Lylla onto that bridge and able to work.

"Captain Wayward," she said, trying to sound innocent despite the effort it took to help the woman stumbling with her. "Not that I have anything against Naomi, because I don't, but wouldn't it be slightly more advantageous to utilize the psychic navigator we happen to have on our ship in a situation such as this?"

"You have a psychic navigator?" Janssen asked. "Is that how you got that little ship away from Ghati Prime so pokken fast?"

"Yep!"

"I don't suppose," Bontemps said, "this psychic navigator is interested in producing some offspring?"

"She's too young," Madison said with a roll of her eyes.

"It was worth asking," someone called from behind them.

Captain Wayward shook his head with a chuckle. "We'll run interference so everyone has a chance to escape. Head to a neutral jump point of your preference. As soon as we have a chance, we'll set up another meeting."

The other captains agreed.

Everyone had to work together to get all the injured and

unconscious people down a ladder. From there, they ran down more corridors until they reached the shuttle bay. All the shuttles sat in a line, waiting.

Including two of Cradok's shuttles.

"Captain Wayward," Madison said as she handed off her injured person. "Do you want to take one of Vane's shuttles or one of Cradok's?"

He grinned. "I'd love to take both, but we're lacking a second lunatic pilot. Let's take Cradok's."

"You heard the captain!" Pirro said. "Wayward crew, into the Oligarchy shuttle on the end."

As they ran, Madison remembered the communicator in her pocket. She should've thought to enable the speaker and hand it to the captain long before this.

Kirehe had distracted her. Every important thought in her head had evaporated at the sight of her warrior princess being a warrior princess.

She checked for Kirehe as she fished the communicator out of her pocket.

Bringing up the rear of the stream of Stardrifters, Kirehe jogged with her maras. Blood spattered all four of them from head to toe. Kirehe traded high-fives with a few members of Roberts's crew before turning to join her own crew.

Madison turned on the speaker for the communicator and handed it to her uncle.

"Violine, so sorry to keep you waiting," Captain Wayward said.

"Captain, the ship is standing in Vane's path, preventing him from jumping. Oligarchy vessels have just arrived. They have a flagship, two cruisers, and a whole salad of smaller ships. The sooner you can get Madison here, the better. All our gun batteries are already firing. Give me the name of that psychic navigator and I'll get her to the bridge."

"Lylla!" Madison shouted as she ran into one of Cradok's shuttles and jumped into the pilot seat. They designed the things for pharedim and qusamadi pilots, which meant humans fit into them without an issue.

The craft had no jack for her eye socket, of course.

She could fly it anyway.

"Be advised we are arriving on one of Cradok's shuttles," Captain Wayward said. "I'd appreciate not being destroyed by my own crew."

"Yes, Captain."

"All in," Gordy called from the back. He thumped on the wall.

Madison smacked a button to shut the back door of the small craft and slammed the throttle forward. They dove out of Vane's ship and into a mess of plasma blasts, shuttles, small fighters, and other garbage.

"A shame we couldn't sabotage Vane's ship on our way out," she said.

"Speak for yourself," Gordy said.

Madison glanced behind to see him holding up a detonator. She faced forward with a grin and wove through the battle already in full swing. "Hang on," she suggested.

"Kirehe," Gordy said, "was there anyone behind you?"

"No. Kirehe follow. All with small ships."

"Oolaang and I paused for about a minute on the way to the shuttles while he rigged up something. No idea what. Didn't waste time asking."

Pirro laughed. "Never mess with Oolaang. I've missed the little guy."

Through her focus on getting the ship to the *Star* in one piece, Madison heard the click of Gordy pressing the button. She had no scanners to report the results.

The tiny ship twisted at her command, flying far too close to an Oligarchy ship to attract fire from a different one. As she'd hoped, plasma blasts ripped across the space. She banked. The blasts hit her intended target.

"Madison, I can appreciate the impulse, but let's get back to the *Star* as soon as possible."

She grinned even though her uncle couldn't see it. "Yes, sir. I will stop having fun immediately, sir."

Captain Wayward chuckled. "You can have fun with the *Star.*"

"Captain," one of the security crewmen said, "I'm sorry, sir. They used hevits. We never saw anything."

"Yes, Dane, I know. I'm just glad we brought Kirehe. Without her, this would've gone quite differently. I wish we had five more of you, young lady. And a lot more of your dragons."

Madison knew he meant it. Despite the fact Kirehe had worked hard on Sanctuary because of her anger at Madison, she'd still proven her worth to Captain Wayward. And the dragons' worth too.

"Kirehe wish more can hear hevits. Oolaang make box?"

"It's worth asking the entire engineering gang to look into," Captain Wayward said. "Eliminating that threat would do wonders for our cause. Not to mention morale."

As they approached *Wayward Star*, the shuttle bay door slid open. Their ship had space for six shuttles. Two spots had small ships already, both with Wayward blue markings. Madison resisted the urge to both try to take out another Oligarchy ship and shove the shuttle into the bay too fast to stop properly.

She eased the shuttle through the force field to set it next in line. Like a proper shuttle pilot not at all in a hurry.

"We're inside," Captain Wayward told Violine.

Everyone stood aside. Madison bolted out of the shuttle as the bay door shut, wishing she could take five minutes to tell Kirehe how incredible and amazing she was.

That fight with the pharedim still awed her.

She sprinted for the bridge. On her way, she disengaged her cybereye.

Someone needed to keep this ship intact.

CHAPTER 34

KIREHE

The captain hurried in Madison's wake. Pirro and Gordy stayed to help with the three unconscious security team members.

"Kirehe do?" Her minimal glimpse of the fight showed her no obvious way to help.

Dragons had no use in a space battle.

Pirro hefted a man over his shoulder. "You can stand by the assault airlock with your dragons in case they try a boarding action. Gordy, go with her. You two work well together. If I find anyone else standing around with nothing better to do, I'll send them to you."

"Yes, sir." Gordy pointed for Kirehe to take a different path than Pirro and the security team.

Pirro paused. "Oh, and expect the ship to slide around. Madison will be flying it." He and the security team left the shuttle bay.

Gordy chuckled. "I think that means watch for places to hold on in case you need one all of a sudden."

The ship shuddered. Metal groaned.

As Kirehe and Gordy sprinted up the corridor with the maras at their heels, the floor dipped to the left. All of them slid into the wall.

"Repair squad delta report to deck five," a woman announced over the speakers.

"Deck five is…" Gordy tugged Kirehe's elbow to help her get moving again. "Weapons? I think? And if they're calling squad delta, that means alpha and beta are already assigned. That's bad."

The ship rolled to the right. Kirehe lost her footing and landed in a heap of squawking, flailing mara limbs.

A siren wailed in the distance.

"Hull breach," Gordy said as he dangled from a handle by one arm. "Madison, this is a capital ship! The gravity generator can't compensate that pokken fast."

Kirehe shoved against a mara flank to extract herself. "She no hear you."

"I know that," Gordy snapped.

The ship righted itself. Kirehe scrambled to her feet and followed as Gordy led the way.

Ahead, the assault airlock iris whined and cracked open.

Hevits streamed onto the ship. Kirehe heard them.

"Enemy!" she shouted at Gordy.

All three maras streamed past her.

Kirehe shrieked to get the hevits' attention. She had to keep them from rampaging through the ship.

Behind the hevits, four qusamadi fired rifles. Two wore jumpsuits, marking them as pilots.

Wayward Star dipped to the left again.

Everyone, including the hevits, lost their footing and slid into the wall.

The maras adapted faster than the hevits.

Blood and feathers coated the wall within seconds.

Kirehe held her shield against the qusamadi. Gordy fired around her.

"Backup," Gordy said.

Two more weapons fired from behind them, held by people in blue coats.

One qusamadi pilot fled deeper into the assault craft. The other three took blasts and fell, twitching.

The threat had passed. One lone qusamadi pilot with a stun rifle stood no chance against them. Especially when Kirehe sent Heetay and Fobi after them.

The two maras returned swiftly with more blood on their muzzles.

"What do ship?" Kirehe asked.

"No idea," Gordy said.

The ship shifted again, righting itself.

Kirehe and Gordy stuck together as they moved to the floor.

"We need a miracle," one of the newcomer crew members said between wheezes.

Jaco lay in a heap on the floor, catching his breath and holding a rifle.

Hennrick, the pilot from the shuttle, lay beside Jaco, also holding a rifle. "Why am I here? Because I can shoot a gun. Great idea, Pirro."

To Kirehe's great surprise, Oolaang clutched the nearest doorway. "Is there anything I can do here? Pirro said you needed help, but he wasn't specific."

Gordy leaned close to Kirehe and muttered, "Pirro did say he'd send us anyone standing around like an idiot."

She snorted.

Jaco glanced from one person to another and scanned the maras. His gaze settled on Oolaang. "I might have an idea."

Kirehe scowled at Jaco. Nothing he said could possibly interest her. "No like idea."

"I already hate it too," Hennrick said.

"Look," Jaco said as he sat up. "We're not doing great. An Oligarchy fighter crashed into my turret, there's been a full hull breach, and Captain Wayward pledged to make sure all the other captains can escape before we leave. At the rate we're going, that'll mean we all die. At least be willing to try something?"

"If it's crazy," Oolaang said, "we're the right people for the job. Spit it out."

Jaco pointed to the assault craft with a mad grin. "We fly this thing back to the flagship. Kirehe and her dragons get us to the engine room. Oolaang sabotages the ship. We run like hell and get back out. Hennrick makes sure the *Star* doesn't leave us behind or shoot us down."

He wanted to execute Madison's original plan. Without the most important piece.

"Need Madison," Kirehe growled. "Not you. Madison."

"I'm what you got." Jaco stood and leaned his rifle against his shoulder. "Besides, it's the least I owe you. Madison is flying the ship or she'd do it in a heartbeat. I'm here to take her place as much as a guy who can't pilot worth a damn can. We have a ship, we have the time, and we'll probably never get a better chance to try this."

With a small smile, he added, "You asked me to prove it."

Suddenly, Kirehe understood. She nodded and matched his smile.

Gordy muttered something about an idiot. He sighed, though, then shrugged and looked to her. "It's no worse than your plan to storm the meeting room. We might even kill Cradok."

Jaco nodded. Either he hadn't heard the first comment or he chose to ignore it. "That would be ideal."

Oolaang shuffled into the ship. "Let's go already. Nothing happens while people stand around talking."

"Rila, can you fight more, or do you need to rest?" Kirehe whistled.

Like a good pack alpha, Rila checked with Fobi and Heetay before answering.

"We eat. We fight. Rest after."

Kirehe nodded. "Cost is one hevit to eat. Do plan." She snared a fistful of hevit and dragged it from the *Star* to the assault craft. "Skila," she chirped, "stay with Madison. This is no place for a kukiri."

Skila bumped her face against Kirehe's cheek. "Kiki best dragon." She fluttered out of the assault craft.

"Skila best Kirehe dragon," she called after the kukiri.

The men followed Kirehe.

She nudged aside the remains of the last qusamadi with her foot.

As he slid into the pilot seat, Hennrick lifted a small box to his mouth. "Violine, this is Pilot Hennrick. I need Adar to tag the assault craft currently attached to the big airlock as friendly."

"Exactly why do you need something as daft as that?" a woman asked from the box.

Hennrick glanced at Kirehe then Jaco.

Jaco shrugged and said, "We're going to perform a Madison maneuver with it."

"But she's on the bridge," the woman said.

"Yes, we know," Hennrick said. "Please just trust me."

The woman sighed. "Understood. I'll see what I can do about the other ships for you. No promises."

"Thank you. Nothing else for it but to go," Hennrick said. "Prepare to disengage." He snapped a harness over his body. His hands ran over the buttons, dials, switches, and levers, using some and ignoring others.

The small ship hummed and whirred.

Hennrick took a moment to gesture for everyone to back out of the cockpit area. "You all might want to strap in or hold onto something. I'm no Madison, but we're going to have to fly through some serious kut."

Kirehe ducked into the staging bay and helped her maras anchor to the wall with their claws. The ship would have to return them all to the *Wayward Star*, so they needed to use some caution with its integrity. The interior wall seemed safe to damage.

The craft bobbed and weaved. Kirehe held onto a strap hanging from the ceiling. Gordy, Jaco, and Oolaang did the same.

Three times, the ship shuddered with impacts. Hennrick swore loudly enough to hear twice. They flipped and twisted.

After an eternity of swinging, swaying, and bumping into each other, the ship righted and landed.

"We're in!" Hennrick called. "They didn't even challenge us. Opening the door."

They let go of the straps. The maras pulled their claws free and grumbled about the rough ride. The door churned open in an empty bay.

"We kill feather machines and bad masters now," Kirehe whistled.

"Yessssss," all three hissed.

Gordy let his rifle hang across his body in favor of the hevit blade. "Oolaang, you're in charge of directions. I'm your bodyguard. Kirehe leads. Two maras in the rear. Jaco and Hennrick in the middle with guns."

"Are we sure I shouldn't stay with the ship?" Hennrick asked.

Gordy shrugged. "What if we can't get back to this ship? What if some hevits come and load up while you're here alone?"

"Good points. I'm coming. Not the galaxy's greatest at security work, but I can not die."

"That's our top priority, yeah. Second is not getting caught." Gordy grinned at them. "Move out, people. Time waits for no one."

Kirehe directed Heetay and Rila to the back. She stalked out of the ship with Fobi. They discovered empty corridors.

Under the circumstances, this made sense. During a battle, Kirehe assumed everyone had a place to go and a thing to do. Hevits had few purposes, and most would send them out of the ship.

Cradok would never expect a Stardrifter boarding action. If Kirehe understood correctly, the Stardrifters never fought back. Or, at least, they fought back only long enough to secure their escape. Engaging the Oligarchy in any meaningful way, especially a flagship, they simply hadn't tried since the war over Sanctuary.

She let one corner of her mouth curl in anticipation and glee. While she wanted to kill Viriok with her bare hands, she had no trouble settling for killing Cradok by blowing up his ship.

They reached a corner and Kirehe heard hevits. Her maras heard it too. She waved for the men to stop.

Hevits marched past in pairs, their feathers a soft white instead of camouflage.

Kirehe and the maras attacked the second row. She'd discovered an entire assault complement, none ready for battle. They lacked weapons. Several failed to react, as if they required orders to function.

Rho had told her to pity them.

This time, she did.

But she still killed them.

The maras tore through the hevits, bathing the corridor in blood and feathers. Kirehe and Gordy helped. Jaco and Hennrick kept watch.

Oolaang held his nose as they hurried through the aftermath.

When they escaped the battle, Kirehe wanted a bath. Tiny white feathers stuck to dried blood on her thigh, chest, and spear.

They reached the door Oolaang wanted. Jaco opened it and held it for Oolaang. Hennrick joined him inside a cylindrical room glowing with red light. Consoles lined an inner ring with a walkway around them.

Kirehe, Gordy, and the maras stood watch.

A pharedim woman's voice spoke everywhere. "Security chiefs, perform immediate internal sector sweeps."

Gordy clucked his tongue. "Sounds like someone noticed your work."

Kirehe shrugged. "Messy."

"Not a lot you can do about that, yeah." Gordy checked his blade and leaned against the wall. "We should expect more resistance on the way out. Once they figure out you're here, they might send some bigger guns."

"Bigger guns?"

"Tougher enemies," Jaco said.

Of course. When Cradok realized his hevits performed well below expectations, he would send enemies with more skill and less reliance on stealth.

She almost hoped he came himself.

Almost. Nihan hadn't killed Viriok. Kirehe doubted she could kill Cradok without the entire team of dragons, specialized weapons, and something else to distract him.

At some point, she would come up with this situation. She had, after all, promised to eat Viriok's liver.

Someday, she would keep that promise. Not today, but someday.

"I'm done." Oolaang stepped out of the round room, snapping shut his toolkit. "It's ready to blow in ten minutes. We should try to get off the ship by then."

"Let's not stand around, then." Gordy helped Oolaang settle on his back.

Kirehe nodded. "We run. Shout if fall or hurt."

They ran.

CHAPTER 35

MADISON

A ship the size of *Wayward Star* could only maneuver so much. Madison's connection to it through her eye socket allowed her to accomplish more than others, but she couldn't overcome basic physics.

This ship as her body rolled to one side then the other as she angled to keep Vane from fleeing before others could escape. As long as Vane's ship stayed between her and Cradok's flagship, she considered the situation a win.

"Exactly why do you need something as daft as that?" Violine said on the edge of Madison's awareness. She paused and sighed like someone had told her something annoying or dumb. "Understood. I'll see what I can do about the other ships for you. No promises."

After a moment's pause, Violine shouted, "Adar! That assault craft stuck to our airlock?"

"What about it?" Adar growled. "It's inside our shields!"

"Designate it friendly."

Adar said nothing. Madison imagined him staring at Violine like she'd grown another head.

The assault craft in question detached from the ship.

"Jaco is in there," Violine said, "and he's going to do something stupid and risky."

Madison snorted. "He learned from the best." No, she would not allow that little squad of fighters to approach using an unprotected angle. This also gave her a good opportunity to protect that assault craft by putting it into their blind spot.

The ship rolled. Everyone dangled to the side, strapped into their seats.

"I'm almost mad he didn't ask me to come," Madison said. Too bad she couldn't do anything to the already-dead pilot whose fighter had hit that one turret.

"He knows we need you here," Captain Wayward said. "I approve his action, whatever it is. Make it happen, Adar. And make sure to let us know when he returns."

"Sure," Adar grumbled. "Like I don't have fifteen hundred other things to take care of."

Madison saw the change of status for the small ship.

"Lylla, Naomi," Captain Wayward said, "we're not leaving without whoever is on that assault craft or confirmation they're all dead. Please keep that in mind."

The bottom fell out of Madison's stomach. Jaco dying on a stupid, risky raid would certainly put the cherry on top of this kut sandwich. "Who else is on that ship?"

"I can only confirm Hennrick, but odds are good he's got a collection of people. He's not a complete idiot."

Oolaang. Jaco had taken Oolaang. Madison knew it in her interior scaffolding.

While tracking everything else and making adjustments to keep Vane and Halsey as contained as possible, she noted the assault craft docking with Cradok's flagship.

What had she expected? For Jaco and Hennrick to fly the thing into the bridge, sacrificing themselves for a chance to maybe inconvenience Cradok? No, they had more brains between them than that.

"They took Kirehe." The words tumbled out of her mouth. Their horror took a moment to register.

"For all we know, they took a full security team," Violine said.

"She's right. Jaco's not remotely stupid. Impetuous and brash, certainly, but not stupid." Captain Wayward tapped his armrest, a mean feat when they all hung sideways. "They're following your example, Madison. We need to buy them time."

"We need to buy everyone time," Adar snapped. "Who buys time for us?"

"Today," Captain Wayward said, "no one. The cost is too high. Madison, can you please stop stressing the gravity engines quite so much?"

She stopped forcing the ship to rotate too fast for the dampeners to correct gravity for them.

Of course Jaco wanted to replicate Madison's idea. Except without Madison, they had to fly to the flagship, get inside, sabotage it, and get out.

The scanners showed her a bigger problem. Moments before Adar announced it, she saw *Good Times* go static.

Adar announced it. "Bontemps is stuck in a tractor lock."

"The flagship is the only ship big enough to catch any of us today." Captain Wayward made a noise that politely tiptoed around the edge of swearing. "Cradok can get seven ships as soon as Halsey and Vane are out of the way."

"Halsey just jumped," Adar reported. "*The Schooner* was using her a shield. Janssen is now taking heavy fire. His shields won't hold long."

"Madison, let Vane leave."

Several voices on the bridge all shouted, "What?"

"Do it!"

"Yes, sir." She dove under Vane's ship, hoping it looked like they had to avoid something. As a bonus, several unsuspecting fighters slammed into his shields.

She also managed to rub the damaged turret across Vane's hull, pressing against his shields and ripping open a hole on both ships.

Madison knew they'd already blocked off that section of the *Star* or she wouldn't have done it.

They all shook from the impact.

"Shields at thirty-six percent," Adar snapped. "We have a fresh hull breach in the section already contained from that turret matter."

"That was petty," Captain Wayward said, though he sounded amused. "Kindly stop damaging the ship on purpose, Madison."

She smirked. "That part already needed repairs."

"Even so."

Vane's bulky ship moved yet didn't jump. Without it between them and the flagship, though, they had no protection from Cradok.

Zanmi's Revenge changed to static. Adar announced it a second later.

"Yes, I expect we're all outgunned." Captain Wayward sighed. "As soon as another one is tractored, Violine, I want you to contact Cradok."

"Cradok?" Violine asked. "What for?"

"To surrender, of course. With three down, there's no chance the other three will escape. That means we have only one chance, and it's those lunatics on Cradok's ship. We're going to buy them some time."

Madison took a deep breath and let it out slowly. She would not panic. Kirehe could kill hevits by the barrel. Jaco had taken her so the mission had a chance of success.

Grand Bear went static.

"Orsino is stuck," Adar said. "That's three."

"Violine, if you please. What's Janssen's status?"

Madison saw the bad news easier than Adar could get it. "*The Schooner's* shields are down."

"Cradok's people have accepted our communication request," Violine said. "Putting it on screen now."

Madison opened her eye. She saw a giant image of Subjugator Cradok. Bile rose in her throat. She hoped Jaco and his team accomplished something other than getting killed.

"Captain Wayward, you seem to have left the meeting before my arrival. Quite rude."

"My apologies, Subjugator Cradok. I had pressing matters to attend elsewhere. These things happen."

Cradok had no appreciation for Wayward humor. He'd proven that months earlier when he'd captured Madison.

"What do you want, Captain Wayward?"

"I wish to formally offer my surrender to you, Subjugator Cradok, in the form of a duel."

Madison slowed the ship to a halt. They had no further need to run or evade at this point. She watched Cradok digest this as she did so. He seemed properly wary.

With so few targets left, the other three ships fell into his tractor beams. He controlled all the ships.

"I see."

"Naturally, I'm offering only myself. I understand your desire to see Madison strung up in some fashion, but I have some conditions, and her escape, along with the rest of my crew, is one of them."

Despite knowing her uncle did this as a sham, Madison believed him. She heard the honest willingness with which he offered his life in exchange for his crew. If he saw no other option, he would follow through with whatever deal he struck.

Captain Wayward would die to save his people.

Like all those souls lost on Irid Prime.

Someone on the bridge lost control of one tiny sob.

"Naturally." To someone else he said, "Cease firing until this negotiation is complete."

Cradok raised his head with a superior sniff of victory. He thought he understood the situation.

The Oligarchy had chased Captain Wayward for over a decade. Cradok had led that chase. Again and again, he'd slipped through Cradok's eight blue-gray fingers. Every time, he'd resurfaced and committed another daring raid against the Oligarchy.

His efforts had become tamer in recent years, but he'd still irritated Cradok like a piece of food stuck between two teeth.

In Cradok's mind, he saw yet another human moron sacrificing himself to save others. Even after experiencing the battle at Irid Prime, he still believed they had no to little ability to lay traps, to lie convincingly, or to work together on this level.

"You have little to bargain with for additional terms, Captain Wayward."

"As I'm sure you're aware, there are six other ships in the area. None of their captains have vexed you even a fraction of the amount I have. I hope you don't deny that."

Cradok smirked. "No, I don't deny that. You are, quite simply, the sum and total of the problem in this sector."

His admission said something to Madison. She needed to think about it.

"As we are agreed on that point, and as it is quite clear you are in a position to prevent their escape, I ask that you instead allow it. Let these seven ships leave."

"I'll do that, and vow not to pursue them for six months, if you bring Madison Wayward with you." Cradok smiled like he knew he offered something neither Captain Wayward nor Madison would ever agree to.

Six months of peace would give people a lot of time to repair and upgrade ships. They'd have a solid chance to organize and prepare. If just one captain had the guts to lead everyone, they could prepare an ambush. Kirehe's help would make it work.

Not that she or her uncle would follow through with this surrender. If they wanted to sell it, though, Madison had to think it through.

"I accept," Madison said. "For a guaranteed six months of peace for all seven ships and their crews, I'll also surrender."

Cradok smiled even broader.

Captain Wayward frowned. "If that's your choice, Madison, I accept it, but I think we're not asking for enough. Cradok, I know you want us both quite badly. What else are you willing to offer? To have us both with a guarantee neither of us will resist or attempt to escape? You were willing to grant citizenship for someone to turn us in. I must ask for an exchange at least equal to that. And, of course, I must ask for a gesture of good faith."

Looking to the side, Cradok said. "Release one of the other ships. The most damaged one will do. Inform them they may leave."

"Yes, sir," a pharedim man said.

He returned his attention to the camera. "Is that enough of a gesture for you, Captain Wayward?"

Janssen's ship lost its static. The scanners reported it had multiple hull breaches.

"*The Schooner* is free," Madison said.

Captain Wayward nodded. "Yes, thank you. Violine, please inform them of the situation and give them instructions to leave as soon as possible. I assume the ship will require some repairs before they can do so."

"Probably," Cradok said. "We won't harass them so long as they don't try to fire on us."

"Yes, sir," Violine said. "I'll tell them."

"As to any further concessions on my part, I believe I can offer a full year of amnesty instead of a mere six months. That seems reasonable to me."

Madison's pulse raced. Jaco and his team needed to get done and get off that ship. Scanners failed to report it leaving. They had to know they only had limited time.

"Then, Subjugator Cradok, I accept your terms on behalf of Madison and myself. Send a shuttle. My security teams will not approach it, and I'm trusting you not to send troops into my ship."

Cradok waved in dismissal. "There's no need for such pettiness on my part." After all, his tone said, he already had what he wanted. "Thank you—"

Though the camera stayed still, Cradok stumbled a step. "What was that?" he snapped.

A pharedim spoke too softly to understand.

The slow turn of Cradok's head and his hard glare at Captain Wayward spoke volumes. "Wayward," he growled.

Captain Wayward offered him a polite, friendly smile. "See you in Hell, Subjugator Cradok."

The picture cut off.

With a sigh of relief, Captain Wayward said, "They succeeded."

Madison pored over the scans.

"The other ships are loose," Adar reported.

"Show me the flagship," Captain Wayward said.

The viewscreen filled with Cradok's flagship. Fire billowed from the center to sputter and die in space. Force from an explosion shoved the ship into an Oligarchy cruiser, ripping a hole in both hulls.

Everyone on the bridge stared in stunned silence for a moment. Cheering erupted among them.

Despite her joy at the sight, Madison needed fewer distractions. She shut her eye and focused on the scans around the flagship. Nothing launched, not even a tiny shuttle.

Jaco, Oolaang, and Kirehe remained on a ship disintegrating before their eyes.

"Run faster," she whispered.

CHAPTER 36

KIREHE

They ran. Every corridor seemed to stretch to eternity. Had they taken a wrong turn? No. Oolaang directed Kirehe. The small man knew which way to go. He had the directions.

They would reach the assault craft in time. The sabotage would wait for them to leave. Everyone would escape the ship.

Kirehe had not come to this ship to watch her maras die.

Finally, they reached the hallway splashed with dead hevits. How long had it taken? Five minutes? More? At least she knew they had only a little farther to go.

As she turned the next corner, another group of people rounded a corner in the distance and saw them.

Both groups paused for a moment. But only a moment.

Four pharedimi, six qusamadi, and the machine hum of several hevits charged them.

"We found the problem," one pharedim said into a handheld device as he rushed forward. He used several words Kirehe didn't know but guessed they indicated the location.

"Hevits," Kirehe chirped, making sure her maras knew where to focus their attention.

Gordy, Oolaang, Hennrick, and Jaco opened fire, filling the hallway with the buzzing blasts.

Kirehe and her maras charged to meet the enemy, trusting the others not to shoot them in the back.

Both qusamadi slowed to try to shoot as they hurried in the wake of the rest of the enemy. Their laser blasts hit the floor and walls. One hit Kirehe's shin. She felt a sting and tingling flesh. Nothing else happened and she trusted the leg to do its job.

Moments before the two groups met, Kirehe planted her feet and held her spear. A surprised pharedim impaled himself. Kirehe plunged the weapon through him. She wrenched it free and kicked him into his allies.

Rila's pack ignored the enemies they could see to rip through those they couldn't.

One qusamadi fell under the hail of laser blasts.

Instead of engaging, the remaining qusamadi stayed back and tried to shoot the maras. They hit hevits.

Swarmed by three pharedimi, Kirehe fought to defend herself. She used her spear as a staff. Her three enemies fell into a rhythm within moments. These pharedimi had trained as a unit.

They each used two blades as long as their forearms. In all their left hands, the blades crackled and buzzed with electricity. The blades in their right hands had dull black metal.

Kirehe had no time to think. She moved her feet, swung her staff-spear, and watched three different sets of shoulders.

Her leg ached.

A charged blade smacked her fingers, sending a jolt through her body.

Gordy slammed into the pharedim on her left. He knocked the woman to the floor and plunged his stolen hevit blade into her shoulder. She screeched.

With one fewer opponent and one fewer hand, Kirehe growled and swished her staff to defend herself.

The blades flew at her in furious arcs. She only needed to hold them off until the maras handled the hevits and qusamadi.

Laser bolts arced past her and missed the pharedimi.

Gordy slashed his pharedim across the neck, stole her charged blade, and joined Kirehe's fight.

"More incoming!" Jaco shouted. "Behind us."

Suddenly facing only one pharedim, Kirehe risked a few glances to assess their situation.

Jaco, Hennrick, and Oolaang backed into the next corridor. Gordy's battle against the other pharedim seemed as much of a stalemate as hers. Beyond them, six hevit corpses littered the hall. Rila favored her foreclaw as she crunched a qusamadi gun in half. Heetay's tail swished in the air. He and Fobi ripped up one qusamadi.

The remaining qusamadi drew a small stick and snapped it to the side. Like the pharedimi's left-handed blades, electricity crawled over the suddenly meter-long stick.

"Rila! Bad stick. Flee!" Kirehe took a slash across her thigh for her inattention. Though shallow, the cut burned with intense fire.

Her maras flowed through the two pharedimi, distracting both.

Kirehe speared hers in the side. Gordy stabbed through his with one blade and slashed across their neck with the other.

Gordy picked up his dead pharedim and used it as a shield for both of them against four new pharedimi pausing in their charge to fire their guns.

"This way!" Jaco called.

With her hand still numb, Kirehe had to shove aside her still-living pharedim enemy without killing her.

The injured pharedim stumbled into the qusamadi with the stun-stick.

Gordy set his hand on Kirehe's shoulder. "Let's go."

She stumbled as she moved. One leg had suffered both a laser bolt and a strangely stinging slash. Numbness and searing pain warred with each other.

"Leg," she said. What else could she say? Feeling returned to her hand, causing extra pain added to the already potent throbbing in her thigh.

"Kut." Gordy yanked her into the second corridor. Laser blasts flew past them to slow the fresh pharedimi. He threw his corpse to focus on helping her. "I didn't know you knew how to get hurt."

If not for the pain, Kirehe would've laughed.

The ship rocked.

Everyone froze, even the enemies.

"Ten minutes!" Oolaang shouted.

So much time had passed so swiftly. Kirehe hadn't even noticed.

With Gordy's help, Kirehe shambled to the next corner.

"Move," Jaco barked. "I'll cover you."

"Don't be an idiot." Gordy shoved Kirehe at Hennrick. He passed his hevit knife to Jaco and raised his rifle. "Hennrick, Get her onto the ship. Jaco, get your dumb ass into the docking bay and make sure it's clear. Oolaang, stick with them."

Jaco followed orders.

"Maras protect Gordy," Kirehe whistled.

With Gordy providing cover fire, Hennrick helped Kirehe limp to their docking bay. She used her spear as a makeshift crutch. Jaco reached the door first and smacked the button to open it.

Gravity shifted, making it feel as if the ship veered to the side. Hennrick kept Kirehe from falling. The maras screeched their distress.

The docking bay door opened. Crates and large-scale tools slid across the bay.

Oolaang sprinted for the ship, dodging debris. Jaco fired his gun from the door, providing cover for Gordy, who hurried backward from the last corner, still firing his rifle.

Hennrick groaned and staggered for no apparent reason.

Kirehe turned to see a qusamadi following through with the blow he must've landed on Hennrick. She flung Hennrick to the side and held her spear ready. With one leg nearly useless and the pain forcing her to gasp for breath, she doubted she could hold her own against a fresh combatant.

"Gordy's hit!" Jaco shouted.

"Maras fetch!" Kirehe whistled.

The qusamadi darted at her with another of the electrical sticks. Kirehe twisted. In better condition, she could have counterattacked. Her leg prevented it. She settled for dodging until the maras arrived.

Her maras dragged Gordy into the docking bay by his shoulders. He still fired his rifle.

As the qusamadi lunged, the ship rocked and shuddered again. The unstable ground fouled his attack and threw Kirehe to the floor.

Jaco flung himself into the fight with the hevit knife. He crashed into the qusamadi. They fell to the floor together.

Fobi pounced on the qusamadi and tore him in half. The stun-stick skittered across the bay.

One of the pharedim from the hall, carrying two blades like the dead ones, lunged through the doorway at Kirehe. She rolled enough to avoid his attack. Laser blasts fired from inside the assault craft.

"Hurry up!" Gordy bellowed, his voice pinched with pain. "Get your asses in this bucket!"

"Your ship is dying," Jaco growled as he scrambled to his feet.

Kirehe kicked with her good leg. With nothing to brace against, she had no power.

The pharedim, still looming over her, raised his dull blade and thrust it at her gut. She had no way to evade the blow and not enough time to knock it aside with her spear.

"No!" Jaco dove into the way.

The dull blade slashed through Jaco's coat, across his chest. He prevented it from hitting Kirehe. His blood sprayed across Kirehe, the pharedim, and the floor.

Fobi leaped onto the pharedim, only a moment behind Jaco.

A moment too long.

The ship shuddered and groaned.

Kirehe scrabbled to her feet. Jaco lay on the floor, wheezing from agony. If his chest hurt half as much as her leg, he had every reason to give up.

Gordy and Oolaang kept shooting at the doorway, preventing anyone else from reaching them.

Taking a fistful of Jaco's coat, Kirehe gasped for breath. She roared her pain and determination with every movement as she dragged him to the ship.

Fobi, drenched in blood, joined her. Her claws dug into his coat and she pulled Jaco by the arm.

He moaned with every inch. "I'm burning," he whimpered.

"We're all in!" Gordy shouted. "Let's go!"

Kirehe heaved Jaco one more yank deeper before giving up and falling to the floor, gasping for breath. "Leg," she groaned. "Jaco hurt."

Gordy dropped his rifle and crawled to Jaco. He muttered some words she hadn't heard before. "What the pokkenspul was on that blade?"

"It burns," Jaco murmured. He sounded weak.

"He's lost a lot of blood already." Oolaang shrugged out of his coat and shoved it at Jaco's chest. "It's bad."

Whatever else Kirehe thought of Jaco, she considered his debt repaid and wanted him to know. She wriggled closer and took his hand. "Jaco good. Prove."

Gordy prodded the wound on Kirehe's leg. She ground her teeth to avoid screaming in Jaco's face.

Jaco turned his head toward her. His eyelids hung heavy. "Love," he mumbled.

She knew. Jaco loved Madison. He acted like her brother because he knew she had no deeper interest. But he loved her with all his heart. Someday, he would find a woman and be satisfied, but she would never take his heart.

"Madison soon," Kirehe said. "See soon."

Gordy shifted closer and murmured to her, "I think those dull blades were poisoned."

Jaco said something else she thought sounded like, "You too," but his voice was too soft to hear over the assault craft engines.

"He won't stop bleeding," Oolaang said. "There's too much blood.

I can't cover it all. It's too much. Make it stop. Jaco, you have to fight! Stay awake. Stay with us. Just keep listening to my voice. You're going to be fine. Everything is going to be fine. We're going back to the *Star*. They can fix this. I know they can. You just have to last long enough."

Oolaang shouted, "Hennrick! Tell them we have serious injuries!"

Jaco's grip on Kirehe's hand failed and his eyelids slipped shut.

The small man kept shouting his distress, goading Jaco to stay awake and fight.

Some battles could not be won.

Kirehe bowed her head and touched his face. "Worthy," she murmured. Her own eyelids felt heavy and she wanted to lie down beside him.

CHAPTER 37

MADISON

The scanners showed several small ships fleeing the flagship. Despite this, Cradok's ship resumed firing all functional batteries. Madison moved the ship into a blind space.

More small ships separated from *The Schooner*. That ship had severe damage. Escaping for them required a miracle. The ship had a chance if the *Star* could prevent the last intact cruiser from giving chase.

"Captain Janssen calling, sir," Violine said.

"Put him on." Captain Wayward stayed on his feet.

Captain Janssen appeared on the viewscreen. Blood dribbled down his face from a cut over his right eye and he had a swollen lip.

"My ship is done, Chris."

"Get to an escape pod," Captain Wayward said without hesitation, "and we'll pick you up."

Captain Janssen chuckled and coughed. "I'm not in much better shape than the ship. Force fields are holding the bridge together. Evacuation order has been given. Whatever I can take down with me, I'm taking it. Pick up as many as you can before you go, Chris."

"We will. Godspeed, Adrian. It's been a pleasure knowing you."

"A pleasure, indeed," Janssen said with a pained, rueful smile. "No regrets. Stick to your dreams, Chris. They're good ones. Tell those boneheaded numbskulls I said so."

"Aye, Captain," the entire bridge said together, including Madison.

They all knew.

The transmission ended.

"*Grand Bear* has entered FTL jump," Adar announced.

The bridge gave a ragged, subdued cheer.

Madison closed her eye again, ignoring the stupid tears rolling down her cheek. Only a few days earlier, that man had tried to take her for the bounty. Crying for his brave sacrifice seemed so stupid.

She did it anyway.

Zanmi's Revenge disappeared a few moments before Adar announced it.

Another cheer rippled across the room.

The data told her when the main bulk of *The Schooner* slammed into the remaining undamaged cruiser.

Cradok's flagship cracked into three pieces. Two plunged into the already damaged cruiser while the third drifted in the opposite direction.

Madison had no ability to track the dozens of small craft filling the area.

"*Good Times* has picked up ten *Schooner* escape pods," Violine announced. "They were closest. Also, the assault craft expedition has left the flagship with all aboard."

More cheers followed this news.

Once she knew, Madison picked out the assault craft among all the small ships. At least the traffic dwindled swiftly.

"Captain," Madison said, "the Oligarchy ships capable of jumping are doing so without picking up escape pods. If we want to capture some prisoners, this is a good time to do it."

"*Good Times* has their bays at capacity," Violine said. "They're preparing to jump."

With Janssen's sacrifice, the battle was over. Everyone knew it. Even the Oligarchy people.

Captain Wayward took a moment before answering. "Leave them. Our people take priority, and I don't want to chance the injuries and deaths they might cause once onboard. We'll have other opportunities, and we have a great deal of data to work with already. Fire on those pods."

"Yes, sir," Adar said. "Picking up our first *Schooner* escape pods now. Violine, ask the others to pick up five each. That should cover them all."

Madison let the clean-up chatter fade into the background. She watched the assault craft slip into a bay and had to force herself to stay in her seat.

Four capital ships spread debris across the area, and their shields could only take so much more damage. She had to keep them clear of large debris while they scooped up escape pods and avoided banging into the remaining Stardrifter ships.

Her job ended when they jumped and not a moment before. No matter what else happened.

"We've picked up the assault craft," Adar announced.

The bridge cheered one more time.

"All friendly escape pods are secured, sir," Adar announced. "And the other three ships are preparing to jump."

"Well done, everyone," Captain Wayward said. "Lylla, show Naomi what you can do. Initiate jump as soon as we're the last ones left. Madison, you can go. I believe we can handle this."

Madison unbuckled her harness before he finished speaking. She flew out of the bridge and ran faster than she'd ever run before.

By the time she reached the cargo bay with the shuttle, the ship had jumped into FTL. She discovered Rho and their medical team already at work inside the smaller ship.

Oolaang sat on his feet on the floor, his shoulders shaking as he wept into two of his hands. Two maras sat with him, both quiet and holding their heads low.

"What's wrong?" As much as Madison wanted to run in and see Kirehe, she paused beside Oolaang. "What happened?"

"They had—" He hiccuped. "They had poisoned blades."

Panic flushed Madison's entire body. "Who," she managed in a strangled whimper.

"Jaco and Kirehe."

She thought someone punched her in the gut, the heart, and the spine at the same time.

"Madison," Rho called, sounding grave. "Come into the ship. We can use your help."

Though she wanted to collapse in misery, Madison obeyed. She shuffled forward. More tears streamed down her face. She wondered if she'd ever stop.

Probably not.

One body lay to the side with a Wayward blue coat over their head and chest. From the shape of the legs, she guessed it was Jaco.

She wanted to lie down and die beside Jaco. Her little brother and best friend had given his life to save everyone else.

A third mara lay beside the body, tended by a medic wrapping gauze over its forelimb. Hennrick sat to the other side with a medic daubing at his face.

In the center, a cluster of people, including Rho, worked with their backs to her.

"Madison, get your ass over here," Gordy snapped.

Drawn by his anger, she fluttered to his side. Where he held Kirehe in a shared forearm grip. Rho and two other medics worked on her leg.

Kirehe chewed on something hard that filled her mouth so she couldn't talk or scream. Sweat beaded on her brow. Her entire body flexed, taut and tense.

"They poisoned her," Rho said, "and she's strong enough to survive it, but the anesthetic isn't working. Even worse, it's doing the opposite of working. We have to clean this wound. It's unpleasant work."

"She's alive," Madison mumbled.

She hated the elation coursing through her. How dare she betray Jaco's sacrifice to rejoice for Kirehe?

"Quit feeling conflicted and help," Gordy snapped. "We tend the living before we mourn the dead."

Of course. She knew better. Madison had lost friends and family before.

Madison dove into the knot of medics. She slipped behind Kirehe and wrapped her arms around the most important person in the entire universe. Supporting her physically took more effort than she expected.

Despite Rho's assertion this had everything to do with pain they had no method to ease, Kirehe looked like she could chew metal and spit rivets.

"They're going to fix it," she said because she had to say something. Even something stupid. "What happened? How did she get hurt?"

"She held off three pharedimi at once." Gordy smirked. "Like a boss. One cut her thigh. It's shallow, but they had some black gunk on the blades."

Madison checked him over. Assuming all the blood on him belonged to enemies, he seemed fine. "Where were you?"

He rolled his eyes at her. "Shooting the hevits, then fighting right alongside her, princess. She was in front because that's where she belongs."

"What happened to…" She tried to say his name. It refused to come out of her mouth.

"I took two stun bolts to the legs, thanks for asking. The maras saved my ass. Didn't see what happened to Jaco, but I can tell you without a doubt one of the maras completely destroyed the pharedim who did it."

Rho filled the short, shallow slash with blue gunk. "We're done but for wrapping it, Kirehe. I'm sorry it had to hurt so much. We'll experiment when you're healed to figure this out."

Kirehe spat out the thing in her mouth and collapsed against Madison. Gordy kept her from hitting too hard. She panted to catch her breath.

The four medics worked together to gingerly wrap gauze around Kirehe's thigh.

"Jaco saved me," Kirehe said in her native language after slowing her breathing. "He traded himself for me."

"I should've been there," Madison said. Tears slid down her cheek again, the stupid things.

"You're not a fighter," Gordy said. "You're a pilot. You can't be everywhere, do everything, and save everyone. We had a pilot, and the captain needed you where you were."

Rho patted Madison's knee. "She needs rest. I promise she'll be fine. We'll get her settled with her dragons. Someone will be here to collect Jaco soon."

They loaded Kirehe onto a stretcher.

"He loved you," Kirehe said. "He did it for you."

Like every other stupid thing he'd ever done, Jaco had gotten himself killed because he wanted to protect Madison.

Madison watched them carry out Kirehe. Her warrior princess whistled and the maras got up to follow her.

Hennrick stood with a small bandage beside his right eye. He left the ship and collected Oolaang.

Gordy nudged Madison toward the body. "You have to look. Even if you think you don't, you do."

She knew that. This had happened to her before.

"I just wish I'd been there for him." She wiped her cheek as she shuffled forward.

"Kirehe was there for him. So was Oolaang, and so was I. He wasn't alone and he knew it." Gordy crouched beside the body and lifted the coat for her to see his face. "He was a good kid. Dumb, but ultimately good. I'll miss him."

Jaco was so unnaturally still. Madison half-expected him to jump up and laugh because she fell for his trick.

But he didn't, and he never would.

She dropped to her knees and cried.

Not long after, crewmen came and collected the body. Gordy supported Madison, helping her find her room so she could sit and be miserable. Her uncle came and sat with her. He shared his favorite stories about Jaco, the ones that always made her smile.

Later, the ship left FTL, then jumped again. After their third jump, Madison sat in the pilot seat again. Six ships remained of the original nine. They met in another empty region of space.

This time, they all spoke by video. Each captain had things to do and repairs to worry about.

Madison watched the viewscreen, split into six pieces. They had cuts, scrapes, bruises, and too much anger to laugh or quip at each other.

"It's unclear if Subjugator Cradok was killed with the destruction of his flagship," Captain Wayward said. "Regardless, we can expect to see more activity from the Oligarchy in our sector. Governor Yuechki will undoubtedly begin a merciless hunt to find us all."

Captain Bontemps cleared her throat. "Captain Wayward, you asked us all to join you and commit to fighting the Oligarchy. I was skeptical we could accomplish anything, and I think that was a reasonable position at the time."

"I agree." Captain Wayward nodded.

Bontemps snorted. "You blew up Cradok's flagship, Chris. I don't know how you did it, but you saved everyone. You and Janssen, I suppose. It was kind of your fault we were there in the first place, but when Vane and Halsey betrayed us, you and your crew pulled through. We're here because of you."

Roberts raised a hand. "Seconded. We have a lot of work ahead of us, and I think we need someone to coordinate everything."

"Someone who's proven he has tactical prowess well beyond what Cradok can anticipate," Zanmi said.

The others nodded.

"I propose we offer Captain Wayward a promotion," Captain Bontemps said. "To Admiral of the Stardrifter Armada."

At once, the rest of the captains seconded the idea. Madison suspected they'd chattered in advance about the idea through their communications officers.

Captain Wayward let silence fall. Madison craned her neck to see him blinking stupidly at the screen.

Jaco would've enjoyed this moment.

Bontemps grinned. "Did we somehow manage to render you speechless, Chris?"

"Yes." Captain Wayward chuckled. "Briefly."

The rest of the captains laughed. Madison heard a low murmur of laughter ripple across the bridge, and among the other bridge crews in the background.

"To say I'm surprised and honored is an understatement." Captain Wayward paused for a moment. "Admiral has a nice ring to it. I accept. We'll have to do some research into how armadas work, I suppose. In the meantime, we have dead to mourn, ships to repair, and outside crews to integrate. There are other captains to contact. Vane and Halsey both escaped and both will be desperate. Our settlements need to be warned to expect reprisals and offered help to either prepare or evacuate.

"Although I'm not sure what an admiral does, I have no doubt that I am nothing without the support of my crew and my captains. As we turn our attention to preparing for war, let us remember that we are not our ships or settlements on planets. We are our people."

After this speech, the captains exchanged some ideas with their new admiral and accepted missions to locate resources or perform research.

Admiral Wayward's crew would soon assemble to honor the dead, of whom they had few bodies. With Kirehe by her side, Madison would say her final goodbye to Jaco.

A hero who lit the spark to ignite a war.

OTHER BOOKS BY THE AUTHORS

STARDRIFTERS
Dragoncaller
A Foundation of Gravestones
The Last Armada (coming soon)

OTHER TITLES BY BOTH AUTHORS
Nova Ranger Academy
Unnatural Dragons: a science fiction anthology
Swords, Sorcery, & Self-Rescuing Damsels
Working the Table: An Indie Author's Guide to Conventions
Clockwork Dragon

WRITERPUNK ANTHOLOGIES
'punk adaptations of classic works·
Sound & Fury
Once More Unto the Breach
Merely This and Nothing More
What We've Unlearned
Hideous Progeny
Taught By Time

LEE FRENCH

Spirit Knights series
Maze Beset trilogy
The Greatest Sin series (with Erik Kort)
Harper Revolution series
Darkside Seattle collection (as L.E. French)
Damsel In Distress
Al-Kabar

JEFFREY COOK

Dawn of Steam trilogy
Airs & Graces trilogy
Fair Folk Chronicles
Gothcraft series
The Accidental Inquisitor series
Unchosen

If you'd like to keep up with Lee, Jeff, and the rest of the Clockwork Dragon crew, sign up for our monthly newsletter on our website, www.clockworkdragon.net.

ABOUT THE AUTHORS

Lee French is a *USA Today* bestselling author living in Olympia, WA with two kids, two bicycles, and too much stuff. She's a frequent visitor to Myth-Weavers, an online RPG site, and also trains in taekwondo. Best known for her young adult urban fantasy series Spirit Knights, she is an active member of the Science Fiction and Fantasy Writers of America and a NaNoWriMo Municipal Liaison.

Jeffrey Cook is an indie author living in Maple Valley, WA with his wife, housemate, and two large dogs. He's written 23 books with more on the way, mostly in the worlds of steampunk sci-fi, urban fantasy, and a bit of space opera. Outside of writing, he's an avid gamer when he can manage the time, a regular attendee on the local convention circuit as vendor and panelist, and a sports fan when he has a free weekend.

He works with Clockwork Dragon, a Western Washington based indie author co-op, and helped to found Writerpunk Press, a small charity press that writes science fiction adaptations to benefit PAWS Animal Rescue in Lynwood, WA.